HOLD
FAST

OLIVIA RIGAL
SHANNON MACALLAN

This book is a work of fiction.

Even if some locations depicted do exist,
the story and events described are completely fictional.
All names, characters, and the events described within
have been imagined by the author.

Any resemblance with reality is purely coincidental.

LadyO @ LadyOPublishing.com
www.LadyOPublishing.com

Hold Fast— 1st ed.
ISBN **978-1535543248**

Table of Contents

The authors would like to thank:

Scarlet- we'd never have met but for you;

*Sophia, Christa, Kim, Jasmine, Sydney, Maria, Nicki, and Erin for
your unwavering encouragements and friendship;*

our Beta Readers and fabulous ARC team;

and Cormar Covers

The only thing necessary for the triumph of evil is for good men to do nothing.

Edmund Burke

People sleep peacefully in their beds at night only because rough men stand ready to do violence on their behalf.

George Orwell (attributed)

The world we live in has a lot of cold, dark, and frequently scary places, and you can't turn on the evening news without encountering some fresh new hell of humankind's brutality.

HOLD FAST is a book firmly rooted in the real world. It is gritty, raw, and intense. We have not shied away from the bad or the evil. But while there are plenty of horrible things done by evil people, there are also Burke's 'good men' who are not willing to let evil triumph; Orwell's 'rough men' who 'stand ready to do violence' for us, and the night is always darkest just before the dawn of a bright new day.

We hope you enjoy our story.

OR / SM
San Diego, CA
July 2016

Chapter 1

Courtney

Sunday Morning, 7 August 2016

Daniel's gentle snoring wakes me early.

It's still ten minutes before six according to the clock hanging on the rough plywood wall; five 'til, according to the cheap digital watch that serves as our alarm clock. *Not that much lost sleep. The alarm was just about to go off anyway, but still. I could have had five more minutes.*

Daniel grumbles when I nudge him. He's cute when he does that, childlike. It makes me want to take him into my arms and cuddle him. Officially he's my husband, but in reality? Daniel's the only child I'll ever likely have.

"Come on, sleepyhead," I whisper, softly ruffling his hair until he's awake. He opens his eyes and smiles at me. The physical resemblance to his half-brother never ceases to amaze me. Twins, if twins could be born so many decades apart, and to different mothers. How can two men look so much alike, yet be so utterly different?

Daniel is kind and sweet, finding joy everywhere in the world around him. He can even find beauty in this hovel we've shared for five years, with its splintery floors and yellowing plastic windows.

Perhaps it's simply time? Perhaps it's the responsibility? His brother Emmanuel is the anointed one, after all. The Lord's chosen prophet.

My Daniel's face is beginning to show wrinkles, but they're from smiling; the light in his eyes is joy. Emmanuel's creases were born from disapproving scowls, and his eyes burn with a terrifying zeal.

Mom, how could you have ever fallen in love with Emmanuel? And how could you bring me here, make me live like this? Can't you see how sick this place is?

"What do you say we go back to sleep and pretend to be sick?" Daniel asks with a wink, sitting up with his back to the wall.

"I wish," I sigh. Forget five minutes. I'd love another five hours. "But I can't. You *know* I can't. Today's a market day and I have to get ready and load the truck and..." I trail off. There's no point in finishing my sentence. Finish my sentence? My sentence is life plus eternity. It will never be finished.

Market days are hard, but they are also a blessing. They get me out of the compound. Every Saturday and Sunday from mid-spring until late autumn, we have a booth at the open-air farmer's market in Greenville. It's tiny and remote, almost the last outpost of civilization before reaching the deep forests of northern Maine, but I get to speak with people.

Normal people who seem to be living *normal* lives. *Normal* people who don't look up to a vicious, manipulative bastard who claims to have a New Revelation from The Lord. *Normal* people who have no need to look at the ground to avoid the wrath of a prophet and his two sons.

Normal people.

Free people.

Daniel claims that those people out there have no more freedom than we do, but I think he's just trying to convince himself that what we have is for the best. But I know better. Daniel was born into this life. I wasn't.

I remember life outside this compound. Life in a city, with houses and paved streets, not this cluster of drafty, converted garden sheds on a sprawling run-down farm deep in the forest. A life centered around friends and family, school and the mall. A life not built around a shabby chapel where an angry old man rants daily about the New Revelation given to him directly from The Lord's lips.

A life where a man like Daniel could be free to openly express his love for Joshua. Where they could get married and live out the happily ever after from whatever fairy tale they build for themselves, if that's what they wanted.

This is the only life he's ever known, and I think he's afraid to leave it, unsure he could survive in the unfamiliar. I can't comprehend that fear of the outside, can't understand why he wouldn't want that life. I'd have run years ago if I were him. But then again, I'm happy that he didn't. If Daniel hadn't asked his older brother for me, God alone knows who Father Emmanuel would have married me off to.

I did run. Years ago, and more than once. But here I still am, so maybe he has a point.

Sitting up for the first time in the cool morning air is always painful, and the first few steps of each day are pure misery. Twenty-three years old, and I walk like I was sixty-three.

"It's bad this morning, isn't it?" my husband asks. We may not be intimate in the way of husbands and wives, but we do care very much for each other. Daniel's eyes lose some of his joy as he takes in my limp, but he can't see the grinding in my hip with every movement, or feel the throbbing ache.

"It could be worse," I tell him with a game smile. "At least I can tell it's not going to rain today." I stare out the scratched and yellowed window at the dawn and yawn.

"You're thinking about it again," he says. "About running."

"Thinking? Yes. Dreaming, even." I sigh. "Always."

"Courtney, you know it can't happen," Daniel says, taking my hands in his. "Next time? The lesson won't be so easy."

"Oh, I know it can't happen. I can't run, Daniel, because I can't *run*. They taught me that lesson so very, very well. Really *drove* it home, you might say." I smile bitterly, and my husband winces and looks away. Yes. Lessons. Friendly little learning aids to help even the slowest student understand things. Like why she shouldn't run.

Yes. Oh, very much yes. I'm still thinking about running. When it comes to learning how to give up, I'm a damned slow learner.

Perhaps the lesson wasn't meant only for me, or even mostly for me. Maybe it was meant for everyone else. And maybe Daniel's not afraid that he can't survive *in* freedom. It might be survival just to reach freedom that he thinks is impossible.

Daniel turns his back to me and we both hurry to remove the long flannel nightshirts necessary even in summer with such flimsy shelter. My husband helps with the buttons on the back of my market day dress. It's the least faded and patched thing in my limited wardrobe, but it's still probably at least as old as I am, and I adjust a bleached-white apron to cover some still-unpatched holes in the front of the skirt.

It's our standard morning routine. We wake up, we dress. We go to prayer holding hands, we eat our meals together. In public, we officially despair every month when we don't have happy news to share with the community of a new blessing visited upon us.

Right, because unless the archangel Gabriel comes down in person for a late-night visit, that is just not going to happen. And even if it did, how could I bring any new life into this place? What kind of person would do that to a child?

It's not the life I dreamed about, but then... does anyone ever get their perfect dream life?

With breakfast and prayers finished, it's time to be about the business of the day. My husband sends me on my way with a kiss on the cheek, and I head for the barn. My mother greets me with a baleful glare—she's already brought the truck around, and I'm late. She and Nathan have been waiting for me.

Loading the truck is backbreaking work for two women and a boy, but we manage. Bushel baskets and wooden crates loaded with fresh fruits and vegetables fill the stake-bed truck almost to overflowing. The bench seat of the truck is nearly as crowded with my mother and Nathan.

"Be careful, Courtney!" My mother gets skittish every single time we drive over the narrow wooden bridge.

"Mom!" I growl back. "I've managed to drive over that stupid bridge ten thousand times already without killing us. Could you please let it go?" I'll pay for that later, I know, but she's not going to risk slapping me while we're driving.

"Actually, it's not even two thousand," she says, rolling her eyes at me. Or perhaps not. Is this going to be one of her good days?

"How did you come up with this number," Nathan asks and I can't help but smile at his genuine curiosity.

"Well, Courtney's twenty-three now, and she got her permit on her fifteenth birthday. She's been taking me to the market twice a week so…" My mother pauses on purpose to give Nathan a chance to do the math.

Wedged in the front seat of the minivan between us, he frowns and solves the problem out loud. "Twenty-three minus fifteen, that's eight. And then there are fifty-two weeks a year. So that would be four times across the bridge a week by eight years times fifty-two weeks." The boy frowns, going back over his work in his head while ticking results off on his fingers. "But no, that's not right either, Sister Heather. You and Sister Courtney hadn't come to The Lord yet when she was fifteen. She was… I don't know how old she was."

"You're right, Brother Nathan! That's so clever of you to remember that. She was sixteen. So go ahead and figure it out now."

My mother nods and winks at me. For all her faults, I have to hand it to her, she's a fabulous teacher. She's just tricked the kid into doing what he claims to hate. I keep my eyes on the road ahead while Nathan counts on his fingers, wondering if she'll eventually remind him that we don't drive to the market during the winter months.

He mumbles to himself, "Four times fifty-two is two hundred and eight... times eight, makes 1,664, but minus... it's 1,456, and it's a round trip so- 2,912!" Eyes narrowed, Nathan bares his teeth at me in a predatory grin. "Courtney," he hisses. "You *lied.*"

I bite my tongue and keep my eyes on the potholed logging road. It's a waste of time trying to explain concepts like exaggeration and nuance to Nathan. All nine-year-olds, even ones raised in a *normal* life, have a tendency to see the world in black and white. *This* one, though? Father Emmanuel's youngest son was brought up to watch everything, to sniff out the slightest, smallest sin in our closed community. In a life where the wages of sin literally are death, that makes him a very dangerous child.

As always, I'm torn between sadness for the little boy and fear of him. What would he have been like if he'd been raised outside of the world according to Father Emmanuel? His quick intelligence, the clever and inquisitive nature, could have taken him anywhere, let him be anything he wanted.

The world according to Father Emmanuel is my private hell, a tiny box with no exit and only a pinprick window where I can see the world on market day, and Nathan is his father's spy.

I can't hate him for it, though. Nathan's just as trapped as I am, and he doesn't even know it.

I can't forget it, though.

Even if Nathan didn't work out the math for the winter months, the fact remains: I drove past the graves of my stillborn sisters this morning for at least the thousandth time. Deep in almost virgin forest, the graves lie unmarked and unremembered but for the small white chunk of granite and perennial wildflowers that a younger, envious version of myself placed there. Every time I drive past the path leading to that small clearing, I want to scream to the world that this man is *Satan*, not the holy man he pretends to be.

But there is no one to scream to.

The Church of the New Revelation, everyone on the compound would swear that Father Emmanuel is nothing less than The Lord's gift to our fallen and sinful world, a witness and a prophet, with a mission to bring America and the world back to righteousness. My mother? Forget walking on water, *she* probably thinks he could breakdance on it if he wanted. The few people in the outside world whose path I cross, they think we're just a quaint relic, a leftover from an earlier time. Like the Amish or the Mennonites, perhaps, but with a little more hellfire and brimstone. They have no idea, and they never will. They won't *see*, because they won't *look*. I've tried to tell them, but they won't listen. *And anyway*, they always say, *it's nowt t'do wi' me and mine.*

That's what they said the first time I ran, when they brought me right back to my mother and her vile holy man.

"Whoever spares the rod hates the child, but the one who loves their children is careful to discipline them," Father Emmanuel explained. "As it says in The Lord's

Word, 'train up a child in the way he should go: and when he is old he will not depart from it.'"

He pretended that it tore him apart to punish me, but there was a sick glee in his eyes as Brother Lucas beat me bloody and bruised with a length of broom handle. For my own good, of course. To train me up in the way I should go. So I would not depart from the way.

I was sixteen then, so much younger and more innocent, but he was right. By the time it was over, I knew I would never forget the lesson. I'd learned that I couldn't count on anyone but myself.

And then the second time I ran... The truck's jostling over deep ruts and brutal potholes covers my involuntary shudder at the memory.

And where would I run to, anyway? My father's dead. The very night he died, my mother drove home from the hospital to get me and brought us here. She wouldn't even wait for the funeral. We had to leave his sins behind, and like Lot's wife, no looking back could be permitted.

Dad was an only child, and my grandparents were gone long before he died. And Sean. I'd run to you, if I knew where you were. The only two men I've ever loved, the only two men I could run to... and they're both beyond my reach.

The deep logging trails give way to graveled dirt roads barely wide enough for the heavy logging trucks to take their loads of tree trunks to the paper mills, and finally to smooth paved roads.

"So you *admit* you're a liar," Nathan taunts. The logging roads are too rough for conversation - too rough for anything but holding on for dear life to anything solid – and I'd hoped that the boy would have forgotten this in the jostling.

Nathan was picked to escort my mother and me to the market because he's strong enough to help us put up the booth, but also because he's smart enough to watch everything we do, and dedicated enough to report even the slightest hint of sin. Even worse, he knows it. His father's flattery and brainwashing have turned an intelligent and curious young boy into a vicious miniature of his father, zealous in sniffing out wrongdoing in others, and he would love nothing more than to demonstrate he's earned his master's trust by having something juicy to report.

"Now, Brother Nathan!" My mother's protest is too weak to be taken as a serious reprimand, but that's hardly unexpected. She fawns over the small monster. Mom, would you have treated your own sons that way if you'd been able to give Father Emmanuel any? Or would you have hated them and ground them under your heel like you did with me? I know the answer, of course. Anything from that twisted man would be a gift from Heaven, in her eyes.

So long as it was a boy, of course.

Not for the first time, I find myself envying my little sisters-that-never-were. Those 'useless girls' never had to live like this.

I shrug off Nathan's taunt, keeping my eyes on the road. I'm memorizing every detail of it. One day I will be running away down this road. One day, I'll be a free woman. One day.

The thought makes me generous toward the little boy who will probably never know anything about life outside the compound.

"What do you say when you're really hungry?" I ask him. He sees the world in black and white, so let's see if I can introduce the concept of a third color: gray.

"That I could eat a horse," he says. His expression shows that the question surprises him but he plays along anyway. "But what does it have to do with you lying?"

"Do you sincerely and honestly believe you could actually eat an entire horse? All by yourself?" I ignore his question and continue with my own.

While he ponders the question, I park in our assigned market space and turn off the ignition. Mom gets out to pull the first of our tables off the truck, leaving Nathan and me alone for a moment.

"Let me answer my question for you," I say, taking one of his hands into both of mine. "You couldn't *possibly* eat an entire horse. It's not true, and everyone around you knows it's not true. But saying that you *could* doesn't make you a liar."

He looks into my eyes struggling to understand what I'm saying.

"You're not trying to deceive anyone, you see? You're not lying, you're just creating a picture, a mental image, to tell your mother that you're really, *really* hungry. Does that make sense?"

Nathan nods, and I can see wheels turning in his head.

"Well, when I said 'ten thousand times' it was just an expression. I wasn't trying to deceive my mother. I just wanted her to know that I have enough experience to know I need to be careful driving over the old bridge and she shouldn't worry."

I give him a few seconds to mull this over as I jump down from my seat.

"Using an exaggeration like that is okay, Nathan," I say pulling on his hand to make him follow me. "When you do that, you're not telling the *exact* truth but you're using it to help someone else understand something that *is* true."

Obediently he follows me, and in silence, helps me unload our baskets and bins of produce onto our table. My mother, picking up on his pensive frown – because, of course, she notices him, right? – waits until he's out of earshot.

"Courtney," she asks, with a fond smile in his direction, "did you break our chatter box?"

"No," I say, shaking my head.

I didn't break him. Quite the opposite, I hope. I may have done something to fix it. I gave the little boy some food for thought. With any luck, he'll take the time to digest it fully.

Chapter 2

Sean

Wednesday Evening, 10 August 2016

Another patrol.

The sun beats down fiercely on Sadr City, and my CamelBak is already empty.

Shit. I know I filled it. Where did my water go?

Whatever.

The streets are empty. They're always empty on these patrols. Where the fuck are all the locals? There's at least a solid fucking million people living in these few square miles of dusty concrete and mud brick. There's not enough rocks for all of them to crawl under, and even if there were – there's only six SEALs walking down the street. It's not like they couldn't squash us like bugs if they wanted to.

"Six of us? You just had to go and fucking count, didn't you?" Saggy spits a brown stream of Copenhagen juice. It kicks up a tiny dust cloud and evaporates almost instantly. So does Saggy. One instant he's there – SO3(SEAL) Jason Higgins, nicknamed Saggy within the Teams – and then *poof.* Before my eyes he fades to a sparkling mist, which winks out as if he had never existed.

One after another, so do Toad, Tinkerbell, Mullet, and Meat. Tinkerbell looks disgusted; Mullet shakes his head sadly.

"You know better than to count, brother," he says. His words echo up and down the street after his misty outline is gone. I'm alone now.

"No, man," I say. "You know why I have to count. You fucking *know* why, Mullet." My voice is raw, harsh.

I miss them. The brotherhood—when you spend enough time in combat with someone, there's a bond—but even more than that, I miss the firepower. Meat's SAW is a force multiplier. The M249 Squad Automatic Weapon spits out a shitload more fire than my M4 could ever manage without melting the barrel.

Doesn't matter. Gotta finish the patrol.

I've got the route memorized. I know this shit like the back of my hand. I've done this same fucking route at least a thousand times. I don't even bother asking why we're patrolling here anymore – SEALs aren't for fucking street-level patrols and everyone knows it.

We do body snatches, grabbing up insurgent leadership as quietly as we can. We kick doors. We do overwatch with sniper rifles, shooting suicide bombers before they can detonate. If they want to go to Paradise, let them do it by themselves rather than in the company of a crowd of strangers. We kill people and break shit.

These chickenshit patrols are what the Army sends its dogfaces to do. There's Marines to pick up the slack as well. But still, every fucking night I do this route, and every night that hot midday sun pounds down on me.

The sun. It's night. Something's nagging at me about that. What? Shake it off, man. Shake it off. Head in the game.

End of the next block, turn north. There's a dog barking somewhere. I don't know where it is – I never know where it is. I hear it every time.

Alley. One hundred meters. Check in on the radio. There's no beep to tell me the crypto is synced, and no voice comes back at me. Still, make the report to silent air.

Check the chamber on my M4 – charging handle comes back just enough to see a sliver of brass ahead of the bolt. The handle makes a metallic *click* when I push it back to the stops and the catch engages. Hit the forward assist a couple times, make sure the carbine is back in battery. I'm going to need all the firepower I've got when I go around this corner. Just like I do every night under the hot Iraqi sun.

I put the rifle to my shoulder and come around the corner. There should be a stack of guys behind me, each with their own sector to cover, but since I'm by myself now, I have to do it all. Lead with the muzzle, sweep from right to left, expose as little of myself as possible until I've cleared the area.

There's nothing here, nobody. I didn't expect there to be. There never is.

The black curtain in the window at the end of the alley shakes. There's no breeze. God, I wish Meat was still here with the SAW.

The red dot of the Aimpoint is centered squarely on the window. Any moment now, it's going to happen. The muzzle of the RPK is going to push the curtains aside, and this time I'm going to light that motherfucker up before he has a chance to open fire.

The coarse black curtain shakes, and there's the gun. I've got the drop on him this time. His head has to be ... there. Right there. Take up the tension on the trigger and ... *click*. Nothing happens. The round has evaporated, just like my water. Just like my brothers. It's the same thing every night under the killing sun in this alley. And just like every night, the enemy's old Soviet-built machine gun barks.

Motherfuckers are learning from us. Used to be they'd just spray and pray, yelling out *Aloha Snackbar* while full-auto recoil pushed their muzzles too high. The safest place to be was right in front of them. If the first two bullets missed you, the rest would too. This guy though, he's using short bursts, controlled. Aimed. I take the first two rounds in my chest plate, the third zips past my left ear.

My brothers disappeared because I'd counted them, and I hoped they'd stay gone. It didn't work, though – they're back now. Their corpses are broken, shattered things lying in the street under the hot sun. Just like every night on this patrol. What's left of Meat's face looks sad.

"You know that doesn't fucking work, bro." His tone is matter-of-fact, resigned. He sighs, and foamy blood burbles out through the holes in his neck. Meat turns his head to look at the others. "Take the SAW, man. You need it more than I do." He looks around at the dusty ground of the alleyway where pieces of his skull and half his brain matter lay scattered. "Shit," he says. "As often as we do this, you'd think I'd be used to it by now," and closes his one remaining eye. He's lying still now, and his hand is loose on the machine gun as I roll and drag it to myself.

No matter how hard I try, I can't change history. I can only repeat it.

My chest plate was never meant to stop heavy rounds at close range, and it didn't. I've got two big, bloody holes in my body in spite of the armor. The twin hammer blows put me on the ground while the unseen gunner dealt with my brothers, but now she – it *is* a woman, the body count guys will tell me this when I wake up in the trauma center at Landstuhl – is coming back to me. I'm still moving, she can't leave me alive.

The SAW is still coming around when she fires. I'm on the ground, prone, and my left calf burns now from a new hole. She aimed high, thank fucking Christ. Only caught me with one round. The muzzle is dropping though; she's coming back on target. My first burst goes low, all three rounds absorbed by the mud brick wall below the window. She fires again, this time stitching me from halfway up my back with the first round. Second one in my ass. The rest of them are high, hitting in the dirt behind me.

My second burst from the SAW hits home, and the RPK is silenced. There's nothing moving now except for the settling clouds of dust and that goddamned curtain. It's still moving with the nonexistent breeze. My ears ring from the gunfire. The smell of blood – and worse things – fills my nose. It's cold here, in the bright nighttime sunlight.

There's a *THUNK-sqeeeeeeeeeeeeeeaaaal,* and I'm thrown forward by deceleration against the lap belt.

Why is my alleyway decelerating?

I jolt awake, reaching for my weapon, but all I find is the armrest of the comfortable first class seat, and it all comes back to me. It's not real. It never is, not any more. That sun and blood-drenched alleyway only happened one time in the real world. One day. It's only in my dreams that it happens every night. I'm on the airplane, headed home, and we've just landed.

A young mother sitting next to me holds a baby on her lap, shrinking as far from me toward the aisle as she can get. Across the aisle is an older man – maybe in his late sixties – that has the look. His eyes meet mine, and yeah—he's been there. He nods once, sharply, in recognition.

My breathing slows as the airplane taxis toward the terminal, and by the time the door opens my hands have mostly stopped shaking. The words tattooed across my knuckles taunt me – HOLD FAST, one letter across each finger. A legacy of my time as a Bosun's Mate before I went for Naval Special Warfare. The tattoo is ancient superstition, a talisman to strengthen the men handling sails and anchors. A spell, even, to ensure the hands would never slip.

Hold fast? I can't even hold fast to my own fucking mind anymore.

First class passengers get to leave ahead of everyone else, thank Christ. I need to get out of this metal can, need different air. The woman with the baby is the first one off – she can't get away from me fast enough, gives me one quick nervous look over her shoulder, keeping herself between me and her child as she hurries for the exit like I'm some kind of fucking monster.

Standing up sucks. After eight years in the Navy – six of them as a SEAL – I've been banged up and broken in more fucking ways than I can count, and after a long flight, it's agony to unroll myself and work stiff, painful joints back to functionality.

I retrieve my green canvas sea bag from the overhead bin, toss it over one shoulder, and head for the jetway myself. I tense up as quick footsteps approach from behind.

"Petty Officer Pearse?" I freeze, turn. It's the man from across the aisle. He seems almost apologetic, and looks like he's debating whether or not to put his hand out.

"I'm sorry," he says. "It's stenciled on your bag. BM3 Pearse. You were a Bosun's Mate?"

"Used to be, a lifetime ago. Got out as a first class, and not a Bosun's Mate, anymore, by then."

"Yeah, had you pegged for something else. Um. My name's Dick. 1st Battalion, 7th Cavalry. Ia Drang Valley, 1965." He makes a decision, holds out his hand. I take it. It's reflex, as much as anything. Dick clasps my hand tightly.

"Sean Pearse. United States Navy. Bunch of things. 2008 until... just now." Avoid the subject of the Teams. People ask too many questions when you tell them you're a SEAL. I don't want to fucking answer questions.

"It gets better, son. It takes time, but it gets better." Dick releases my hand, claps me on the shoulder. "Thank you for your service," he says, then he's gone down the jetway. I hear more footsteps behind me. The rest of the passengers are starting to deplane now. I don't have any interest in getting stuck in a mob, so it's time to get moving myself.

I don't have any checked bags – most of my stuff is in storage while I figure out where I want to settle down now that I'm a civilian again – so I can skip wading through the crowds at baggage claim.

My ride's here already, waiting for me. My mom's standing anxiously at the curb on her tiptoes trying to see me over and around the mass of people. Melissa Pearse – no, Melissa Dwyer now. She's remarried. I was in Afghanistan when she married Bill. Her face lights up when she sees me, and I feel a little better. A little closer to normal. Whatever the hell normal is.

My mom is a compact woman, solidly built, and her fierce hug rocks me back on my heels.

"Welcome home, Sean." Her face is buried against my chest, and as my arms go around her, I feel her shaking, sobbing. She's relieved, I guess. I'm home. If a stranger knocks on the door, it won't be someone stopping by with condolences from the Secretary of Defense and a grateful nation. One visit was enough, and now she won't need to fear a second.

Home. The World. Diesel smoke from shuttle buses lies thick in the air, bringing with it memories of the bases and airfields scattered around all the shitholes in which I've spent the last eight years. The smell is the same, but the sounds are different. There's still rumbling diesels at idle, but they don't have the deep grumble of a Bradley, and no badly-greased tracks squeal wherever I turn. The crowds of people are happy families meeting loved ones, not sergeants corralling misplaced troops.

My mother releases me, steps back to look at me. She scans up and down with penetrating eyes, pausing at the long, knotted white scar on my left cheek, the tattoos on my forearms. Another white crease of scar runs down the length of one of them, breaking the brightly colored ink there. She shakes her head – whether at the ink, the scars, or my general gauntness, I can't tell – and pops the trunk for my bag.

"Thanks for coming to get me, Mom." It sounds lame, but I'm at a loss for what else to say. My bag goes in the trunk, and I close the lid behind it.

"Let's get you home, Sean."

My mother doesn't push me to talk, and the ride home is a blessedly quiet one. I can feel her watching me though, silently scrutinizing me out of the corner of her eye, and I turn to look out the window. I haven't been home since I left for the Navy eight years ago, and it's going to take me a while to get used to Maine again.

The airport is on the outskirts of the city, and streetlights are few and far between until we get back into a busier part of Portland. Familiar low brick buildings line the streets, brightly lit stores and restaurants with plenty of business traffic on the sidewalk. The buildings are the same, some of them centuries old. Maine doesn't take easily to change.

But things have changed a lot in the last eight years. I've changed. My family has changed. All those years ago, Bill was a husband and father, a neighbor. He'd been a good neighbor, always there for us. He'd tried to help us out as much as possible, back when my widowed mom and I needed it most.

The next time I see him, he'll be a husband and *step*father. *My* stepfather.

I never got the full story on what had happened there. What had changed with his wife? And what about his daughter?

I'm suddenly glad of the dark as I feel a flush run up my neck at the thought of Courtney, Bill's daughter, and the hard, angry kiss she gave me before wiping her eyes and turning away, refusing to watch me get on the bus for boot camp. It's been eight years since I saw her, too. She sent me letters for a while after I left, but they stopped after her parents divorced and her mom moved away.

I'd like to see her again. I'll have to ask Bill about her.

Lost in a happy reminiscence of first love, I'm startled when the car stops and the headlights go out. I grab for the door handle in a brief panic, ready to roll out and take cover, but this isn't an ambush. We're home.

Chapter 3

Courtney

Thursday Morning, 11 August 2016

At first glance, this community appears vibrant, full of life. Bustling and noisy. Men and women, children and animals, each one with a place to be, a task to complete. Everything is in motion as complex as the gears and wheels and levers of a clock.

The analogy is apt, perhaps heartbreakingly so. The parts of that clock do the same thing, the same way, over and over and over. Day after day, week after week, month after month. Year after year. There is no variation, there is no change. The minute hand cannot become something better, something more.

And so it is for us. Tightly regulated and restricted, we each perform our function in accordance with The Lord's Plan. Each of us has our own part to play, Father Emmanuel tells us, and we must content ourselves with fulfilling our purpose in His work.

Most things we do together – meals, services in the chapel, work in the fields – but there are some things done in smaller groups as well. Everything is done in groups. I've never seen it spelled out anywhere, but it's very clear that nobody is ever to be left completely alone and unattended for any length of time. No one, that is, except Father Emmanuel and his two sons, who do whatever they damned well please. Daniel, brother of our anointed prophet, gets a certain lenience as well.

It's harder to spread dissension and disloyalty when you can't do it in secret, I guess. Judas couldn't have managed his thing if everyone was watching him all the time. The Lord's Word says 'be sure your sins will find you out,' but you'll be caught a lot quicker when there's always eyes on you.

That's why my Mondays and Thursdays are so special. They're my favorite days, my bee days. On those days, I'm almost my own person. It's the only shred of Daniel's allowed lenience in which I'm allowed to share. I can't think of any other reason I might have gotten so lucky, unless... okay, fine, so everyone else is afraid to go near the bees. That's the real reason. I tend to twelve clusters of hives, spread out around the compound.

Of course, I still have to get up early for prayers, and I have to play my part as Daniel's dutiful wife over a bowl of some gray mush at the communal breakfast, but after that? I'll be blissfully alone. For hours. I hum tunelessly while making a sandwich to take with me for lunch.

What a lovely day. It's sunny, warm but not miserably hot, and I'm going to be free all day.

"Sister Courtney. You're full of cheer today." Brother Jeremiah's voice startles me.

"I am!" I answer. "And why shouldn't I be, when I'm so blessed."

My answer is too perfect. Jeremiah frowns at me suspiciously, and he looks *exactly* like an angrier, bigger version of his brother Nathan. Do they both stand in front of a mirror and practice their father's disapproving scowl every morning? I have to bite my lip to keep from giggling at the idea, but this is going to be so *perfect* a day, and I couldn't bear for anything to ruin it.

Father Emmanuel's oldest son is twenty-five. Jeremiah is his father's successor and he knows it. He's arrogant, so puffed-up and full of himself that I almost expect to see him explode any day. He's also viciously sadistic, as mean as a junkyard dog. I don't think there's anyone other than himself that Jeremiah truly loves, and he views the world through a lens of suspicion and petty spite that colors everyone and everything in shades ranging from absolute indifference to utter hatred.

He was the boy who started by pulling the wings off flies, and would probably have graduated on to torturing kittens if he'd lived in the outside world. The semi-feral barn cats got lucky—Jeremiah has other outlets, better things to torture. People.

The three people that Jeremiah hates most in this world are his little brother Nathan, his uncle Daniel, and me. He's not particularly smart, and he's hopeless even at little things like making correct change at the market, but Jeremiah has a sly cunning that lets him instinctively know the best way to hurt someone.

As soon as Nathan was born, Jeremiah lost his specialness, and he recognized a threat to his position as he watched his little brother grow and recognized that the boy was on the verge of being truly brilliant. Daniel is less of a threat to Jeremiah's future status, but he is standing in the way, blocking Jeremiah from something he wants almost as badly.

He wants *me*.

"You don't fool me for a second, Sister Courtney," he says, smirking. Uh-oh. This is dangerous territory. My plan to have a good day is on very, very thin ice.

"Brother Jeremiah, I have no idea what you're talking about." It's true. I really have no clue what he means. Even if he doesn't *really* have anything on me, Jeremiah will never waste an opportunity to hurt me, just to remind me he's higher in the food chain than I will ever be.

"I know the truth," he says, caressing each word. "I know why you're still barren after all these years. Why you've never whelped a little mongrel for my dear uncle."

"The Lord works in mysterious ways," I respond lamely, my pulse racing as a runaway freight train of sudden fear slams through me. "He'll send us a child when it pleases him to do so." What does he know? Does he have any proof?

"Oh, Sister Courtney." Jeremiah sighs, shaking his head in mock sadness. "The Lord may be almighty, but my uncle's name isn't Joseph, and you're no Virgin Mary," he sneers. "Or at least, you're no *Mary*, anyway." My heart drops as I meet his gaze. Jeremiah is studying me intently, and the permanently annoyed expression he usually wears is gone, replaced by something new. Anticipation. Jeremiah leans forward, reaching out to push my hair away from my ear.

"If he's going to get a brat in you, he's going to have to *touch* you first," he whispers. I will myself to stillness, but I can't suppress a shuddering ripple of terror and disgust at the feel of his hand caressing my cheek, my neck. His breath, warm and wet on my ear.

"I swear to you, Brother Jeremiah, that I lie by your uncle's side every night," I say, and I'm not lying. I *do* sleep by his side, and during the brutal Maine winter, we snuggle for warmth. There may be no lust between us, but the affection and caring are very real.

"Does this mean you don't mind sharing him?" Jeremiah lingers over each word, savoring the taste of my fear. I shake my head, raising my eyebrows in surprise and opening my mouth to protest but he speaks over me.

"I know where his preferences lie, Sister Courtney, and when the time is right, my father will know as well. And on that day..." Jeremiah pauses for effect, hoping to terrify me.

It works, but I'd rather die than let the vampire feed off my fear. I turn away from Jeremiah to wrap a cloth around my sandwich and stuff it in my bag. I don't need Jeremiah to tell me what will happen to my husband if one day Satan should find out about Daniel and Joshua. Or what will happen to me. I know very well how our lives will change on that day.

"You're not even a little curious?" he taunts me. I shrug, keeping my mouth shut. Nothing I could possibly say would help the situation, and there's no way I'd be able to keep a steady voice anyway.

"Well, it might happen soon anyway, even if my beloved father doesn't have a... let's just call it a *revelation*, shall we? A *revelation* about my dear uncle and his *good friend* Joshua." Jeremiah's lust rolls over me in waves even stronger and more disgusting than his fetid breath. I close my eyes, unable to look at his predatory grin any longer. He snakes a strong hand behind my head, locking his fingers tightly, painfully in my hair.

"The Lord has commanded us to be fruitful and multiply," he says, in a flinty, hard-edged voice. "The Lord is patient, but he will *not* tolerate your disobedience much longer, and he will reveal his disappointment in you to my father. And on that day, you *will* be *mine*."

My back is against the wall, and Jeremiah presses close against me, crushing my breasts between us, grinding his crotch against my belly and hip. I push him away, slipping to the side and cross shaking arms over my breasts as much to steady the trembling as to cover myself. Having him so close leaves me feeling dirty, and I feel a wave of nausea rising. Jeremiah cocks his hips, and the motion draws my eyes. I can't *not* see the obscene bulge there, and his pleasure as my face twists in revulsion is the final straw.

Jeremiah jumps back as I retch, grabbing at a bucket by the sink and pushing it in front of me just in time. I drop to my knees in front of it, vomiting again and again until there's nothing left but sour bile.

When I'm through, Jeremiah gently helps me to my feet and gives me a glass of water.

"Thank you," I say. My voice is raw. It hurts to talk but I still have to ask. "Why are you being nice to me now?"

"Because you're going to be my beloved wife, soon, and I... I don't want you to be unhappy." There's something new on his face now, overlaying the lust and anticipation. It's something softer, something I've never seen on his face before. Something that on any other person I'd say was—sincerity? No. No way.

"So, what, this is your way of wooing me?" Disbelief shocks me into unwise boldness. "By threatening my husband? By threatening *me?* You think you can terrify me into falling in love with you?" Jeremiah's face stiffens. "I will *never* marry you, Jeremiah. *Never.*"

"You," he says, his voice coldly furious, "will submit to The Lord's Will, which will be revealed to His prophet."

"Not if it's His Will that I submit to *you,*" I hiss at him, turning my back on him and striding toward the kitchen's back door. I know that antagonizing him is a dangerous mistake, potentially even deadly, and I need to get away before I make my situation worse. I've seen how vicious Jeremiah turns when he doesn't get what he wants, and right now he wants *me*.

I tense up as I hear his quick footsteps behind me, flinching away to avoid the hand I just *know* will reach out to grab me, but not quickly enough. Jeremiah's hand lands on my arm, his grip on my sleeve spins me around while he pushes me backwards. My back is against the wall again, and Jeremiah crushes me against it, pressing his vile mouth against mine as if he wants to eat me alive. Without thinking, I push him away with all my strength and he falls back on the floor.

If looks could kill, I would be a bleeding corpse, but Jeremiah's eyes slide past me and the rage on his face stills in an instant as if it had never existed. My back is to the door, but I don't need to turn around. There's only one person who can leash the mad dog.

My only question is how long has he been standing here.

"What's happening?" Father Emmanuel asks in the warm, sweetly seductive tone he uses to make new converts. It drips with honey and molasses, so sweet I always hope they will realize he's a phony.

Jeremiah eyes dart from his father to me and back as he slowly gets up. Like me, he must be wondering how much his father saw.

"It's my fault, Father Emmanuel," I say, turning to look at him. If Satan came in while Jeremiah was on the floor in front of me, he couldn't have seen enough to be dangerous, not from where he's standing. I'm stuck between a rock and a hard place. Tell the wrong lie, the rock will crush me. Tell the wrong truth, the hard place will grind me to dust.

"I was feeling ill, and Brother Jeremiah – bless his heart – went to fetch me a bucket so I wouldn't make a mess. When I was done, he brought me water." I gesture in the direction of the *evidence at hand. The best lies are the ones that stick closest to the truth.*

"Just now I felt sick again, so I pushed him away. I didn't want to—*oh no!*" I reach for the bucket and pretend to retch again, but stress and fear turn my acting into reality.

"After so long, could you have finally received the blessing?" he asks.

"I have fervently prayed for it, Father," I reply, bowing my head and slowly standing. "I'll empty this outside, and then I must tend to my chores."

The self-appointed prophet frowns, studying my face as I walk past him toward the door.

"Do you want Jeremiah to accompany you?" he asks.

I pause as if giving the question some thought and then decline as politely as I can. "Oh, Father Emmanuel, I don't want to waste any more of your son's precious time. I'm sure I'll be fine."

"Fine," he says after a long moment. "You may go on your own." Turning to his son he continues, "And now, young man, you and I need to have a talk."

I pause at the door hoping to catch the beginning of the conversation but Satan notices, "You are now excused, Sister Courtney. Please close the door behind you."

I obey, lingering longer than necessary outside the heavy wooden door. I don't know if they are speaking in low tones or waiting for me to walk past the window before they begin, but I can't hear a thing. Frustrated, fearing for Daniel as much as for myself, I walk away.

So much for Monday being one of my favorite days.

While rinsing the bucket with a hose, I realize I need to confront my mother about what I've just learned. Does she know about this plan to throw me in that monster's bed? I know she's bent around Father Emmanuel's little finger by faith and belief, but I just can't wrap my mind about this. She fawns over his sons, caring for them in a way she never showed me, but I know she loves me. Yet, she brought me here, and here I still am. Because it's The Lord's Will that I'm here.

Trudging painfully off to the first set of hives, I ponder on The Lord and His Will. Each step is a reminder that it's His Will that I not run away again. My mind shies away from the memory of the terrible pain of that lesson, blurring and glossing over Father Emmanuel's look of satisfaction, blocking out my mother's role in that horrific day that left me like this. I want to be sick again.

But as harsh as my mother has been in seeing to it that I submit to His Will, she's been so much worse on herself. Father Emmanuel is obsessed with male heirs, almost to the point of madness. My mother became infected, twisted by it too. Every time the ultrasounds showed her carrying another daughter, she turned suddenly clumsy, throwing herself down stairs and out of haylofts. Her zeal to please him, to please The Lord, made sure she didn't waste any time with girls. She needed them out of her as quickly as possible so she could try again to please The Lord by giving his prophet a son.

Those losses almost killed my mother, but the fire of a twisted, misplaced faith sustained her through it. The worst part of it, though, is that she doesn't blame him, doesn't see that he's an impossible tyrant. She blames *herself* for being incapable of giving him the boys he so desperately wants. She's convinced herself that she's failed him. That she's failed The Lord. You may not blame him, Mom, but I sure as hell do. And I blame you, too.

On a normal day, I'd save this cluster of hives for last, but this has not been a normal day. I need peace, I need to think, and that means I need to go to my hillside first. The crest of the hill is covered by trees, and my hives are just at the edge of the woods, hidden from the view of the miserable little cluster of buildings by a large boulder. I set it there not only because it's a perfect spot for my bees – the shallow slope is covered with wildflowers - but also because it's my favorite place in the compound. From there, I can see far away, and with my eyes lost in the horizon, dream of better days.

Today I dream about my mother deciding to run away with me. She should want to do that if she is as horrified as I am by the very idea of my marrying Satan's son.

How would it happen? Would she just wake up one day and realize that this was *wrong?* That handing me over to that sadistic monster was *wrong?* I sigh. I'd best just gloss over that part of the daydream. Get to the part where we leave, and Daniel and Joshua come with us.

Of course, there's the question of where we'd run away to.

For a long time, I dreamed about just going home. Even if my father was dead, the house hadn't vanished. It would have passed on to Mom and me. After the second time I was forced back, during the long healing, I learned otherwise. Father Emmanuel showed me a printout from a title search. My home was gone, repossessed by the bank. Could it have been fake? Perhaps. I don't know. I have no idea what a genuine title search would look like.

If I knew where Sean was, I'd go to him in a heartbeat. When we were little, he was my protector. When my dad came back from war with only one leg, there were kids that made fun of me for having a cripple for a dad, or who asked how many babies my father had killed. Thanks to Sean, none of them did it more than once. Would he still stand up for me today? It's been so long since then.

Where is he now? What is he doing? Is he even still in the Navy? Lying on the grass in the shade of my boulder, I look up at puffy white clouds overhead. White, like a sailor's uniform. I have to giggle at the thought of oh-so-serious Sean Pearse, coming home to me from work all dressed up in a sailor suit. It seems fun and silly, but then a whole different idea hits me: what about Sean coming home from his ship to me, and I meet him at the door wearing his uniform?

In my mind, I see his eyes light up as my hips sway to a beat only the two of us hear, and I slowly discard each piece of the uniform, one at a time, leaving a trail of white fabric all the way to our bedroom. And when my beloved can't wait until we get to the bedroom? Well, truth be told, neither can I.

Living on a farm for all this time has left me a solid working knowledge of the mechanics of the act. I've seen the cows and the sheep and the goats, and I've helped in birthing calves and lambs – but anything beyond the physical side? A woman married five years should have no mysteries or curiosities left in the bedroom, but then, very few women have had a marriage like mine.

What would he like? What would make him happy? What would make him want me most? I don't even know anymore, but I try to guess in my daydream. But that's all it is: just a daydream. It's not real. In my mind, he comes home to me every day, and I have nothing to fear with my protector there. In my imagination, there is no pain when I walk, and when I dance for him, I do it on two perfect, straight legs. Two legs I can wrap around him and … *mmm.*

Oh, Sean. Where are you now? I hope you're well, and happy, wherever you are. I miss you so much.

He's not here, but I won't let that bring me down. No. I'm twenty-three years old. I still have an entire life ahead of me. It doesn't really matter if I don't know precisely where my next home will be. What really matters is that I know it's somewhere out *there*, because one thing is absolutely certain: it has never been and never will be here in this godforsaken community.

Chapter 4

Sean

Thursday Morning, 11 August 2016

Mom's gone to work by the time I get up in the morning, and I'm alone in the house with my new stepfather.

I've known William Dwyer my whole life. He and his wife Heather—ex-wife now, I guess—were our neighbors. I babysat for their daughter Courtney when I was in junior high and high school.

Bill and my dad grew up together, went to high school together. They joined the Army together. They got out together, bought houses next door to each other. They got jobs at the shipyard, repairing and refitting the McGuire Line's ships. After 9/11, they both signed up for the Maine Army National Guard with the 172nd out of the Brewer armory. They volunteered for active duty augmentation, and they went to Iraq. They got blown up together in the Second Battle of Fallujah in 2004.

But they didn't come home together. Bill Dwyer went to Landstuhl in Germany where the docs patched him up enough that he could go to Walter Reed Medical

Center, then back to Maine. Dad made it home a lot faster than his best friend. He was a week in the ground in the Togus National Cemetery before Bill was airlifted to Walter Reed.

I come downstairs, drawn by the smell of coffee. Bill's in the kitchen – I hear dishes clinking.

"Morning, Sean. Welcome home." Bill's graying now, and smaller than I remember. When I was a kid he was a bear of a man – hugely strong, solid. Tough. A dark haired, bearded lumberjack's reflection of my dad's clean-shaven blond runner's build. He's wasted away now, scarcely bulkier than I am. The prosthetic left leg he earned in Fallujah sticks out below the hem of his shorts, and he walks over to me with a cane.

"Hey, Bill. Congratulations. On the wedding, I mean. I wish I could have been there." He nods, his face serious.

"Thank you, I appreciate it. I wanted to come with your mom last night to pick you up, but I had to work."

"What do you do now?"

"Pretty hard to drag a toolbox around a shipyard with this leg. I'm still working for McGuire, though. I supervise the night shift security where the tankers unload. Pay isn't spectacular, but with the VA check, it's not too bad, and your mom's still a nurse at Maine Med, of course."

"Huh." No idea what to say, there. "I'm glad you're doing well."

"Well enough. Better than some of the leading alternatives, I guess." He reaches into the cupboard for a coffee mug and passes it to me. It's my dad's mug. On one side is the United States Army seal, on the other, old English letters spell out my father's rank and name: SSGT KEVIN PEARSE. Bill fills it about three-quarters full. "What do you take in your coffee?"

"Nothing, thanks. Just black."

"I wasn't talking about cream and sugar." He hooks a thumb over at the counter where a bottle of Jameson's rests. "This is nighttime for me, remember? There's the Irish, and I've probably got some bourbon around."

"Ah. Yeah, Jameson's works. What the hell, I don't have anything big to do today."

"Yeah, I was gonna ask about that, see what your plans are."

"Don't have any, right now. I haven't taken any time off in the last four years, so I've got sixty days of terminal leave and the other sixty days of leave cashed out. Got some time to figure things out. Hadn't really counted on the whole job search thing just yet, y'know? I'd planned on doing my twenty, at least. Military's drawing down now, cutting troop strength. They offered me a medical retirement. I asked what my other option was and they said wait until the end of my enlistment and go home without anything. So, here I am. Medically retired at age twenty-five."

"At least you're home alive. Melissa worried about you so much. Every single day you were gone she was over at Immaculate Conception lighting a candle for you."

"Really? She stopped going to mass after Dad died." Bill shrugs.

"She didn't want to lose another man."

"Huh." We drink our coffee – and whiskey – in silence for a time. I'm comfortable around Bill. I always have been. Now there's another level to it; he's been there, done that, got the scars. He gets it. Bill breaks the silence first.

"Your truck. You might want to put some new tires on it, but I've kept up the registration. Insurance is good to go. It's got a new inspection sticker. Oil's fresh, got a tune-up last week. Tires were too expensive though, I'm sorry. Couldn't afford them. I've driven her around a little bit, just a few miles a week to keep everything lubricated and running right."

"I appreciate what you've done, Bill. It means the world to me. Not just what you've done for me, but for Mom, too."

"Your mom's a good woman, Sean. I love her dearly." I nod. "Brings up another point. Just because your mother and I got married ... what I'm trying to say is ..." I wave my hand at him.

"Don't worry about it, Bill. It's cool. I'm glad you've both got someone. Speaking of which though, what happened? With Heather? That was all long after I was gone."

"Heather didn't want me to go back to the Army. That was one thing." Bill finishes off his coffee, and after a long look at the pot through narrowed eyes he skips the caffeine and goes straight for the Jameson's instead. "After I came back from Iraq like this--" he waves a hand at his prosthetic "--she put up with it for a while. A few years. She up and left about a year after you enlisted." He cocks his head to the side. "How much do you know about Heather? About before we got married?"

"Nothing, I guess." I shake my head with a shrug and Bill nods.

"Right. She's a lot younger than your mom and dad and me. Heather was a runaway. She grew up in one of those fundamentalist splinter group things, but she never really talked about it much. They had a compound, some kind of a farm thing, but she wouldn't go into details, didn't ever tell me where it was." My new stepfather frowns down at the table, tapping a finger as he considers how to tell the rest of the story.

"Anyway," he finally continues, "Heather couldn't ever get her head really straightened out, never dealt with it. She threw herself into being a wife and mother, but something was always, I dunno, just not *right*. She wanted to be happy, wanted it *so* badly, but something was missing inside her, or broken. She tried. God knows she tried, but it didn't work." Bill sighs, raps the table with his knuckles once then turns his head away as if he can't bear to look at the table or the mug in his hands any longer.

"After Iraq, after I came back a cripple, Heather started to fall apart. She stopped going to mass, but she spent hours and hours every day with her head buried in a Bible. King James Version, the Protestant thing, not the Douay-Rheims or one of the other Catholic versions. She got obsessive, 'the wages of sin is death,' right? So, your dad and I were sinners, obviously. I was spared because of *her*. Because she was working to *redeem* me." Bill snorts derisively. "This leg, well, it was a warning. Anyway, I tried to humor her. We started going to church, but it just wasn't going to work. It took a while for it all to finally come crashing down, though. She finally left about a year after you went off to the Navy."

"Sorry, man."

"Is what it is, Sean. It is what it is."

"How's Courtney? Do you ever get to see her?"

"Fuck if I know." He shrugs fatalistically. "I haven't seen her since Heather left. Heather drove me up to the VA hospital again. It was supposed to be a two-day thing, more work on my leg, but soon's I got checked in, she hands me this thick yellow envelope, tells me she's leaving me. She's not willing to stand by and let my- how did she put it? Oh yes, my *obstinate sinfulness* drag her and Courtney down too. So, divorce papers. And she drove straight home and picked up Courtney and they were in the wind. I've never seen them again."

"Not once?" I'm incredulous. "Nobody can just disappear completely. And you've got rights, don't you? I mean, what happened during the divorce?"

"Well, as for the divorce, she never showed up for court. Judge asked me what I wanted, and of course, I was hurt and angry and so I said fine, gimme the divorce and I wanted everything. Judge ruled her in default and gave it to me. So, I had full custody technically, but it's awfully difficult to exercise your custodial rights when you have no idea where your child and her mom are. Even the cops couldn't find them. That's ... actually sort of the start of how your mom and I got together." Bill smiles faintly, fidgeting with his mug, intently studying the pattern on the tablecloth. "That was actually the one bright spot to come out of the whole mess."

"How's that?" I'm uncomfortable prying, but I have been curious.

"I spent every penny I had on private investigators, trying to find my daughter. Every single penny and then some. Mortgaged the house and lost it. Your mom gave me the spare room here, helped me get back on my feet. No matter what I've done for her, what I've done for you, it can't ever even start to make the smallest dent in the debt I owe her." Bill's face is carefully expressionless, his voice is matter-of-fact. Only his eyes give away any hint of how deeply he feels the truth of what he says.

"Did you ever find anything? Any trace of Courtney?" *Best to change the subject.*

"Couple hints, here and there. Heather grew up on some sort of church farm, a cult compound sort of place, so that was the first thing I tried to find. There was some talk about a farm somewhere back in the beginning, maybe some sort of Jonestown thing. Couple investigators thought it was over in Vermont, maybe upstate New York or over the border in Canada, but nothing ever panned out. I even sent people out west, poking around Arizona and Utah, out where some of the polygamist groups are."

"And nothing since then?"

"Heather's off the grid. Totally." He pauses. "There was ... one thing. It's just a maybe, and at this point. Courtney's been an adult for a long time now, Sean. She's, what, twenty-three? Couple years younger than you are. She's free to come and go as she pleases now." He shrugs, staring down into his coffee mug morosely. "If she wanted anything to do with me, I can't believe she wouldn't have reached out to me by now."

"What was it? The 'one thing' you got?" Bill stands with difficulty, and using the cane he limps heavily to the china cabinet and pulls a folded sheet of paper out from under a stack of plates.

"This is it. Seven years, just over seven years now. This is the only sniff." He slides the paper across the table to me and I unfold it. It's a picture printed out on an inkjet, probably taken with a cell phone camera. It shows a table at what looks like a farmer's market. There's a variety of early produce on the table – rhubarb, mushrooms, green onions, some tomatoes and cucumbers that probably came from a hothouse. Wild fiddleheads.

"Looks like springtime stuff at a farmer's market? Fiddleheads, you can only get those in what, April? May?"

"Yeah. Saw this picture in the Press-Herald back in early May, and yeah – the article was about farmers' markets. Went to the website, printed it out. But look here." He taps on the paper. There's an indistinct, slightly out of focus view of the next table over. Two women are standing there. I haven't seen Heather or Courtney in eight years, so I can't really say if it's them or not.

"I don't really remember Heather all that well, Bill. Courtney... It's hard to make out details, especially when they're facing away from the camera."

I remember Courtney vividly, though, the shape of her, the feel of her in my arms, of her body pressed against mine that day at the bus station. Every day for the past eight years, I've remembered that.

The girl in the picture is facing away from the camera, I can't see her face. She's got the right blond hair, though.

"I know. Just, something about the way this one's standing. It makes me think it's Heather. Looks thinner'n I remember, but it could be her. Can't see their faces, but if that's Heather then ... is the girl my daughter?" I look again, trying to reconcile the girl in the picture against my memories of the bright, funny girl I grew up with. At seven, eight years old she'd been a precocious little terror tagging along after me, and by the time I'd left for the Navy, she had developed a fearsome intellect and a heartbreakingly beautiful set of curves that eight years of war couldn't drive out of my thoughts.

"I can't tell, man." I fold the picture again, give it back to Bill. "Where was it taken?"

"I talked to the reporter about it, but he didn't know who they were, what farm they were with. He couldn't even remember much about them at all, other than what market he'd taken it at."

"Sounds like a pretty lousy reporter," I observe. "Didn't he keep notes or something?"

"Well, yeah, but the guy wasn't talking to them," Bill tells me. "He was talking to the people running the next booth over, those two were just in the background."

"Right," I say. "Makes sense. So, where was it?"

"Greenville. Up north, near the southern end of Moosehead Lake."

"Huh." I don't want to pick at old scabs, pry at old wounds, but at the same time, I don't really have anything planned for the next couple of months, and I do know the area. My dad and I, and my grandfather when he was alive, used to camp around Moosehead for hunting and fishing, though I haven't been since Dad died. Maybe I could take a run up to Greenville and have a look. Can't say anything about it though. Don't want to get his hopes up. I'll have a talk with Mom about it after Bill's gone to work.

"Well, lad, that's about it for me for the day. I'm off for bed, I think."

"Yeah. I'm going to check out my truck, go have a look around Portland. Get some new tires, maybe." Another idea perks me up. "Also, they don't have a lot of Dunkin' Donuts in the shitholes I've been visiting lately, and I've got this odd urge for a cruller." Bill laughs at that.

"You're a Mainer, right enough." We both stand, and he clasps my forearm. His thumb lands on the gnarled ridge of scar tissue that runs from my wrist nearly to the elbow of my left arm. "Shit," he says, looking at it. "What was that one?"

"Shrapnel, I guess." I shrug. "Caught a piece of something or other." I say. I know exactly what it was, and when it happened, and where. It was a Russian-made 122 mm artillery rocket, part of a quick hit-and-fade by Taliban forces. Just thinking about it brings to mind the line of white-hot pain as the fragment creased my arm. I don't really feel like talking about it, but if there's anyone I would ever be able to share that shit with, it'd be Bill Dwyer.

Once he's gone upstairs to bed, I chug the rest of the mug of high-octane coffee and head out to the side yard after rinsing my dad's cup. My truck is parked under an awning, and it looks like Bill did take good care of it. It's a 1987 Chevy Blazer, one of the big K5 models. The two-tone blue paint sparkles with a fresh coat of wax. It must have been a lot of work for Bill to reach everywhere to do that with his prosthetic – the lift kit isn't huge, but there's some very high places on The Beast. I appreciate him even more now.

The big 350 V8 kicks over easily and catches on the first crank. I love this truck– I've had it since I got my license. I saved up my money for three years prior – babysitting, mowing lawns, summers in the blueberry packing sheds near my grandparents' house. Every spare penny I could scrape together went into buying The Beast. The four-wheel drive, ground clearance, and solid axles have gotten me into – and out of, fortunately – a whole variety of stupid situations, and I wouldn't trade it for anything.

The tires, yeah, they're pretty rough. Paulin's over on Forest Ave should have just what I need in stock, and while I wait, there's another priority mission to undertake. Should be an easy one though. No matter where you go in Maine, there's almost always a Dunkin' Donuts within walking distance.

I have plenty of time to think while I wait for my truck to be ready.

I'd been looking forward to my cruller for so long, but my first look at the twisted-up golden-brown pastry puts me in mind of a long-ago early summer afternoon, and a wrist-thick braid of golden-brown hair. Lost in memory, my cruller is gone and I'm licking sticky glaze off my fingertips before I even realize I've started eating.

I'd been fourteen when the roadside bomb killed my father and maimed hers; she was twelve. We'd been playmates as children, and though we'd drifted apart in junior high, we crashed back together tighter than ever, clinging to each other desperately for support. The next three years brought us ever closer, and she almost always spent the night in our spare bedroom whenever Bill had to suffer through another procedure on the long, hard road to recovery.

At some point, and I can't remember when it happened, I began to notice her as more than my best friend. I'd been desperately in love with Courtney Dwyer for all of high school, but I was painfully shy, and she was younger than me. Two years difference? In your thirties, that's no big deal, but in high school, it's enough distance that it might as well have been the Grand Canyon between us. I'd never said anything to her, and never imagined she might have felt the same about me, but that kiss at the bus station...

An entire world of fantasy rolls itself out in my head. What might have happened had I not left? Hazy and indistinct at first, but details settle out. I've followed in my dad's footsteps at the shipyard instead of the military. It's hard work, but it's let us buy a small house, and Courtney can stay home with-- children? Maybe.

I can almost feel the doorknob in my hand, coming home at the end of the day, and hear the slap of tiny feet against wood floors. Small children barrel into me, looking for hugs, just like I did to my own dad. And Courtney's there, smiling, greeting me with a kiss and an impish smile.

"Hey, Sean," she says. "If you'd just sign here, I'll give you your keys."

My what?

Keys.

There's a pang of regret as the homey scene in my imagination vanishes, and a man with greasy hands is holding a clipboard to me, jingling my keys with his free hand.

"Sorry, man." I'm embarrassed to have been caught daydreaming like that. It's been happening too much since I've been home. I'm not as alert as I should be. One quick scribble later, I'm back behind the wheel of my truck, but I'm not ready to drive away yet. Sitting there in the parking lot, watching cars go by, there's still a remnant of regret.

Why do I feel a sense of loss? That life was never real. I never had it—her—to lose. A silly daydream shouldn't affect me so much. It does solidify something for me, though. That out-of-focus picture wasn't much to go on. I couldn't tell if it was Courtney or not, but I want to find out.

Bill's pain and hopelessness affected me this morning, and I'd already been half-seriously considering the idea of going up to Greenville to chase the wild goose on his behalf, but now? I won't lie, not even to myself and pretend I'm doing this just for him. If I can find something that will help ease Bill's sorrow, that's great, but I'd like to see Courtney Dwyer again for my own reasons. I need to know if there really is a reason I should regret leaving her behind all those years ago.

But what happens when—no, if—I find her?

Chapter 5

Courtney

Thursday Evening, 11 August 2016

It's already dusk when I wake up.

Jeremiah took a toll on me this morning. I laid down in the shade for five minutes to daydream and it turned into sleeping away the whole day.

For the briefest of moments, I consider spending the night here and just going back in the morning, but that's probably not a good idea for a couple of reasons. First, someone spotted a mama bear with four cubs out here just yesterday. Second – and perhaps more importantly – if Daniel sees I didn't come home and he starts asking around after me, they'll think I've run. The last thing I need is for that to happen. The last thing that *Daniel* needs is for that to happen.

I hike back down the hill, through a field of berries and back to the flimsy garden shed I share with my husband to change clothes. It's already time for evening prayers, and it wouldn't do for me to show up with grass stains all over my dress. I'm about to join the crowd of worshipers in the chapel when I notice a door ajar on the low north wall of the refectory building: the shower.

When I push it open, the air is still misty but all the booths are empty.

Should I indulge in a special treat? An afterhours shower? With no one around to tell me I have to be miserable, forcing me to be quick about it? I'll be able to enjoy the luxury, make it last.

A glance at the shelves in the corner finds there's one dry towel left. I snatch it up and undress quickly in a stall. Obviously, this is a sign that The Lord's Plan calls for one more shower to be taken tonight. As a true believer, I have no choice but to follow His Will.

A light turn of the faucet and a quick step back-- that's the start of the shower roulette ritual. The temperature and the pressure are inconsistent, variable. It's anyone's guess whether you'll freeze or boil on that first try. I wait a few seconds and continue the ceremony, by testing the water with my fingers. I'm in luck, the flow is steady and warm. Silent thanks go to whomever was here before me for not using up all the hot water and I ease into the sinfully delicious warmth, savoring the pounding droplets on my neck.

I rest two hands on the slimy walls while the water rushes through my hair and down my back. With my eyes closed, I can almost believe I'm back in the house where I grew up, back in the shower in my pink tiled bathroom. I was so spoiled then. I had no idea what an absolute luxury it was to enjoy something as simple as comfort and privacy in a modern bathroom.

By the time I'm finished rinsing, the water is going cold. I'm still a bit damp when I slide back into my clothes and wrap the towel around my hair. I'll return it tomorrow.

Detouring around the main house and the chapel to avoid being seen coming from the showers, I double back to my home around the far end of the row of pathetic shacks. Light seeps through the wood cracks around the door of the pitiful hovel that was our wedding present. With a greeting and a smile on my lips, I open the door to go inside.

Everything in the shack is upside down, and my mother stands in the middle of the wreckage. Her face is serene, but her eyes are on fire. Her hands are clasped in front of her as if in prayer. This is the mother that terrifies me. This is the one who brought me here, who screams about sin and penance and salvation. This is the woman that stood by and watched that day after the second time I ran.

Jeremiah stands beside her, and Daniel is nowhere to be seen.

My thin mattress is a tattered ruin, and the intricate patchwork quilt that I spent months sewing by hand has been shredded. Stuffing from both covers the floor like an obscene snowfall. All my hard work, gone in an instant, and I won't have time to make a new quilt before winter.

Everything in my home has been opened and torn apart. Clothes lie everywhere, the small chest of drawers is smashed and broken. The old battery-powered clock on the wall is destroyed. Even the wooden pallet frame that raised the mattress off the floor is a splintered ruin.

Nothing of mine has been spared, not even my Bible. Pages lie scattered, and the cover hangs, sad and empty, off the edge of the shelf. I notice that even the cover has been ripped apart, and the note my father had written to me on the inside is destroyed. They'd never have dared to desecrate what they thought of as a *real* Bible, but mine carried all the 'pagan superstition' and 'heathen apostasy' of the Apocrypha. It was the only thing I had left from my father, and now it's gone too.

My eyes slowly fill with tears as I try to make some sense of the destruction around me, and I take a deep breath. No. This is good. I have nothing left to lose here any longer. My heart hardens with a new resolve. Right. I don't care how, but I will get away from this place. Away from these insane people. Willing away my tears, I brace and glare at the two people standing in the middle of my ransacked home.

"Why?" I ask, proud of the steadiness in my voice.

Jeremiah looks away, but my mother stares back at me, stepping closer. From this distance, the insane sparkle in her eyes is even more disturbing. What happened to you, Mom? Was this something that was always inside you? Or did Emmanuel do something to you to bring you over to the dark side?

"We know," she says, so softly I hardly can hear her. "We know everything. Just tell the truth, repent now and I promise Father Emmanuel will make it all better." The sweet pleading in her voice is meant to be reassuring, but overlaid with that fire glowing in her eyes, it's only more disturbing.

"Mother," I say, hiding my anger and fear under the calmest voice I can manage. "I have *no* idea what you are talking about."

"Don't you lie to us, woman!" Jeremiah finally speaks, and I shake my head in despair.

The tiny room is silent for a few seconds while I wait for him to say more. He bides his time, but my mother runs out of patience first and gives me a hint, "Nathan saw it *all!*"

"He saw all... of..." Oh, Daniel, I begged you to be careful. What did you do in public?

"He saw you stealing from us!" Jeremiah yells.

I'm so lost in my private terror for my husband that his words don't register immediately, and when they do I have to fight to keep the puzzled look on my face. Finally. They're talking about money. The little shit saw me making change and pocketing dollar bills. I'm ready for this. Oh, I'm so ready for this. If I wasn't talking with crazy-Mom? If it was good-Mom here with me, or at least not-as-crazy-Mom, I would have had a hard time fighting back a smile.

Of course, I've squirreled away money, and of course, I've stolen it from you. I've been keeping back a few dollars here and there, saving toward the next time I ran. I'm not stupid, though. I don't keep it here in my home, and I don't set it aside when anyone is around to see me doing it!

"He saw me do what, now?" I ask. I've already got a plan in place to deal with this one, so let's just get it over with. I need to get my mother calmed down, and then I need to find something to sleep on.

"I saw you put money in your pocket," Nathan is standing by the door behind me. He's not alone. His mother is with him, holding a small bottle of water and some pills.

Rebecca pushes me aside, ascertains the condition of the room with a quick look around and walks past Jeremiah, shaking her head at him as if he was an unruly child. She reaches my mother and gives her the water with a pill to swallow. Mom obediently takes the medication. It's like a game they play. Rebecca has to hunt my mother every day to make sure she's medicated. I don't know what Satan has her on, but tonight I hope it's some sort of tranquilizer. She seems about to explode.

"Come now, Sister Heather. Tonight you can sleep in the infirmary," Rebecca says as she escorts my mother out of my ravaged home. I watch them start to walk away, and Rebecca turns to call her son. The little snitch is still glued to the door, not wanting to miss even a second of the showdown he's orchestrated.

Just as I hiss at him, he silently shakes his head. His lips move, soundlessly mouthing *I'm sorry* before running away. He may have been raised to be a miserable little monster, an inquisitor ferreting out the tiniest scraps of sin, but there is still good left in him, some shred of conscience, of empathy. I hate myself for thinking the worst of him. Could he even understand what he'd set in motion here?

"So you were looking for money?" I ask, turning to look at Jeremiah.

Jeremiah nods, and a wicked smile flickers across his lips.

"But that's not all that Nathan will see," he whispers, inching his way closer to me, so close I can feel his breath on face. "It would be awful if he were to witness an *abomination*. No child his age should ever have to see a thing like that."

I can guess what's coming next. Now that my mother and Rebecca are gone, now that there's nobody to see or hear, Jeremiah can use all the leverage at his command to get what he wants out of me. Hopefully all he wants tonight is the money. From the look in his eyes, he's expecting to enjoy this.

Jeremiah clenches a fist, starting to cock his arm back, and I press a hand against his chest to keep him at arm's length. It's pathetic-- his arms are so much longer than mine, and my attempt to protect myself will not matter if he swings at me. Just before he strikes, I try to pacify him by telling him why I had put money in my pocket instead of in the cash box.

"It's for Brother Jonathan," I tell him, naming the church's bookkeeper. "I don't know why he needs change, but he always asks me to break down some of the larger bills for him, and I do. You know I'm always happy to help. I'll do anything for the good of the community."

His arm slowly comes down and the anger on his face eases back to only mild annoyance and suspicion. My explanation is so easy to check. It would be stupid of me to lie to him about something like that. And the best part of it is I'm not even lying. It's the exact truth. Brother Jonathan really *does* want change in small bills. I simply don't give him all the change I bring back.

"So, yeah, Nathan saw me set some money aside, but it wasn't for me..." I keep on pleading because his mood could swing back to anger in a flash. The truth of my explanation will save me from consequences *later*, but nothing will protect me from a black eye or a bloody nose if I piss him off *now*.

"I see," he says as he turns away, absently surveying the devastation in my home. "So. I'm pleased to discover that my dear little brother simply misinterpreted what he saw. I would hate to know my wife was a thief."

His detached tone fills me with dread.

"Where is Daniel?" I ask, softly. What are you plotting now?

Jeremiah turns his back to me and reaches for the door. For a moment, I think he's going to ignore my question and just leave, but he's only pausing for dramatic effect.

"He and my father are having a serious talk about the future tonight," he tells me, without even a backward glance.

As the door swings halfway shut behind them, I want to scream. My knees are weak, shaking. They won't support me much longer. I lean against the doorframe, hugging myself for comfort, and let myself slide to the floor. For one brief instant, I'm tempted to kick over the kerosene lantern and set this miserable little hell on fire.

Resting my head on my knees, I sob quietly. I can't take this anymore. Daniel, how can you be so perversely loyal to your brother? Do you think he'll hesitate to pay you the wages of what he says is a sin? I couldn't bear to see you stoned to death, even if it didn't mean I'd be given to that monster afterward!

My getaway fund isn't huge, not yet. I've only managed to hide away a couple hundred dollars. I don't know what a bus ticket costs, but I'm sure I don't have enough to get away even to Portland, never mind somewhere far away, and certainly not enough to live on for more than a day or two. Portland isn't far enough, not to get away from these people. Boston, maybe. Or New York City? I don't know if even London or Berlin or Shanghai would be far enough away to hide.

I need to go. Somewhere else. *Anywhere* else.

I need to be free.

Chapter 6

Sean

Thursday Evening, 11 August 2016

It's been a busy couple days. I've got a mission, and that means I need intelligence and supplies. Google makes a hell of an intel shop, though, and Portland has plenty of shopping available. It's a good thing the Navy paid me out a lump sum for so much of my unused days of leave. I've burned through a big chunk of it today.

My mother is home by the time I get back from my expedition, and dinner is ready.

"You're just in time. Grab a plate," she says, waving a large brown box in front of me. I hadn't realized how hungry I was, but the smell of my favorite pizza sets my stomach rumbling. Amato's has the best you'll find in southern Maine, handmade in a chain of local delis that still use real ground beef instead of the rabbit-shit-looking processed pellets the national chains use. It's good stuff.

"Just a minute – my hands are pretty full here. Let me drop this off. I'll be right there." I put my bags in the living room for the moment, and when I come back to the kitchen, all I have left are two boxes each with a dozen mixed Dunkin' Donuts in them.

"Had a bit of a craving today, did you?" My mom is amused.

"Yeah, not sure what happened there. Why don't you take those with you for the other nurses tomorrow?"

"Thank you, they'll love that."

The pizza is just as good I remember, and when we're done, my mom asks about my shopping.

"Saw a couple bags there from Cabela's," she says. "You planning to go camping?"

"I'd sort of thought about it," I say, shrugging vaguely. "Might head up to Moosehead this weekend. It's not hunting season yet, but I picked up my license today and thought I might scout out some areas up there for November. Too late for the moose lottery this year, though."

"Scouting, huh?" She frowns, looking past me at the china cabinet where Bill has the picture stashed.

"Yeah. Blueberries are in season now, too – thought maybe I'd stop at a farmer's market and get some on the way back. Wouldn't that be nice? Fresh wild blueberries? Haven't had those in forever."

"That's all you're looking for? Signs of deer and some blueberries?" My mother has always been able to read me like a book, and her raised eyebrows say she doesn't believe for a single second that's *really* all of it.

"Of course not," I say. "You know just as well as I do what I'm thinking about here. My question is, why hasn't Bill gone up there himself?"

"I think he's afraid to." Mom sighs. "What if it's not them? I mean, he doesn't want Heather back, but he wants to at least know his little girl is alive and okay. If he goes up there and he doesn't find them? Or if he *does* find them, and it's not Courtney? I think he feels like he'll have lost her all over again." It makes sense in a sad sort of way.

"What if it *is* them?"

"What if it is?" She shrugs. "What if she doesn't want anything to do with him? That Heather was always a poisonous little bitch, and who knows what she's done to that poor girl's head. I think he'd rather just believe that it's Courtney and go on suffering, rather than risk confirming it and having her reject him."

"Tough spot there," I say.

"That it is." My mother nods sadly. "So what exactly are you planning to do?"

"Pretty much exactly what I said." I shrug. "I *do* want to spend a little time in the woods. Go to some of the places we used to camp with Dad. The farmer's market in Greenville happens on Saturdays and Sundays. I'll check it out, see what I see, and then come home with whatever I find out."

"If you want to hunt this fall, why not go up to the camp?"

"I think I'd like a little more wilderness than that, right now. I'll probably stop in there on the way home, though, check on things." The hunting camp on Tilden Pond in Belmont has been in the family a long time. Buried deep in the woods of Waldo County, it has a comfortable little cabin with a well and easy access to the small lake. Good fishing there, too. "Plus, of course, I'm curious about Courtney myself. She was a nice kid. I'd kind of like to know what happened to her, and I owe Bill that much at least for taking care of The Beast for me. Never mind taking care of you." My mom blushes a little, but smiles softly.

"We've taken care of each other." She clears her throat. "I miss your dad, and Bill will never replace him, but he's not trying to."

"Yeah, I know." Jesus, this conversation went depressing all of a sudden.

Mom sighs, then smiles wistfully at me.

"And what about you, Sean? You're not going to all that trouble just on Bill's account." Her knowing look makes me feel like a guilty six-year-old again, caught in some transparent subterfuge. I stay awkwardly silent, shifting uncomfortably and Mom chuckles.

"My Lord, the two of you." Her smile grows and she shakes her head. "Even a blind man could see you were pining over each other for years. Everyone except the two of you, I guess."

"Was I that obvious?"

"Oh, honey, you have no idea." Her laughter is bright now, cheerful. "You were her hero when you were just six or seven, and she had a wicked bad crush on you *years* before you ever started to think about her that way. Your father," she breaks off, making the sign of the cross before continuing, "God rest his soul, he and I always thought the two of you would wind up together."

"Never underestimate the stupidity of teenagers, Mom."

"Well, who knows? Maybe you'll actually find her," she says. "Maybe there'll still be something there?" Another laugh, hearty, full of humor. "But, oh, Sean," she gasps. "There might be a problem with that."

"Problem?" I ask. "You mean, a problem aside from the whole needle-in-haystack, Lost City of Gold, forlorn hope, aspect of it?"

My mother bounces with anticipation, smirking wickedly at me.

"Sean, what do you call a girl when your parents are married?" Delighted peals of hilarity pour out of her as my jaw drops.

"Oh, *shit.*"

"Watch your mouth, Sean." There's no sting in her rebuke, though. Only warmth and happiness.

"You know, I hadn't even put two and two together on that point. Sh- sorry, Mom. *Crap*, I mean. I really had not thought about that. She's my stepsister now." That's a cold bucket of water right in the face.

But my mother takes pity on me.

"I'm sorry," she says, a contrite expression on her face. "I shouldn't have made a joke out of it like that." Another giggle. "I just couldn't help myself."

"God." I put my head down, face in my hands. "Why'd you have to bring that up?"

"Relax," she says. "It's not like you're actually *related*. You two were head over heels in love *years* before her father and your mother ever had even the first impure thought about each other."

"Christ, Mom! Like this wasn't already an awkward enough conversation."

"Oh, get over yourself, Sean." She smiles warmly at me, then walks over and hugs me. "Who knows what'll happen if you ever do meet her again. Maybe you'll just purely hate each other now."

"Never know, I guess." I laugh. The awkwardness is broken. "But, yeah. *If*. I'm not really getting my hopes up on this. I'd like to see her again, yeah, but I know the odds are against finding her this weekend." I shake my head. "This is all pretty fu- *messed* up. Why didn't you ever tell me what happened to Courtney?"

"First off, I didn't really have anything useful to tell you, and second—why didn't *you* ever ask?"

It's a good question. Why *didn't* I ever ask? "She never answered the last letter I wrote her. I always figured she'd just moved on." I shrug. "It's true, as far as it goes. I didn't want to be pushy, didn't want to keep bothering her if she didn't want the attention. If she wanted to write to me, she could have. Or so I always thought."

"Idiot." Mom stands on tiptoes, reaching up to cuff me fondly on the back of the head. "So you just sat there suffering in noble silence for all these years?"

"Like I said, never underestimate--"

"Yeah, yeah. Whatever." Mom waves her hand and rolls her eyes at me.

"Okay, let's take a look at the stuff I bought today." I get up and bring the bags back to the kitchen table.

"Oh, you got a new phone?" My mom picks out the bag from the AT&T store right off.

"Yep. Might as well, right? My old one... I carried that thing all over Afghanistan and Iraq, figured I deserve an upgrade. According to the coverage map, I should be good to go in the whole area around Moosehead, so that's something." I shake my head – I can still barely believe the north Maine woods has cell service. There's a population density of somewhere around two people per square mile up there.

"Oh, fancy. Look at you, all rich with a new phone!"

"Yeah, not rich for long at this rate," I say. "I've got a pension, but it's not enough to just lay around on the couch all day. I'm going to have to find a job at some point."

"About that," she says. "Bill can probably pull some strings, get you on at McGuire, in their security department. Big tough SEAL? You shouldn't have any trouble getting in there even without connections."

"It's something to think about." I shrug noncommittally and she drops the subject.

"What'd you get at Cabelas?" she asks, poking at the next bag.

"GPS, one of the ones they make for hikers and hunters. Some cheap night vision, a few other things. New pocketknife. Some clothes. Nothing really interesting." I try to shuffle things around so my mom doesn't notice the bag from CVS, but it doesn't work. Why did I want to look at my purchases with her around? That was just a stupid idea.

"What'd you get at the drug store?"

"Oh, ah, batteries mostly. Some ibuprofen to take along." I try to push that bag to the side and keep it closed.

"Awful big bag for that," she says, opening it up, and I cringe as her eyes go wide. "Now Sean, you know I'll love you and be proud of you no matter what, but is there something here you want to talk about?" She laughs as she pulls out the box of tampons, another box of overnight maxi pads, and the pantyhose. "And oh, look at this! Condoms! You're all set for a nice weekend here!"

"Yeah, great, Mom. I'm glad you find this so amusing." I really have no reason to be embarrassed by this, but for some reason I am. "Okay, so condoms are good for waterproofing things. Batteries. Detonators. Get the unlubricated ones, you can put things inside and tie off the end. They're useful, and the ones in the kit in the truck are probably all dried out and worthless by now. Pads and tampons? Best first aid supplies ever. Some quick work with tampons saved my life in Iraq, plugging up a couple bullet holes and stopping the bleeding. Pantyhose make great tourniquets and compression for bandages."

"You're not expecting to actually need this stuff are you?" Mom's face is suddenly serious.

"No, but it's better to have it and not need it than to need it and not have it. Speaking of which, I want to get into the toy box." Wordlessly, my mom digs in her purse for her keys and pulls one off the ring, hands it to me. "Mom, I'm not *planning* to get into trouble, and I'm not looking for it. I just want to be ready if it finds me."

"Son, you've had enough trouble already to last you a dozen lifetimes," she sighs.

"You wear your seatbelt every time you get in a car, right? Not just when you're planning to crash it?"

I stand, ready to head for the basement where my dad's gun safe lives, but Mom catches at my sleeve. "Take your shirt off, Sean. I want to see how the doctors did putting you back together."

She's all business now--my mother, the nurse. Professional fingers probe at the puckered scars of entry and exit wounds on my chest, back and abdomen, the slashes of scar where emergency surgeons removed my spleen and one kidney. The line through the sleeve tattoo on my left forearm. Another, a big one, twisted and gnarled, on the right side of my chest.

"They did good work. Crude, but good." I shrug.

"I'm still alive, so they must have done okay."

"Last night," she begins, then hesitates, biting her lip. "I heard you, when you were asleep. Are you having nightmares?" There's concern in her eyes, worry. Love.

"What, me? Big strong SEAL? Stone cold killer having nightmares?" I look away. She doesn't need me to answer. She already knows, and sighs heavily. I don't want to get into it – how could I ever tell her about the terrible beauty of that alley? The pain, the fear. Seeing my five closest friends chewed up by machine gun fire in an ambush? The symmetry of shooting back, the guilty adrenaline rush. Killing.

"If you need someone to talk to, Sean – at the hospital, we've got some people. The cops go to them, after..."

"No, it's fine. Time, that's all I need." Yeah, that's not going to fucking happen. A cop shrink? What good's that gonna do me?

"Okay. Just ... take care of yourself, okay?" She yawns, stretches. "Oh, my Lord. I need to go to bed – four o'clock comes early. These twelve hour shifts are killing me." Another yawn. "Overtime's nice, though."

"Wake me when you get up, okay? I want to get an early start tomorrow. I'd like to spend a little time by myself in the woods before, y'know, Saturday. Before I go and, um, buy some blueberries."

"I will." My mother hugs me tightly, kisses me on the cheek. "I love you, Sean. I'm so proud of you, and so happy you're home safe again." Her face crinkles a bit, though, and she says, "You ought to shave. You're getting scruffy."

"I thought about that. I think I'm going to keep it for a bit. Might be a good idea to be less recognizable, in case ..."

"... in case that *is* Heather," she says, and I nod.

"Yeah. I'd rather she not recognize me right off if she is there. I'd like to feel things out a little bit first."

"Good thinking. Okay, I'm going to bed now. You'd best go soon yourself if you plan to get up that early tomorrow." Mom pats me on my scruffy cheek.

"I will. I want to get the truck packed up tonight, and I still need to get some stuff out of the toy box."

The basement is a typical New England cellar. It stays cold year round, and it's damp. Musty. When dad set up the gun safe here, he had to go to some extraordinary lengths for dehumidification to keep the guns from rusting. The key easily pops the lock open allowing me to turn the handle and retract the locking bolts, and the heavy door swings smoothly. Racks and racks of rifles and pistols lay within.

The pistol is an easy choice. My dad's old Beretta 92FS lies on the top shelf of the safe, and I snatch it up along with three spare fifteen-round magazines and two boxes of 9 mm cartridges.

Rifle's a tougher call. What am I going to take with me? I'm not expecting trouble, but it's pretty standard practice around here to have a rifle under the back seat of a truck, or on a rack in the back window. My fingers linger over the cold blue steel of the old Winchester I used to take down my first deer when I was ten, but then I skip over it to the next option, an AR-15.

It looks a lot like the M4 I carried as a SEAL, but the Colt AR-15 is a civilian weapon, not a machine gun like its military cousin. It's also a little longer to meet minimum-length laws. This should suit my needs perfectly – the M4 was my closest companion for six years as a Naval Special Warfare Operator, and the AR is close enough that I'll be okay with it. Five magazines, thirty rounds each, go into the bag with my pistols mags, and a half-case of cartridges come along for the ride, too. Five hundred rounds should be enough to handle anything short of Canada invading. Might get some time for a little practice out in the wilderness, too.

Packing the truck is easy – my camping gear was all carefully stored before I left for the Navy, and the bags go in the back of the Blazer in a specific order I still know from long practice even after long years away. I'm as ready as I can possibly get.

Mom was right, though: it *is* getting late, and four in the morning *will* come far too early. I need to get some sleep. When I finally close my eyes, I know I'm heading straight back to that alley in Sadr City, again.

Maybe this time it'll end differently?

Chapter 7

Courtney

Friday Morning, 12 August 2016

"Courtney! Courtney, wake up!"

Startled out of my sleep, I jerk up and hit my head against the frame of the upper bunk.

Upper bunk? What upper bunk? I'm in the women's dormitory. Why'm I not at home with Daniel? I rub my sore forehead and shift on the bed. As I sit on the edge, mindful of the metal frame above me, flashes of yesterday come back to me.

Kneeling next to me, little Jennifer covers her mouth with a chubby hand. She's trying very hard to hide a giggle. You are too sweet, so innocent. Seeing you smile always fills me with joy.

"It's okay, baby," I tell her, grinning ruefully. "You can laugh. When I was little, I'd have laughed at a grownup who did that, too." I look around, but no one else seems to have noticed my presence. The other girls are walking to or from the bathroom with their toothbrushes and towels. The teenagers are chatting away and the younger girls jumping around, oblivious to anything that could come and spoil this wonderful summer day.

"What are you doing here?" Jennifer asks. "You never stay here in the summer. You say it's too hot in here at night!"

"You're right! It is too warm," I say, grabbing the little girl and tickling her. "There's almost fifty little monsters like you in here and that's just way too many people in this small space!"

"So why were you here last night?" She's not one to be easily distracted, my little Jennie. She gets hold of a question, she's not letting go.

It saddens me to realize that her inquisitive nature will be dangerous for her, growing up here. "Daniel couldn't come home last night," I tell her. "He was doing something important and had to stay out very late." Is that the truth? I hope it's the truth. I want it to be. Please, God, let it be the truth. Let him come back today, safe and sound. "I didn't want to be alone so I figured I could spend the night here and count on you to give me my morning hug," I finish, holding out my arms to her.

Jennifer's smile grows as she jumps on my knees and we snuggle.

"I swear you must have been a cat in your last life!" I laugh, rubbing her back.

"Meow!"

Jennie's parents are not bad people, they're just... they're *dedicated*. They believe, absolutely and utterly, in the divine inspiration of Father Emmanuel and his New

Revelation. They throw themselves so fully into this life, into serving their prophet, that they barely even remember they have a child. Do they not see how much their daughter is starving for attention? How much potential she has? She's so bright--this little girl could be *anything* when she grows up, if she's only given the chance. Jennifer will probably be the only person I will truly miss when I finally am able to leave here.

"Sister Rebecca came up a little while ago looking for you," Jennie says, pulling away from me, concentrating very hard to remember the words. "She asked me to say that she wanted to see you at the infirmary before you started your chores," she recites in an adorable sing-song.

"Thank you, Jennie," I tell her, planting a quick little peck on her cheek.

She giggles, refreshing as a spring shower, but the sound of her laughter stops suddenly when she frowns. "Is Brother Daniel coming back soon?" she whispers. Yeah, she *definitely* won't let go of a question. "And is your mommy very sick?"

"I'm don't know when he's coming back, baby. And I'm not sure about my mom. Now hop down," I say, patting her on the butt. "I guess I'll find out about my mom when I see Sister Rebecca."

Jennifer makes a face, looking around for nearby eyes and ears before putting her lips to my ears. "I don't like Sister Rebecca!" she whispers.

None of the children like Sister Rebecca. She gives them shots, and the only kind of love she knows is *tough* love, given freely with the sharpest edge of her tongue. That makes her a most effective nurse: no one wants to spend time in her infirmary if there's *any* way to avoid it.

Some of Jennifer's little friends come and drag her away, chittering excitedly: rumor has it that if her crew of tiny hands finishes picking their quota of wild blueberries early enough, they will be allowed to spend the rest of the afternoon splashing around at the lake. That's exciting news for the youngest children.

Left alone, I go through the morning motions. I splash lukewarm water on my face, but I don't have my toothbrush. Even if I could find it in the wreckage of my sad little home, it would probably be beyond use now. I shrug, put some toothpaste on the corner of my washcloth and scrub my teeth as best I can. I still have a few moments before morning prayers and breakfast when I'm done. If I hurry, I can make it to the infirmary before joining the crowd for morning prayers and breakfast.

"Blessed morning, Sister Rebecca," I say to Nathan's mother as I enter her petty little kingdom of misery.

"Blessed morning, child," she answers. Her usual condescension is somehow even more unbearable than usual.

"May I see my mother?" I ask, and her face changes. Rebecca's usual look of smug superiority has vanished, replaced with... pity? Concern? She's never acted the least bit concerned for anyone before. What's wrong with my mother?

"Not right now," she tells me, not unkindly. "Maybe tonight. She's resting, now. I've given her something. To sleep." Rebecca hesitates, as if debating how much to tell me, then looks away, frowning. "She's had a very bad night and I think it's best if she's left alone for now."

"Fine." What else can I say? "So I'll be on my way, then, and come back before dinner time? If that's all right with you?"

Rebecca nods, and I'm halfway to the door before I stop and turn back to her.

"Sister Rebecca? What's wrong with my mother?" I ask. "I know that she has the, the-- I guess, mood swings?"

Rebecca looks out the small, grimy window and frowns thoughtfully, pursing her lips. She spends such a long moment in thought that I'm not sure she'll even answer my question.

"Your mother," she finally answers, "hears the voice of The Lord perhaps a little more strongly than the rest of us. A little more clearly."

"She's always been like that, all my life," I say. "But the changes, they've been worse, lately. More extreme."

"Father Emmanuel was here earlier to check on her," Sister Rebecca says, changing the subject. She turns away from the window, meeting my eyes. What're you really trying to tell me, Sister? "He was... *displeased* with her behavior last night." The nurse's gaze remains steady on mine. "*Most* displeased."

Is this why I can't see my mother before tonight? Did he hit her again? Does he want her tucked away until the swelling subsides?

"And something else, as well. Father Emmanuel suggested that I should have a look at you as well. A *thorough* look," she says, raising her eyebrows at me. "He mentioned that you were unwell yesterday morning. Is there something, perhaps, that needs to be checked out?"

"I- I sincerely hope so, Sister Rebecca," I answer, dropping my eyes and blushing.

"Well, we'll see, I suppose. Oh, I nearly forgot," she says, and her nose is right back in the air, just as high as ever. "Father Emmanuel also said to tell you to go by his office this morning. Before you go out to pick berries."

"Do you know what he wants?" I ask, suddenly nervous. If they think I'm pregnant, then that may give Daniel and me some breathing room. It won't be much, though-- my mother keeps that damnable calendar! In just a few more days that breathing room vanishes and the chains will be heavier and tighter than ever.

"It's not my place to question the anointed prophet of The Lord, Sister Courtney, and it is *most* certainly not *yours*." And the moment is over: she's back to normal.

After thanking Rebecca with nearly unbearable courtesy, I make my way to the refectory. I can't imagine why Satan would want to see me this morning, unless it's to follow up on some unfinished business from last night. What more could there possibly be? The only things they didn't tear to shreds are my cheap canvas shoes. Has the disgusting false prophet guessed that I really *am* stealing money from him? That I really am working towards a third bid for freedom? Nathan *did* catch me stealing, but they weren't able to prove it. I'm safe, I think... for now. And where is Daniel? What has Emmanuel done with him? Done *to* him?

Nerves and fear make every bite of breakfast pure torture. Fear for my poor sweet fake husband, fear for myself. The lumpy gray porridge doesn't want to slide down, and swallowing the disgusting mush is even more difficult with the lump in my throat.

Jeremiah delivers the morning sermon while we eat. I try to listen to the message he preaches, hoping for some distraction from fear, but it doesn't work. Why did I think it would? Is there anyone less likely to be a reassuring presence for me?

His sermon is mostly incoherent, just halting rambling, linking one scripture to another through some ridiculous leap of logic, and using it to draw some inane conclusion or other. I can't even tell what his actual message is, but the adults gathered for their meal listen raptly, nodding as if he's said something profound. Are you people all really this stupid? The emperor isn't just naked, he's also a complete idiot!

Being the center of attention like this makes the prophet's eldest son glow with pride. There's no doubt that he loves the spotlight. He's the closest thing these poor folks will ever have to a rock star, and he's eligible bachelor *numero uno* to the older teenage girls, who sigh and blush prettily every time his gaze passes over them just like he was one of the Jonas brothers or James Marsden at the Teen Choice Awards that year. That year. 2008. Is any of that even still relevant?

Jeremiah's preaching may not have distracted me from my fear, but reminiscence does. I think back to the music I liked then, the poster of Justin Timberlake on my wall. I was already growing out of that at sixteen, already looking for the next big music phase. Something more grown-up. Something more like what Sean listened to. I smile at the memory of listening to his favorite radio station while writing him letters in my bedroom. I never really got a taste for the classic rock on WBLM, but it was a connection to him while I poured out my heart on paper to him, then added a drop of perfume and a kiss with pink lipstick.

Of course, I'd throw that letter away immediately, unsent, and then write something simple and sensible, and *that's* what I'd send instead. Formal, boring, and safe. It's a wonder he ever wrote me back.

I found a distraction from my fear, but it doesn't last. Jeremiah's eyes, roaming the room, make contact with each person in turn. Eventually, of course, it's my turn, and the tiny smile he bestows on me chills me to the bone, setting my stomach churning around the leaden mass of porridge. I push away the bowl, closing my eyes, willing my insides to calm.

When I open them again, several of the other women are looking in my direction, talking quietly, their mouths shielded by their hands. I can't hear what they're saying, but I don't need to. Word has spread, and everyone thinks they know some good news. This is terrible. When the truth comes out, it's going to be worse on me – and on my poor Daniel – than if the rumor hadn't ever spread! Why couldn't I have held my stomach down yesterday?

After the final *amen*, I rush away from the long trestle table to my appointment with Father Emmanuel, knocking on the frame of the open door to his office.

Satan's personal representative on Earth doesn't look up right away, giving me a chance to study him when he's not putting on a show. He frowns down at something on his desk as if he doesn't understand what he's reading. Uncertainty, confusion--those are expressions he would never allow in front of his flock. For us, his default expression is a mocking half-smile that says *I know everything, especially what you're hiding.*

Standing at the threshold of the room and watching him, I wonder for the gazillionth time what it is that my mother sees in him. Thinking back to what Sister Rebecca had said about my mother, I wonder if the answer could really be that simple. Did my mother simply hear the voice of God commanding her to be with Father Emmanuel? I don't know what kind of God would want that, but it's one I'd have no part of.

I knock again and he looks up. The puzzled look on his face intensifies before it clears when he remembers asking me to come.

"Blessed morning, my child," he says.

"Blessed morning, Father Emmanuel," I dutifully answer. "I was told you wanted to see me?"

"Oh yes, it's about your hives," he says pointing in the direction of the screen on his desk. "I want you to show me where they are," he says, and my heart is in my throat. "You see, if you *are* in a... *delicate* state, it would simply not *do* to have you in a position of such danger. I couldn't bear the thought of exposing my little nephew to such a hazard."

"You seem very sure that I will have a boy," I say. It's a dangerous game I'm playing. I've got a weak hand, but it's the one I've been dealt. "But what if I were to have a girl? Or what if I'm not pregnant at all?"

"I feel confident," he says, smiling thinly, "that if you are to give my brother a child, it will *not* be a girl." His eyes grow colder, and he continues with one final word: "*If.*"

"Yes, Father Emmanuel," I say, bowing my head. "I hope to have received The Lord's blessings, but it's still early."

"Early indeed. I hope, however, that you *have*." He shifts his attention to the computer at his desk. "Now then. You will show me where your hives are located."

Three steps and I'm by his desk. In the old days, I had a computer of my *own* on my *own* desk in my *own* room, so I'm familiar with Google Earth, and it takes me no time at all to locate each of my hives.

The grip of his hand on my shoulder tightens with every pin, and by the final one his hand is a talon, claws digging deeply into my flesh.

It takes me less than a minute to set all the pins at the proper locations. I grit my teeth. I will not give you the satisfaction of knowing you're hurting me.

More or less, anyway: I've misplaced all the pins, just slightly. Most of them are close, within a couple hundred yards at least, except for one: the cluster of hives on the hillside, the one where I've hidden my stash of getaway money. I've misplaced that pin the most, putting it much further down-slope, and on the wrong side of the mountain. It's not that far away, in absolute distance, but I hope it will be enough.

When I'm finished, he releases his hold, allowing me to extricate myself from his claws. I swear, I'm going to have the trace of his five fingers on my shoulder for a week.

"Is there anything else you need from me, Father Emmanuel?" I ask, bowing my head in what I hope is convincing mock humility and hoping the interview is over.

His *I know it all* smile spreads on his thin lips as he slowly answers, "That will be all for now, my child."

This is the green light to take my leave. Normally I would rush out of his office, but today I can't: I have to find out what happened to Daniel.

"May I ask something, Father?" My eyes are lowered and my hands folded in front of me. My body language screams submission.

"You may, dear child. Certainly you may." His tone is one of grand and benevolent leader but when I raise my eyes to look at him again, I see a more mature version of Jeremiah's sadistic gleam in his eyes. His cruelty has refined with age; his tortures have grown more sophisticated. He knows what I'm about to ask, but he will not volunteer any information. It pleases him to make me to beg.

"Would you know where my husband is? Brother Jeremiah said Daniel was with you last night but-- Father Emmanuel, he never came home. I'm worried."

Satan's hand waves casually at me, and for a moment I think my question will be dismissed or he'll torture me with some cryptic answer. I am astonished when he gives me a straight answer, a complete one.

"I have been in communication with another community," he tells me absently, already turning back to the papers on his desk. "They are an Amish group, living in the town of Unity. They have a fine young bull, and I have arranged to purchase it from them. The Amish are, of course, base heretics, but they are far closer to God than most of the sinners out there."

"And my husband..." I hardly dare to feel hope, but it seems that I may have something to hope *for*.

"Brother Daniel drove down last night with the money and a truck, but no bull. He will return tomorrow with a truck and a bull, but no money. I despise the necessity of dealing with these heretics, but our cows must be bred if the herd is to survive." He looks up from his papers at me, smiling thinly, eyes cold. "And if my flock is to survive, the ewes must also be bred."

A chill runs through me. In just a few short days it will be exceedingly obvious that I am *not* pregnant. I can't bluff my way through that. On Tuesday, maybe Wednesday, at the absolute latest. The hand will be over, and I will have lost, unless I can draw something better this weekend.

"One last thing, my child," Emmanuel says. "I very nearly forgot to tell you!"

I hold my breath waiting for this additional piece of news. If he's kept it for last, it must be bad.

"Since your mother is... *indisposed*, Sister Leah will be accompanying you to the market tomorrow, in addition to Brother Nathan. Actually, *both* of my sons will be going with you. As of tomorrow Jeremiah will be in charge of handling the money," he tells me. "It will help to prevent any further... misunderstandings."

"Why don't you send someone else if you don't trust me?" As soon as the words are out of my mouth, I want to kick myself for saying them. I can't allow my only window on the outside world to close!

If I run on a bee day, I'll have a six-hour head start before they notice I'm gone, but six hours in the wilderness won't get me far at all. On a market day, they'd know instantly if I was gone, but if I can hitch a ride?

They'd have no way to chase me instantly, and I could be a hundred miles away before they could even effectively begin a pursuit.

"Now Courtney, child," Satan scolds. "Pride is *not* your guide, nor is vanity. Think of the good of the flock!" What is he talking about now? "You're our best representative at the market. All the customers love you, and you bring in more money than anyone else we've ever sent." My eyes shoot wide open as what I fear is confirmed. The man has been spying on me.

"Oh, yes, I've been watching you at the market. You're *very* good with customers; it's just our *cash* you may have a small problem with. Now, go. Be about your work." A dismissive flick of his hand sends me scurrying out of his office.

I lean against the wall of the main house once I'm outside, my stomach churning worse even than yesterday. Unless something major happens this weekend, unless Fate or the universe or some god *other* than the monster that this church worships drops something in my lap over *this* weekend, I'll be doomed by the *next* one.

I trudge off toward the distant fields of low, wild bushes with a stack of buckets in my hand. Those berries aren't going to pick themselves and mindless work is all I can handle right now.

Chapter 8

Sean

Saturday Morning, 13 August 2016

With all the empty forest in northern Maine, it's not hard to find a good place to camp overnight. About an hour past Greenville, there's a nice spot on paper company land that my dad and I used more than once as a base camp for hunting. That's where I wake on Saturday morning under the open air with the first hints of light on the horizon in that time between dark and light called morning nautical twilight.

It's not going to take me long to pack up—the weather was nice enough last night that I didn't bother to set up a tent and slept under the stars instead – so I can afford to take the time to make coffee on the camp stove using the old percolator. It was my dad's, and his father's before that. Three generations of Pearse men have used this on hunting and fishing trips. Realistically, it makes shitty coffee – there's always grounds in it, and you can't help but burn it every single time – but there's absolutely nothing I'd rather have when I'm out in the woods. It tastes like family. Like tradition. I can almost see the ghosts of my dad and grandpa sitting on the other logs around the cold fire pit with me.

Maine's come a long way in the years since I've been home, and nowhere is this more evident than in the cell phone service. The lady at the store had assured me that my phone would work up here, but I'd never more than half believed her. Pulling out my brand new iPhone though, I'm pleased to find she's absolutely correct. Time to review my maps and plan for today's mission, and a solid data connection brings me on-demand overhead imagery.

Obviously Greenville is not hostile territory, but it's still best to treat every mission like you're walking straight into the heart of darkness. Always remember the seven Ps: *Proper Prior Planning Prevents Piss Poor Performance.*

I'm back in Greenville shortly after sunrise, sitting in a decent observation post at Auntie M's restaurant across the street from where the farmer's market sets up. Sitting in a standard folding metal chair at a table by the front window, I watch as farm trucks unload people and produce in the parking lot of the Camden National Bank and the small green common area next to it. It's a perfect vantage point.

By the time I finish a plate of corned beef hash and eggs, it looks like everyone's set up. All the obvious spaces for stands are filled, and there's a little bit of a crowd starting to trickle in. Yuppies on their way to one campground or another, produce buyers from local restaurants or the old resorts filter through. Two more cups of coffee and I judge that there's enough of a crowd for me to blend in at least a little.

A flannel shirt, Red Sox hat and few days' growth of beard are all I need for camouflage in this environment. I'm reasonably certain that neither Heather nor Courtney – if they're even there – would recognize my face. The last time that either of them saw me, I was a beardless seventeen-year-old on his way to boot camp, my mom's signature still wet on the parental consent forms for underage enlistment. Before I stand, I check to make sure the Beretta at the small of my back is secure in its holster. A few dollars left on the table covers my breakfast and a generous tip, and then I'm on my way across the street.

I start at one end of the line of farm stands. I'll have to buy things here and there to stay inconspicuous, so at the first stand I pick up a cloth bag and some-- what the fuck is bok choy, anyway? I have no idea, but it's leafy, it's green, and I buy it just to have something to carry. At each stand, I paw through the produce like everyone else. It strikes me that I definitely want to wash anything I plan to eat – not the bok choy though, that's going straight in the trash – after seeing at least three people pick their noses before handling the food.

I'm always looking at least two or three spots ahead of the table at which I'm standing. I can see the people tending each stand out of the corner of my eye; get a look at people without being obvious about it.

Most of the stands have at least one woman working, but none of them so far is either Heather or Courtney. I'm halfway around the semi-circular layout before I get my first glimpse of what might be the target area. The stand is one of the larger ones, and it's certainly distinctive.

From a good distance away I can see there's three people working there – two women and a boy. A fourth person comes around the side of a truck, and it's a man this time. The truck has a cross on the side of it, and a bunch of badly hand-painted letters. Bill did say that Heather had a fondness for the particularly crazy flavors of that old-timey religion. Could that be the right one?

My next stop is at a small refreshment stand set up in the gazebo in the middle of the green. From here I can drink a bottle of soda – it's Moxie, possibly surpassed only by Allen's Coffee Brandy as the state beverage of Maine - shaded against the mid-morning sun, and observe the stand without looking like I'm staring.

The banner above the table and the lettering on the truck proclaim this stand belongs to The Church of the New Revelation, whatever the fuck that is. The man looks younger than me, with a patchy beard and lank hair, and he has powerful shoulders. Farm work will do that to you, I guess, but his movements are gawky, awkward. Not a serious threat.

Next, a boy, young, with a strong family resemblance, probably a brother or a cousin. He's got shifty eyes and a face like a weasel. Matching greasy black hair. He's watching everything, observing. He can't be more than ten or twelve - maybe even younger - but there's a cunning in his eyes; a light that speaks of cruelty.

One of the women has gone around to the back of the truck and out of my sight, but the other one is still up at the table hawking what looks like goat cheese and vegetables. Mostly carrots and corn, but there's some cucumbers, tomatoes and eggplant, as well as blueberries. She's definitely not Heather – she's too short for one thing, and her hair is a salt and pepper that started out far darker than Heather's light brown. Mother to one or both of the guys? Dark blue gingham dress with an apron. She looks like she stepped off the set of a movie about the frontier.

I'm already mentally writing this lot off, moving on to the next stands when the other woman comes back struggling under the weight of a heavy load of more... something. Some sort of unidentifiable food product that gets grown in dirt and manure. Beets maybe? She's definitely younger, and she's wearing the same sort of shapeless dress-and-apron rig that the older woman has. She moves awkwardly, bowed under the weight of the baskets and limping. I can't see her face, but she looks unremarkable enough and my eyes are already slipping toward the next stands.

I've already given a cursory once-over to the rest of them, and I've just about given up this trip as a bust, but something drags my eye back to the young woman at the church stand. There's something about her, something calling me back. I need a closer look.

I finish off the bottle of Moxie with one last long swallow, wincing at the taste. As a native Mainer— *Mainah*, if we're going to be precise with the accent—I should love this stuff, but it tastes like pine needles dissolved in fucking cough syrup, and one bottle per decade is about my limit. Bottle goes in the blue bin, and when the older woman is several feet away from the table talking to the older of the two males, I approach.

I *did* tell Mom I'd pick up some blueberries after all, and I handle a few small paper cartons of them while studying the girl out of the corner of my eye. I haven't seen Courtney in years, and there's a lot of changes that happen between fifteen and twenty-three.

This young woman is above average in height, which makes sense. Bill is tall, well over six feet, and Heather came pretty close to six feet herself. The shapeless blue-and-white checked dress – might as well be a gunnysack, really – does a good job of hiding the shape of the body underneath, but as she arranges the new batch of produce on the table it stretches and moves against her and I get the impression of soft, sweeping curves beneath the fabric. With the load of vegetables set down, the awkward movement has not gone away. She walks with a pronounced limp, one leg dragging slightly behind her.

The young woman looks down intently at the table. From this angle, I can't see her face, but her hair has been bleached by long days and years of farm work in the sun. She's naturally gotten the sort of highlights for which housewives and office workers pay hundreds of dollars. I need to get her to look at me, get a better look at her face. I grab two of the cartons of pea-sized berries and turn to face her.

"Excuse me, miss?" She sighs, and her shoulders slump for a moment before she straightens and looks at me.

It's her.

She has the same strong chin, the same wide expressive mouth. The freckle-spattered nose that was always just a little too big as a child, looks just right on her now that she's grown into it. The bright blue eyes that always used to follow me inquisitively when we were young are dull, without the spark I remember, but there's no mistaking them. She looks tired now, drawn. Haggard and worn. Lips that smiled often and questioned everything are pinched tightly with- what? Worry? Fear? This is definitely Courtney Dwyer, though.

"These berries, can you tell me about them?" Fuck, what am I supposed to ask about blueberries? They're berries, they're blue, they're tasty. What else is there to know about them? C'mon, man, come up with something. "Ah, are they organic?" There. That sounds like a not-stupid question. Jesus, those lips. The last time I saw those lips, I was reeling from a kiss that might as well have been a baseball bat to the gut.

"Yes, sir. They're wild berries. They grow as a gift from God, and are hand-picked by the brothers and sisters of the Church of the New Revelation." She speaks so softly, I have to lean closer to hear.

"But are they organic?" I ask. Hell, in a farming context I barely know what that even means. I seem to recall from chemistry class that organic just means that something contains carbon. Why didn't I prepare better? My knowledge of and interest in chemistry pretty much begins and ends with how to blow shit up using improvised explosives.

"The berries are wild, sir," Courtney sighs. "They are not planted, nor are they fertilized or treated with any chemicals. They have nothing more than The Lord's divine blessings to help them grow." Her brow furrows, she's looking at me hard now. Some of the old light has come back in to those blue eyes now, but I can't tell if she recognizes me. Time, tattoos and the beard have done a good job of disguising me.

"Okay, that's good then. How much do they cost?"

"They're eight dollars per pound, sir." Her eyes go wide as she finishes the sentence, and her mouth snaps shut. She starts to look behind her at the others at the stand – the moment I recognized Courtney, the other people at the stand were redesignated in my head as targets Alpha, Bravo and Charlie – but catches herself before turning too far toward them. There's recognition in her eyes, but also fear. More than fear. Terror. Who is she afraid of? Surely not me? Them?

"Courtney?" I keep my voice low. "Are you okay?" There's a barely perceptible shake of her head, and she speaks again.

"If you buy three pounds, there's a discount, sir. One pound for eight dollars, three for twenty-two."

"Oh, that is a much better deal," I say as I fish for my wallet. "Do I pay you?"

Her face turns panicky, and Courtney puts her hands behind her back. "No, sir, I don't handle the money. Please give that to Brother Nathan over there." She turns, pointing at the younger male that I've labeled as Target Bravo. "I'll box these up while you pay him, sir." She looks back at me, her eyes pleading. "Your purchase will be ready when you come back to me."

"Thank you, miss."

Target Bravo is still down at the far end. He's on the tailgate of the truck, sitting on what looks like a cash box. I stretch out my hand toward him with a twenty and a five and he approaches to take the money.

"Three pounds of blueberries. She said that's twenty-two dollars?"

Beady eyes squint at me as Bravo takes the money wordlessly. I leave my hand stretched out for my change, and the edges of the sleeves of colorful ink are visible past the cuff of my dark plaid flannel.

The older male subject, Target Alpha, speaks up.

"Ye shall not make any cuttings in your flesh for the dead, nor print any marks upon you," he says with a sneer. "Leviticus. Nineteenth chapter, twenty-eighth verse."

Cuttings in my flesh for the dead? I have a sudden urge to roll up my pant leg and show him the inked names of my dead brothers from the Teams. I've barely met this arrogant greasy-haired prick, but I'm already taking a strong dislike to him. I paste a forced smile on my face, biting back the desire to give him a much closer look at the 'printed marks' on my knuckles.

Bravo gives me back my change along with a mimeographed tract of some sort. The blurry purple-blue ink takes me all the way back to kindergarten, back in the dark days before Portland's public schools had photocopiers.

"Thank you very much," I tell them with the same false smile. Their eyes are still on me as I go back to Courtney to pick up my berries.

She's arranged it so that her back is to Alpha and Bravo, and she speaks to me in a hushed whisper. "Sean, is that really you?"

I nod slowly.

"I need help. Can you help me? Please."

I nod again, and Courtney hands me the plastic-wrapped package of berries. "Can you wait for me, meet me behind the restaurant?"

I look down, playing the part of your standard issue customer, fat dumb and happy, while putting the fruit in my cloth bag.

She continues in a louder voice. "Please enjoy these berries in the light of Christ's redemption and salvation, sir." The fear is still in her eyes, but there's also a note of hope now. Because of me?

"I will do that, miss. If these berries taste half as good as they look, I'll *come back soon* for more."

Courtney's small, tight smile says she understood the subtle emphasis. She had always been a nice kid, clever and bright. The old protectiveness I'd always felt for her is roused again. Along with... other feelings.

"Ten minutes, maybe fifteen," she whispers again.

It's only a couple hundred feet to the back of the restaurant, but it's the longest short walk of my life. I'm impatient, and the numbers on my phone's clock don't move fast enough while I wait for her.

"Sean?" Her voice is a whisper from the side of the building.

"Courtney! I'm over here," I call out. Courtney comes around the corner and an instant later she's on me in a furious hug that rocks me back on my heels.

"Oh my God, Sean." Her face is buried in my neck, and her arms are locked around me as tightly as any bear trap. My own are no less tightly wrapped around her. She's shaking.

"Is everything okay, Courtney?" I'm pretty sure I know the answer already.

"No. Nothing's okay. I mean, it is now. You're here." The shaking slowly subsides, and she looks up at me, bright blue eyes misty with unshed tears threatening to flood out of her at any moment. My heart skips.

"Do you want to leave?" I ask. "We can leave here, right now."

"Oh, Sean, there's nothing I'd rather do," she replies. The light in her eyes fades. "But I can't go with you. Not now. I mean, not *today*." Courtney purses her lips; her eyes go distant. "Tomorrow, though. Yeah," she says, nodding furiously. "Can you come tomorrow?" Her eyes are bright again, full of so much hope and relief.

"Why tomorrow? Why not today?"

"It's complicated," she sighs. "My mother, she's sick. She's not well..." Courtney's voice trails off, brow furrowed as she tries to find the words. "I think *he* hit her again, and she's finally lost it. It's been, like, two days now. She just stares into space and she won't look at me."

"He? Who's *he*?" I have a low tolerance for people who abuse the weak.

"Look, it's- let me explain. No, there's too much. Let me sum up." Courtney pauses for a deep breath. "She's ashamed that she hasn't been able to give *him* another boy, another heir, and now—Sean, she wants *me* to—"

"She wants *what?*" My voice is a deep growl.

"No," she shakes her head. "Not with *him*, but... look, it's complicated. It's a big mess. It's—she! No. He, he—hasn't promised me to *him*, but I think they're going to arrange for another marriage soon." Courtney swallows hard, and takes a step back. Her palms press flat against my chest, and her eyes are full of pleading.

"They're going to force you to marry someone? Wait, you said *another* marriage. You're already married? They *already* forced you to marry someone?" Rage. Destruction. Fire. Pain. These are the things that await whoever hurts this woman.

"Yes," she begins, but stops and puts a hand on my cheek, laughing softly. She always could see right through me. "No, Sean, it's not- it's okay. Daniel cares for me, and I care for him, but it's not a *real* marriage, not for either of us. It's just security. An alibi. For both of us."

"So, you want to go back there tonight, then? To, what, see your mom? See him? This *Daniel*?" I'll let my questions go unanswered, for now, but I will do some *serious* digging later. There's no way in *hell* I'm leaving all of this alone.

"Yes. I want to- no, I *need* to give Mom one last chance," she says. "Or I need to say goodbye, at least. Have closure. And I want Daniel to come away, too."

"Well, that's a new one on me," I tell her. I'm trying to keep it light. "Here I am plotting to steal away the girl of my dreams, and she tells me I need to steal away her husband, too."

"Well," she giggles with a coy little smile, "I don't think he'd fight too hard if you did try to steal him."

"Huh?" I'm confused.

"I told you, we've been each other's alibi. And I'm not judging, Sean, but the *Navy*?"

I can't help it: the tension and fury in my head evaporates in laughter. I take her in my arms again, hugging her tightly. Whatever has happened to her over the years may have worn at her, but it hasn't broken the sweet, funny girl I knew.

"It's so good to see you again, Courtney."

"And you too, Sean. You'll never know how much it means to me. How did you find me?"

"There was a picture in the Press-Herald, a picture from here at the farmer's market. I wasn't sure, but I wanted to come up into the woods for a couple days anyway, and I thought I'd check it out."

"I'm so glad you did. Listen, I don't have much time: I've been away too long already. They're already suspicious of me, I've tried to run before, and—it didn't go well."

"What do you mean, 'didn't go well?'" She doesn't answer, but looks away, shifts her hips away. *The limp. She was limping.* "They hurt you?" Her silence is answer enough. My rage is back, even hotter than before. "They will never do that again, Courtney. I guaran-fucking-*tee* you."

"I know. But listen, Sean, that's why I have to give Daniel the chance to come away." Her mouth sets in a hard line, her eyes grow serious as she grips my hands. "My," she begins, then swallows hard. "My *body* may be in danger there, but Sean, Daniel's *life* is on the line. I don't *love* him, I'm not *in* love with him, but I care about him. He's protected me for almost five years now."

"Okay," I say, then dig in the bag where I'd kept my old phone, just in case I actually did find her. "Take this. It's got a full battery. I'm here for you, overnight. If you need emergency extraction, just call me. My number's programmed in." The girl cradles the beat-up iPhone uncertainly. "I won't be far, and if you need me, I *will* come and get you out of there. I just need to know where to go." I pull out my new phone, open up the maps, and hand it to her.

"Let's see," she says, fingers quickly moving over the screen. I chuckle at the sight: to look at her appearance, she's straight out of the nineteenth century, but she's working technology like an expert. "Yes, I know what a touchscreen is, Sean." She scowls at me, but there's no real malice there. "I didn't always live in the back end of nowhere." Her face brightens. "Okay, look," she says. "Right here." As I look over her shoulder, she drops a few markers on the map.

"So. What are these?"

"This one is my... it's where I live." She points. "This one, it's where I go sometimes if Daniel's not there. It's the women's dormitory. Over here, they call it an infirmary or a hospital, but it's just a slightly less filthy hovel where you go when you're sick. That's where Mom is. I'll probably be in one of those three places."

"What's this one?" I ask. "The one a ways off to the south?"

"That's the missing beehive," she says. I raise a curious eyebrow, and Courtney shows me a thin, hard smile before continuing. "I take care of the bees for the community. This hive isn't on Satan's map, and I've hidden a little bit of money there. My getaway fund." She sighs. "It's not much, but it's all I have. And it's why they're watching me so closely. They know there's money missing, and they think I have it, but they can't prove it."

Satan? Who the hell is she talking about? That's more digging to do, but *later*. Essentials only, for right now. "Can you get to it tonight?" I ask.

"No," she says. "I won't be able to go to my hives until Monday. That's when I take care of the bees." Courtney looks up at me with a nervous question. "Sean, how close are you going to be?"

"Close enough," I tell her. In fact, that might be a good location to stay tonight: it's on the north slope of a low hill, looking over the- what do you call a place like that? She said community, but is that really the right word? "Yes. I'll try to get it for you."

"It'll be dangerous, Sean. If they catch you, they won't like it. And you'll like it even less. And you weren't a Marine or anything, you were just a *sailor*."

"I'll be okay, Courtney. Don't worry about that for a second," I say, with a fierce grin.

She hasn't seen me since I went off to the Navy, and we lost touch before I went to the SEALs. "I've been in far scarier places than this."

"*COURTNEY!*" It's a woman's voice, screechy and raspy, booming from around the corner of the restaurant.

"Oh, shit!" Courtney says. "It's Leah. I have to go, Sean!" She pushes me away quickly. "Stall her? Please? And be here tomorrow?"

"I will," I tell her. "Both questions."

"*COURTNEY!*" She's close now, and I hear footsteps crunching in the gravel of the parking area.

Courtney smiles gratefully at me as she ducks around to the other side of the building. That limp. Someone needs to pay for that, with interest. Lots of interest.

Courtney vanishes just as Target Charlie appears. Leah, Courtney said her name was. Malevolent eyes squint at me out of a face red with anger. The little that Courtney has told me makes me think I might not like this Leah person very much at all.

"Where is she?" It's a demand, not a question.

"Where's ... who?" I was a junior enlisted sailor long enough to be a master of the slightly confused expression in response to questions from authority. It rarely pays to admit to knowing as much as you actually do know.

"The girl. Blond hair," she says. "Stupid. Fat." Oh, well now. Might not like Leah? What was I thinking? I definitely do not like Leah at all. It's an effort to keep my face relaxed.

"Not sure what you're talking about," I say. "I haven't seen any stupid fat girls today." It's the truth – Courtney is far from stupid, and while I might have noticed some generous soft curvature against my chest when she tackle-hugged me I'd *definitely* not call her fat.

Leah holds eye contact for another long moment. You think you're intimidating me. Oh, that's *adorable*. I can't help it – something primitive inside me responds to the challenge. I don't move a muscle. My posture doesn't change, nor does the expression on my face, but the quizzical good cheer drains from my eyes, and I allow the deeper things to show through.

Every human being has the capacity for violence inside them, but after years of training and application, mine is much closer to the surface than most. Leah is used to being a big dog in a very small yard. She might think of herself as a wolf, but she's never actually met the true stealthy wild killers before, and she cannot hold the eye contact for long.

"All right then." She backs a step, drops her eyes. A few more steps backward, then she's around the side of the building. She recognized the threat and declined to turn her back on me. Perhaps I should have stayed dumb and cheerful, ignored the challenge? Too late now. What's done is done. Time to move on.

I didn't have enough time with Courtney to get a good feel for what's going on here, but a couple of things have been established. First off, she is unquestionably in danger. The meeting with Leah just now underscored that. That woman has a definite tendency toward sadism, and that makes me far more likely to believe what Courtney said about – at an absolute minimum – her mother's beating, and Courtney herself picked up that limp somewhere. Little girl Courtney was never given to lies, and I have no reason to think that grown-up Courtney would have changed that much.

The whole forced arranged marriage thing, though. Does that shit actually still happen? Obviously, she has reason to think it does. The fear in her eyes was genuine.

That fear. All the old memories of her, the feelings, flood in again. She's never going to be afraid again. I'm back.

I return to the map, scrolling around the area to get a feel for things. I'd love to be able to hang out here and keep an eye on Courtney for the rest of the day and then drive there, follow their truck, but that's not going to be possible. It's just paper company roads, logging trails really, between Greenville and the site. No, the *compound*. That's the best word for it. It would be too obvious that I was following them. No, I'm going to have to park somewhere, hump it in on foot.

The hike looks like twelve miles, maybe fifteen if you count the over-and-around bullshit. Courtney will be safe enough here in town, I think: Maine folk may keep to themselves and ignore a lot of shit that's none of their business, but I can't imagine anyone letting a young woman get abused in public without starting up some shit of their own. Old habits, old manners—chivalry is not dead yet, not out here, anyway.

It's going to be a long day, and an even longer night.

Chapter 9

Courtney

Saturday Evening, 13 August 2016

Sean's back! He came back for me! My heart soars and I want to sing out with the purest joy I've ever felt.

Even in spite of the day's emotional highs, I'm utterly exhausted. I'm pretty sure that today was a record-breaker in terms of sales. All the quilts are gone, and most of the produce as well. I'm actually grateful when Leah takes the keys of the truck and announces she's driving. Grateful even in spite of being squeezed in between the door and Jeremiah, with Nathan across our combined laps.

The prophet's youngest son falls asleep on the drive home and I cradle him in my arms. I can't bring myself to hate him. He's just a misguided little boy, seeking approval and love that he will never receive from his father or his brother.

We make it home in time for the end of the evening meal and the beginning of the prayer session. I'm tired and I've been on my feet all day. My leg hurts, and when it does, my limp is even more pronounced. I wonder if Sean noticed it? Of course he did; how could he not?

Jeremiah sure doesn't seem to see it. He watches me struggle under mountains of baskets and bags, putting everything back in storage without so much as offering to help. He does manage to get in a grab at my ass, and under the heavy load I'm not quite able to dodge it.

You don't want a wife to love, you want a slave. A brood-mare. But then again what do I know about love? I thought Sean loved me, but he left anyway, all those years ago.

I regret the uncharitable thought instantly: Sean may have left before, but he's back now. Sean's *back*! He came back for *me*!

Nathan barely manages to follow us and instantly falls asleep again at the table even while his father preaches. Wedged between Leah and Jeremiah, I gobble up scraps left over from the communal supper: the pieces of chicken that nobody else took, dried out or bony, carrots and onions too misshapen to sell to tourists.

Father Emmanuel's ranting is long and loud. He screeches out a rousing sermon full of fire and brimstone, loaded with sin and damnation. America will fall, he proclaims, because she has lain with the Whore of Babylon. He goes on and on about the abomination of desolation, about Gog and Magog, prophesying rivers of blood covering the land, and the gathered community eats up every word with as much gusto as they eat their supper.

If they nodded in approval of the son's ridiculously poor logic at breakfast yesterday, the father's insanity has them ready to light the torches and march on Manhattan, Washington, and Hollywood with The Lord's cleansing purge of fire.

Only at the end, when Father Emmanuel orders us to bow our heads in repentance and pray for The Lord's forgiveness and mercy am I able to hear myself think again.

I close my eyes and lower my head dutifully while I replay my conversation with Sean in my head. A smile blooms on my lips and I bite it back. It's nearly impossible to keep the appropriate mask for the circumstances when all I want to do is shout from the highest mountain peaks, scream to the world that I am the happiest girl on earth. Sean came back for me!

For eight long years, I've waited and prayed. I've gone so far beyond any possibility of hope, and now? My prayers have been answered. Sean is back! He's back home, back in my life. Back for me! All I want to do is shout my gratitude to the heavens, praising a God in whom I'd almost lost all faith. I want to dance and show my joy to the world. But I don't dare.

My *amen* at the end of Satan's final prayer carries only the barest shadow of the bliss and ecstatic exultation I feel inside, but still—I'm showing *too* much happiness. Leah's deep-set eyes fasten to me, but even her sharp-edged gaze, slicing away layers of secret, probing to find the hidden truth of sin, cannot do anything to bring me back to the ground. And what can you say anyway, you nasty bitch? That I'm too fervent in my worship? That I'm too caught up in praising The Lord and His Plan? His utterly magnificent Plan, which has brought me my deliverance?

Once the hymns and prayers are complete, I manage to pull Nathan away from the table. He's dead on his feet, drifting off to sleep almost at every third step, but eventually we reach his mother in the infirmary.

Sister Rebecca reads the Bible at her desk, the leftovers of her own supper on a tray next to her. She's barely touched her food. Satan likes his women on the skinny side, but the woman is already so thin that she looks sickly. She's barely a few pounds away from my gaunt mother.

Nathan's mother looks up from her book as we walk in and for the barest fraction of an instant she smiles. Not at me, but at her son, and even in his exhausted haze the little boy seems to catch that fluttering sign of love and approaches her. Everything in the way he looks at you screams that he wants a goodnight hug. How can you not see it? Or do you just not care? The briefest touch of her lips on his forehead is all he gets as she sends him to bed. There are no open arms, no show of affection. How much longer will he still look for love and tenderness in the world before he fully embraces the stern asceticism of his father? Or is it too late already? I have to believe that he could still be saved.

That's one thing Rebecca, Leah, and my mother have in common: they're not touchy-feely mothers. I know that they must love their children, but they do not show it. Is it something about them that's broken or missing? Is it something about us? Or is it just this place, this church and our vile prophet?

Unlike Jeremiah and Nathan, I was lucky to have a father who made up for it while he lived. The memory of those moments still warms my heart, and I try to share that warmth with the little ones here as best I can. With Jennie, with the others. Even with Nathan, when he lets me.

When the door to their room closes behind her son, Rebecca looks at me again.

"I won't lie to you," she says, shaking her head as she stands and chases imaginary crumbs from the front of her dress. Rebecca motions for me to follow her. "Your mother is not well, Sister Courtney," she tells me as we walk.

My mother seems shrunken, laying in the small cot. The sound of our voices pulls her out of her torpor and she turns slowly in our direction, but there's only disappointment in her eyes when she identifies us. Of course. She wanted *him* to come and visit her.

I'm torn between anger and sadness. How many times will she have to be kicked before she can break that compulsion to crawl back to him? Even a dog has more sense than this. Even a dog will eventually run away, or learn to fight back. Why can't you do the same thing, Mom?

A nightstand by her bed holds another tray of supper. It's just as full as the one that Sister Rebecca had left almost completely untouched.

"She didn't eat anything, did she?" I don't need to look at Rebecca to know the answer.

I help my protesting mother to sit up. She resists, trying to turn her back to me, but gives in at Rebecca's insistence.

"Call me if you need me," she says, pulling the door mostly closed behind herself.

I pull over a stool, and coax my mother into eating. One spoonful at a time, the soup vanishes until half of the bowl is gone.

"Oh, Mom," I sigh. "Where are you?" She turns her bruised face to me when I speak to her, but her eyes are empty, unfocused, and I feel as if I'm transparent. Does she even know who I am?

When she's too tired to eat anymore, I take her in my arms and help her get up. She trudges in silence to the bathroom and back, and I tuck her back into bed.

"Why are we here, Mom?" I know she has no answers for me, but I need to ask anyway. "Why did you bring me to this place? Why won't you leave here?" I look away from her as I stand, staring at my feet as I ask one final question in a bitter voice. "Why won't you let *me* leave?"

"Because *He* commanded it." My mother's whisper stops me in my tracks, and when she reaches out to me, her grip on my wrist is as strong as any steel manacle. "*He* willed us to be here, and so we are here."

"Is this what you want?" I ask. I'm torn between incredulity and anger at her answer. "For yourself? For *me?*"

"It doesn't matter what I want, Courtney. It doesn't matter what we want. It only matters what He commands," my mother whispers softly. "When He commands, it must be done. We must purge ourselves of sin, of wickedness. We must be worthy of Him."

"But *why*, Mom?" Prying her hand off my wrist, I lay it against my thigh. I know she can feel the damage through the threadbare skirt, and in a sudden burst of fury I wish I could let her feel it firsthand. "Why couldn't you just let me *leave?* You ran away, yourself, Mom. Once upon a time, *you* ran away from a place like this."

"If the sheep run away," she says, "then the shepherd cannot protect them." There's a hint of sadness in her voice, in her eyes. Is it truly there, or am I only imagining it? Do I see it because I *want* it to be there? "The flock must grow," she finishes, echoing what Father Emmanuel had said to me in his office.

"Is that it, then?" I ask, sick horror in my stomach. "You're with him on this? You want to see me married to Jeremiah?" I recoil from her touch. "Do you know what that will *mean* for me?"

"The flock must grow," she says again, and it's not my imagination, now: her eyes do express genuine sadness, regret. "*He* commands, and we must obey. It's the only way we can be saved from our sins, from this sinful world. I thought I could live out there, I thought I could protect you myself, but I couldn't. I hear His voice, and I must obey him. *You* must obey him." My mother's blinks several times, each one slower than the last, until her eyes simply stay closed.

I sit again, staying with her until her breath settles into the steady rhythm of sleep. Carefully avoiding the bruises, I brush graying hair from her face. How can you look so old, when only in your forties? My mother seems so fragile, so frail, but her grip on my wrist was stronger than I could have expected.

This is the most open she's ever been about these things. Medication and exhaustion must have given me the key to open her, but they still weren't enough to make her speak plainly. Or perhaps they were too much, combined, to allow it? Every other time I'd asked *why*, she'd simply flown into a rage. Before long I learned to avoid her slaps, and it didn't take much more time before I learned to avoid those inconvenient questions. Even *I'm* as smart as the dogs, Mom. Why can't you be? What did you mean? What did any of it mean?

"Goodbye," I say to my sleeping mother. I've received all the answers I'm likely to get, tonight. I want to tell her about tomorrow, about running away with Sean. I want to tell her everything, but I don't. If she's truly asleep, it's a waste of my time. If she's not? It would spell disaster.

I thank Rebecca as I leave the infirmary, but I hesitate on which direction to go. Left or right? Sleep in my ransacked hovel one last time, or go back to the dormitory for a final night?

Jennie pops out of nowhere and jumps into my arms.

"You look sad," she says, slipping her arms around my neck. "I thought you needed a goodnight hug."

I hug her back with false, joyless smile on my face.

"Oh, but I'm not sad! Not at all," I tell her. "And I'm not in a hugging mood! I'm in a *tickling one!*" As I say the words, I wiggle the fingers of my hand right over her belly. I don't even need to touch the little girl for her to squeal with laughter, flailing dirty bare feet in the air. I laugh with her, hoping she can't pick out the note of sorrow, the loss that I hear. I miss her already.

I walk with her to the dorm. I could stay there with her. There's safety in numbers. Surely Jeremiah or his father will leave me alone if I'm with the other girls. Yet, I need to speak to Daniel.

"Run along now, sweetheart," I tell Jennie after giving her a goodnight kiss on the forehead. "If I can, I'll come to check on you a bit later."

Quickly I make my way back to the converted garden shed. I shudder at the idea of returning, but there's a ripple of glee as well: it's the last night I'll call the miserable little thing *home*. It wasn't much of a home to begin with, but it was shelter. A place where Daniel and I made each other feel safe for a while.

Gathering my courage, I pull the door open, startling Daniel. He's sitting on the shambles of our bed, taking a break from restoring some sort of order. As soon as he sees me, he stands, opening his arms to me. I run to him, and he folds them around me.

"I was so scared for you," I murmur against his chest. "I thought you'd never come back."

"You worry too much," he says. Daniel pats my back gently and *shushes* me. "Don't you have any faith in my brother? He'll never let anything bad happen to me."

"*No*, Daniel!" I gently pull away and look in Daniel's eyes, wondering if he really believes this or if he's just trying to reassure me. "I *don't* have any faith in your brother." I shake my head in disbelief. Maybe a different angle? Even if he's in full denial about his brother, he has to realize that his nephew is dangerous.

"What about Jeremiah?" I ask. "Do you trust *him* as well?"

The smile vanishes from his face. "So you know that he's trying to have you for himself."

"How exactly would I *not* know?" I ask. Daniel looks at me in confusion and I snort. "Your nephew explained it to me in great detail. It's on hold though. For the moment, at least. Didn't your brother tell you? He thinks I might be pregnant. This is, of course, *not* the case. But like he told me: *the ewes must be bred.*"

"Ah." Daniel squeezes me tighter, rests his forehead against mine. "I... did not think he was ready to move on it yet. I believed there was time, yet."

"Time for what? For you to, y'know... *that?*" My voice is hysterical and I hate it. "*That's* not going to happen, and you know it." I choke back a sob. "Daniel, your nephew wants me. And he'll have me, one way or another."

"Oh, Courtney, I'm so sorry," Daniel says pressing my head against his chest. "I know you have no feelings for him, but he's not a bad man. You could learn to love him. What else can you do?"

"Daniel. Husband. *Listen* to me. Even if, somehow, I do turn out to be pregnant? Jeremiah isn't a danger only to *me.*" How can he be this blind? Jeremiah? Not a bad man?

"If he can't take me away from you this way? He'll turn you in. You and Joshua both. And you know what the penalty will be! He may do it anyway, even when he has me. For revenge. You stood in his way too long."

"Again," he says, his voice barely a whisper. "What. Else. Can. You. Do?"

"We can run! That's what we can do," I say, looking up at his face. His eyes are closed tightly, and the lines of laughter around his mouth make him seem old, tired. Has all the fight gone out of you? Can you not see how much danger you're in? "If you won't do it for yourself, think about *Joshua!* You're not the only one in danger, here."

"I know you still dream about your Prince Charming," Daniel says, holding me tightly. "Some nights you call out to him in your sleep, and it breaks my heart, but you have to face reality."

He leaves that statement hanging, and it takes every shred of my willpower not to tell him that I *saw* Sean at the market today. I want to tell him that my Prince Charming is *back* and he's going to rescue me. But I don't.

I trust Daniel, of course. It's not that, not at all. I'm sure he would be happy for me, but I don't dare tell him, so long as he stays behind. Who knows what they will do to him when they realize I'm gone? If he stays behind, the less he knows, the better. For both of us.

I take a deep breath and look into Daniel's eyes.

"Please. *Please*, Daniel. *Run* with me," I beg.

"You know I can't. You know *why* I can't." He sighs, gives me a smile that's so tired, so sad, that my heart breaks for him.

"Bring Joshua with you!" I plead, but I know it's not that. Or, not *only* that. They've never lived in the outside world, and they're more scared of it than they are of Father Emmanuel. They're more afraid of living in the outside than they are of dying here.

"But if you feel brave enough to give it a go, then now's the perfect time," Daniel says, surprising me with the joyfulness in his voice. He's grinning happily as he explains. "Don't you see? After last night? After Jeremiah and your mother did this?" He waves a hand around the scattered wreckage of our life together. "It's perfect. You were scared of Jeremiah, that's why you ran. It even takes the heat away from me."

"You think so?" I ask. I hadn't even considered it that.

"Yes," he says, squeezing me tightly again. "I can even be furious that Jeremiah would be intimidating my beloved wife like that, scaring her into running." Daniel growls, deep in his chest. It's the first time I've ever heard this gentle, sweet man show the slightest hint of anger. "And I *am* furious. Our 'marriage' may be a sham, Courtney, but you've meant a great deal to me the past five years."

"Are you sure?" I ask him one last time. I have to give him just one more chance. "Please, both of you. Run with me."

"I'm sure," Daniel says. He kisses my forehead and opens his arms, releasing me. It's a literal release, but also a symbolic one. "Courtney, don't worry about me. I'll be fine."

I'm overwhelmed. I'm going to miss him, so much. His kindness and quiet strength have been a rock for me for so long. Unable to speak, I reach out to him, and Daniel takes my hand in his.

"Our marriage, Courtney? It's not even legal out there," he says, nodding his head in the direction of the outside world. "There's no paperwork, no licenses. It doesn't mean anything except here on this farm. I release you from your vows," he says, kissing the back of my hand, and then he looks me in the eye.

"If you truly believe your happiness is out there," he says, turning and walking to the door, "then go. Find it. Grab on to it. And all my hopes and prayers will go with you." Pausing at the door, Daniel looks back at me, meeting my eyes one last time. There's no cheer there now, none of the self-mocking humor I'm so used to seeing from him. "But run far, Courtney. Run fast. Don't let them bring you back here again," he finishes, and he's no longer looking at my eyes, but at my leg instead.

Daniel's eyes are shiny with tears, but there's a smile on his lips as he walks out through the door of our home. He's a good man, trapped in such a bad situation. My heart is heavy: I've just said goodbye to one of my dearest friends.

As I watch him walk away, I wonder if I'll ever see him again.

Chapter 10

Sean

Saturday Evening, 13 August 2016

It's late afternoon by the time I'm in place on the north slope of Trout Mountain. Infiltration and stealth are a SEAL's hallmarks, and I've tucked myself into the edge of the tree line, about a hundred yards above Courtney's beehive. The low hill barely deserves the title, but at least it gives me an elevated vantage point where I can see the whole... compound, I guess that's what I'd call it. My dad's binoculars bring everything up close and personal.

The place looks to have been built up around an old farm. There's a sprawling main house, expanded haphazardly with additions over the years, and a ramshackle pole barn with a distinct lean to its structure. Outbuildings – shacks, really – of cinder block, sometimes even just simple plywood or sheet metal garden sheds, are scattered around the grounds. Depending on how comfortable everyone wants to be, they've got housing for a couple hundred people at least, maybe as many as four, if they pack 'em in like sardines.

A few vehicles sit near the house, inside a fenced yard. In a place where most folks feel comfortable parking their car outside overnight with the keys in the ignition, these people have a hurricane fence with a chained locked gate around their vehicles. Guess they don't want anyone going anywhere.

I haven't been watching long enough to get a solid head count, but I'm starting to get a feel for who's who in the compound. I spent a lot of time on overwatch in Baghdad, looking at crowded city streets through a scope for any hint of trouble and sorting out the sheep from the wolves. This evening, I only have my dad's old binoculars. I don't see any signs of suicide bombers or insurgents, but that doesn't mean there's nothing to worry about.

The society I see before me is heavily stratified, that much is obvious from first glance. The women invariably walk a few paces behind the men and look down when speaking to them. *Almost* invariably: some few older women receive a certain wary deference from everyone, not just the other women.

However, the men are not all at the top of the food chain—there's a definite hierarchy there, too. Some men seem worn, tired, beaten down by the hard labor of working on a farm. Others—well-fed and well-rested—move around the compound in a wide bubble of space. Everyone, men and women alike, avoids them. I've seen this behavior before: enforcers. Local tough guys in a position of power.

I study one of the tough guys through the binoculars. In spite of the magnification, it's hard to guess his age. Even with his local status and privilege, a life of farm work ages you early. The man glares at everyone. They avoid his gaze in return. Everyone, that is, except for a swirling knot of small children playing some game with a dog and a ball, laughing merrily. But the ball comes loose from the children and drifts across his path with the dog close behind.

The man is forced to break his stride as the dog tumbles to a halt in front of him, the ball in his mouth. It wags its tail triumphantly, looking around for approval from its young masters and mistresses. The next thing the dog catches is a heavy boot in the hip. From this distance, I can't hear the mutt's yelp of pain. It was a hard kick, though: the dog drops the ball and stumbles away, one leg dragging awkwardly behind. Motherfucker.

There are people around, but nobody says a word. Turning the binoculars from person to person, I find faces that are studiously blank; eyes that focus anywhere but on the injured dog. The group of children follows the example of their elders. One little girl's shoulders heave as she cries, wiping at her nose.

But, no: a small boy stands up, his face dark with fury. He can't be more than six years old and probably closer to four. In another setting if would be funny to see that tiny bundle of rage shaking his fist at a grown man. But not *now*, not *here*. I'm powerless to do anything, and it's hard to watch from a distance as the child runs up to the man, untrained fists flailing wildly. The enforcer grins broadly, dropping to a knee in front of the boy, batting away his blows.

A small crowd begins to gather. Four other men—no, five now. These are more of the tough guy types, the men the others defer to. They're laughing, slapping each other's backs. It's a grand joke, isn't it? Assholes. They're joined by a sixth person: a terrified woman runs up to the group. She's not in on the joke.

The woman—his mother?—reaches out for the boy, trying to pull him away from the danger he's in, but one of the men catches her by the hair first. Her head snaps back sharply as she hits the end of the long, thick braid and it looks like he's twisted her arm behind her back now too. Motherfucker.

The first enforcer, the one who'd kicked the dog, looks up at the woman, a nasty smile on his face. He's distracted, and the boy lands a flying fist straight on his nose. This time the sound carries, the distant howl of pain lagging behind the movements of the asshole's mouth. He jumps up, and when he brushes a long-sleeved arm across his face there's a red streak on the white fabric. The boy stands there, shocked by what he's done, visibly shaking in fear even from this distance. His face is dirty, but tears have cut streaks of brilliant white through the mud and dust. I can't tell if he's frozen in terror or if he's being brave.

The man turns on the boy, bellowing again. The sound hasn't even reached me yet by the time he lands a furious backhand on the side of the child's head, leaving him motionless in the dirt. Takes a real man to lay out a kid that age. I've seen your type a thousand times, in a thousand third-world shitholes, and I've left them with fewer teeth every chance I got. I can't do anything about him right now: my mission priority is Courtney, and intervening here would have a negative impact on the most important thing in my world. Dear sweet baby Jesus, please let there be a reason for me to go down there tonight for Courtney, because I very much want to hurt that man. Badly. I've already labeled targets Alpha, Bravo, and Charlie. This guy is on the list now: Target Delta.

The tough guy rounds on the woman, screaming at her, but falls silent at the touch of a hand on his shoulder. Someone else has joined the crowd.

He's an older man, tall and thin, with a wild halo of shaggy white hair. He carries a cane, but there's no sign in his gait that he needs it for anything: it's an affectation. He wears the same plain white long-sleeved shirt and denim jeans that seem to be the men's uniform here, but carries himself with an aura of authority. The toughs, the enforcers, yielding to nobody at the compound, show him respect: slightly bowed heads, tipped hats. He's in charge. Could this be Courtney's *him*? Her own personal Satan?

At his gesture, the woman is pushed to her knees in the dust. She tries to reach for her son, but another tug at her braid turns her face back to the old man. He's facing toward me, saying something. A quick flick of my thumb cranks the magnification to maximum, and I can read his lips.

"Sister Andrea," he asks, "what's the meaning of all this?"

Her back is to me; I cannot read her answer. The old man shakes his head sadly, though.

"No, Sister. No. 'He that soweth iniquity shall reap vanity, and the rod of his anger shall fail.' Your young Matthew, he 'sowed iniquity' when attempting to strike Brother Lucas, and 'the rod of his anger' certainly did fail. Brother Lucas merely corrected this iniquity, this vanity."

The old man turns to the little boy, weakly attempting to sit up. That must have been one hell of a backhand. He turns back to the mother, smiling. "You see? He's just fine. And he's learned a powerful lesson today. 'Train up a child in the way he should go, and when he is old, he will not depart from it.' The Lord's Word tells us this, my dear."

I hadn't expected an education today: Theology One-Oh-One: How to Twist the Bible, taught by Professor Crazy Asshole. Can't wait to fill out the end of term critique on this guy.

Again, I can't tell what Andrea says, but she lunges toward the old man against the grip of the men holding her to her knees, and a brief flicker of anger crosses his face before he settles back to an expression of calm.

"Now, Sister Andrea, I believe you may need to be reminded of a few other things as well. Does not the apostle say 'wives, submit yourselves unto your own husbands'? And does he not also say 'for the husband is the head of the wife'? You have forgotten yourself." He holds out a hand to-- what was his name? Brother Lucas?

I think I like Target Delta better.

"Brother Lucas," the son of a bitch says, "if you please? We certainly cannot fail in our duty to correct error where we see it."

Target Delta, Lucas, has an evil grin on his face as he strips off his belt and steps up to the kneeling woman. That old bastard was quoting verses about husbands and wives. Delta and Andrea are married. And that's her son? This son-of-a-bitch hit his own kid like that? Oh yes, I do want to do very, *very* bad things to him.

My mood doesn't improve as I watch him lay several dozen hard strokes of a thick leather belt on his wife. She huddles, trying to shield herself with her arms, but it's futile. An arm to shield her face leaves her breasts vulnerable to the lash; covering her chest leaves belly and face open.

I can't protect everyone, and I can't avenge everyone, but Andrea? I vow to you: this ends.

With her whipping ended, Andrea keeps her head down and crawls to her child. The old man steps back up in front of her, and again I read his lips.

"'All the wives,' and this is from the book of Esther, Sister Andrea, 'shall give to their husbands honor.' Can you remember this, from now on, Sister Andrea? Will you give Brother Lucas your cheerful submission and obedience?"

Andrea's body shudders, racked with pain and sobbing. Even if I'd been close enough to hear her speak, I doubt she could have formed coherent words.

"Still," the old man says, "it's best to be certain. To be truly sure. As The Lord's Word says: 'it is better to dwell in the wilderness, than with a contentious and angry woman,' and though we have plenty of wilderness around us, I simply can't spare Brother Lucas for the next few days." He shakes his head sadly again at the weeping mother and child. "Therefore, I think it best if we remove *you* for a while, instead." He steps back, turns to her husband. "The penance box is empty, I believe, Brother Lucas?"

"Yes, Father Emmanuel." Lucas nods fervently. Father Emmanuel. Now I have a name for him. There's nobody else that could be Courtney's *him*. You're on my list too, you evil bastard.

"Then it's settled!" Emmanuel beams, spreading his hands wide. "Jonah's redemption required three days in the belly of the whale. That should be plenty to bring the woman back to the path of righteousness." His gaze turns cold upon Lucas before he continues. "And take care, Brother Lucas. Your position requires you to set a good example. You would do well to ensure your wife and child do not stray from the path again. If you cannot keep your own family pure and in line with the Word of the Lord, then how will the rest of the flock trust you as a shepherd?"

Forget Theology One-Oh-One. This is a post-doctoral class, taught by the 2016 Nobel winner for Advances in Insanity!

Target Delta bows his head in assent. I can't see his lips, can't tell if he makes a response, but he roughly pulls his wife to her feet by her long, dark braid. She's still cradling Matthew in her arms as her son of a bitch husband drags her to a small wooden building standing alone in the middle of an open area in front of the main farmhouse. It's not much bigger than a phone booth, and with the walls and roof painted a very dark brown it must be miserable there in the summer.

Lucas pushes his family inside and slides the door shut. There's no lock on it, only a simple latch on the outside. Apparently they don't expect anyone outside to interfere. If I get even the smallest reason, I'm going to make sure you fucking regret that.

A rumble and a dust cloud half-hidden by the trees to the west announces the arrival of a vehicle. It's the truck from the farmer's market, by the sound of it. Sure enough, it's the ugly farm truck painted with these sick assholes' obscene church slogans.

I watch her limp away from the truck, and my fury seethes. Calm, Sean. Calm. Maintain. You're in mission mode, now. Stay frosty. Gotta keep this cold. Hot rage leads to mistakes, and you can't afford mistakes.

No, *Courtney* can't afford for you to make mistakes. Not after that shit.

The greasy-haired prick from back in town, the target I've named Alpha, is following closely behind her. The truck is between them and the older woman, and he thinks nobody can see him pawing clumsily at Courtney's body. She glares at him, venom dripping from her gaze, and he just laughs. My right forefinger curls, taking up the slack on an imaginary trigger. You're lucky I'm looking at you through binoculars, Alpha. If only this was a scope instead.

Alpha's hands are empty, but Courtney is carrying something heavy. Almost at the steps to the farmhouse's front door, she stumbles, but recovers, resting her burden against the large shape of a full-size propane tank next to the house. I wonder if that's full? I wish I'd thought to pack some flammables. Fire and explosions make nice distractions, and this place would look so much nicer in flames.

I follow Courtney in the high-powered binoculars as she goes from one building to another, making sure I don't lose track of her. There are no alerts to my phone, though, and no immediately obvious threats appear.

I watch as Courtney goes to the so-called hospital, and is there for nearly an hour. Visiting Heather, I guess. Heather always was a piece of work. I suppose it makes sense that she'd descend back to her natural level. She carries a small girl around the compound in her arms, one of the children I'd seen playing with Matthew and the dog earlier, and they smile and laugh at jokes I can't hear.

Courtney is so good with the little girl, so natural, and if I didn't know better I'd think maybe it was her daughter.

Courtney's daughter. What a thought. It's been such a busy day, and I've been spending so much time alternating between horrified and enraged by the things that I've seen and heard that I've not really had time to process what I'm thinking and feeling about Courtney herself. And what does she think of me?

The idle daydreams during the too-brief and too-infrequent downtime from combat operations in Iraq and Afghanistan had often featured marrying Courtney, having a family with her. Hell, just the other day while waiting for my new tires I'd thought about it. Here, tonight, watching her carrying around that little child, it hits me again, more vivid than ever before.

I could absolutely be happy like that, so long as it was what she wanted too. But would she? Eight years have passed, and we'd only had a few short minutes together today. People change a lot in eight years, and there's no way that her experiences here won't have affected her in some way. For that matter, I'm not the man I was eight years ago.

The pair stop in front of the building Courtney had marked as the women's dormitory, and she sets the girl gently on the ground. With a kiss on the top of her head and a gentle swat on the butt, she sends the child, laughing, toward the front door before trudging back toward the door to her own little hovel.

It's full dark by the time anyone emerges again from the shed where she lives. It's a man. The fake husband? What'd she say his name was? Daniel, I think? The man closes the door of the shed gently, carefully, and his face twists up in the throes of intense emotion. Grief? Sorrow? It only lasts a moment, and he's carefully composed by the time he walks from the shed toward the main house, wearing an open, friendly smile.

It's too dark to see anything below, now. Lights glow from the windows of the main house and from the building-- what'd she call it? The building with the food. The refectory, that's it. The only other place that's lit up is the penance box, encircled with a ring of floodlights. The cheap night vision monocular I bought at Cabela's isn't effective at this distance. You get what you pay for, I guess. What I wouldn't give for a box full of my old equipment right now.

Frustration sets in at the visibility. Definitely need more light down there. Wouldn't that fire be just lovely right now?

This is going to be a long night. I have to stay alert, and I've got a long hump back to my truck in the pre-dawn hours if I'm going to make it back to Greenville in time. I've stood tougher watches before, and longer ones, but I've never stood watch over something I cared about this much.

Eight years had certainly changed me. I'm covered with scars now, filled with metal fragments and nightmares, but one thing has definitely remained constant. I'm still in love with Courtney Dwyer. Absolutely, completely, and totally.

The only thing that's changed is that now I can admit it, and I won't ever run from it again.

Chapter 11

Courtney

Sunday Morning, 14 August 2016

This time I get up before Jen does. I haven't slept a wink.

On Sundays, everyone gets to sleep in one more hour. Everyone but those who have Sunday chores such as me. I tiptoe to her bunk and watch her sleep. I want to hug her one last time, just to say goodbye. I want to, but I don't, it would be cruel on my part to tell her I love her and then vanish from her life. I walk out of the silent dorm with a heavy heart. This baby girl is the one I'll miss the most. More than Daniel.

More than Mom.

The very thought of her brings tears to my eyes. The parts of my mother I miss have been gone for so long, I can hardly remember who she once was. I'm sad but strangely with my newfound resolve the relief washes away the guilt. I will no longer have to watch her waste away.

The refectory is almost empty. Nobody from the market crew is here yet, only a few of the people that tend to the livestock. I mumble a vague greeting to the sister ladling out breakfast, and armed with my bowl of lumpy porridge, I take a seat at an empty table. Looking at the lukewarm mud-like substance in front of me, I promise myself that if I ever have kids, I will *never* force such dreadful food upon them.

Too soon Jeremiah, Leah, and then a half-asleep Nathan join me. We make quick work of breakfast and load the truck in silence until the kid finishes waking up and starts chatting up a storm. Oblivious to the tension between Jeremiah and me, Nathan speaks about some sort of drama that occurred last night before we returned. His friend Matthew tried to protect a puppy. Poor kid, he learned the hard way that in this community, it sucks being at the bottom of the food chain. Child abuse masquerading as discipline is just as common as cruelty to animals.

Leah mumbles between her teeth, "Stupid brat got his mother in trouble."

"Sister Andrea will be in the penance box for three days," Jeremiah says, as indifferently as he might note the weather was pleasant. I look at him and shudder. The penance box is a drafty shack where you freeze in winter and fry in the summer. Today the temperature is pleasant enough. I look up at the sky. Thank God it's clear. It's terrible in there when it rains.

We set up our booth and it takes all my willpower to act normally and not look around for Sean. I have no doubt he'll be here. I know he'll be here. I fight back the smile that threatens to break across my lips as I remember how I swore to myself just a week ago that I would never trust anyone ever again and here I am, ready to put my life in Sean's hands. This is one of life's delicious little ironies.

The earliest customers trickle in and I do my best to act as if it's business as usual. It's hard, but I do a half decent job of it until I see a big blue Blazer drive by. Is that him? It looks like Sean's truck, but it's been so long! I can't quite tell for sure. My heart stops and starts again as the vehicle rolls away too quickly for me to get a look at the driver.

I finish bundling up purchases for a customer when the Blazer comes around again. This time the windows are rolled down and I can clearly see Sean. He slows down, looking for a place to park, but there's no empty spot right next to us. He pulls off to the side of the road and stops as close as he can. It's in the general direction of the restaurant that lets us use their facilities but too far away from a direct line for comfort.

I consider making a break for it, but I can't. Sean parked too far away from our booth. I turn around and look at Jeremiah who's sitting at the back of our truck. He's observing me. With this leg, I can't move fast enough to get away. Jeremiah would effortlessly catch up with me before I reached safety.

I paste a needy grimace on my face and shift my weight from one leg to the other, pressing my knees tightly together. Jeremiah notices and frowns.

I turn to Leah and ask, "Can you hold the fort alone for a minute? I *really* need to go."

"Why didn't you go before we left, you stupid little cow?" she growls, eyeing me suspiciously.

As meekly as I can, I whisper, "I'm sorry, Sister Leah. I didn't need to go, then, and the roads..." With my hand held out, I mime the bumpiness of the logging roads.

She sighs, calling out to Jeremiah. "Brother Jeremiah? Go with her, if you please," she tells him. "Make sure that's *all* she does. Watch *everything*."

I make a beeline in the direction of the restaurant and in barely three seconds, Jeremiah is on my heels.

"Come on, Jeremiah," I say, my tone light. "You don't need to come with me. I'm sure you have better things to do than to hold the door for me." Please, please, *please* show one shred of decency in your miserable life.

"Who said anything about holding the door," he replies with an amused smirk. "You heard Sister Leah. She wants me to keep my eyes on you. At *all* times."

"Seriously? You want to watch me pee?" Cold sweat drips down my spine, but I would rather eat shards of glass than let him see how terrified I am.

"Yeah," he says, the smirk broadening into a cruel grin. "I think I'm going to enjoy it."

I have no doubt this sadistic bastard is telling the truth.

"You filthy pervert," I hiss. The words are out of my mouth before I can stop them. "You will *never* get to see between my legs."

"You still don't get it, do you?" Jeremiah shakes his head, chuckling at my anger and determination. "You belong to *me*. My uncle will be dealt with, Courtney. Get used to the idea of being my wife. I will have a *lifetime* of enjoying every single part of you, and I'll have you any time I'm in the mood for it."

"I'd rather die than be married to you," I tell him through clenched teeth.

"Well," he shrugs, "I didn't say it would be *my* lifetime."

We've reached the curb, and Sean's truck is about twenty feet away. I won't get any closer to it. Time to make a break for it.

I stop and bend over as if to re-tie a loose shoelace, and Jeremiah keeps on walking ahead of me. He's four steps away when he finally stops, fists on his waist, giving me an exasperated look. I take a deep breath and gather up all my courage and- *thank you God!* He's turned away! It's now or never. Go, go, go! Don't stop, don't look back!

I can't run, but I move as quickly as I can. As quickly as my twisted leg will allow, and a stunned Jeremiah takes a moment to react. I've made it three paces before he turns back to look at me and notices I'm moving, and three more before he starts after me. Only another five, maybe eight until freedom!

Behind me, too close for comfort, I hear Jeremiah call my name, but I ignore it. Keep going! You're almost there!

"You stupid bitch! You don't even *know* what kind of trouble you just got into," he snarls, grabbing a fistful of my loose hair. It hurts like hell, but I can't give up. Freedom is so close! I stop abruptly and turn around, mustering up all my strength for one good kick. I aimed for his knee, but I'm out of breath and off balance and my foot catches him in the shin instead. My heart sinks for a moment but then he stumbles and drops. Jeremiah instinctively lets go of my hair, using both hands to break his fall.

The Blazer's passenger door pops open – Sean must have leaned across and pulled the handle for me – and my foot is barely on the running board when the big truck starts to move.

"*Go! Drive, Sean! Drive!*" I scream, struggling to pull the heavy steel door shut.

The tires squeal and the big engine roars as Sean guns it. Jeremiah grabs at the door, teeth bared and eyes wild as he pulls at it, trying to grab at me and keep me from freedom. I hold on for dear life to keep the door from swinging wide, and as soon as we're clear of the roadside parking space, Sean floors it and Jeremiah falls, tumbling to the side of the road. I watch him roll to a stop, dazed, as we make it through the intersection and on to the blessed open road to freedom ahead.

Only when he's out of my line of sight do I dare to breathe again, and I reach for my seat belt. The last thing we need now is to be pulled over for something as stupid as a ticket! My hands shake so hard that it takes me almost a full minute to latch it, and another to stop hyperventilating.

"Where are we going?" I ask, shifting on my seat to look at him. My breathing may have calmed down, but my pulse still races.

"The camp, I think. If they look for you, they'll go home first." His eyes are on the road. He's concentrating, but seems so calm, it's almost scary. It's as if he did this sort of thing every day.

"Home? *What* home? My father's dead, my house is gone. There is no *home.* What's left there for me to go back to?" A maelstrom of emotion swirls through me and the very thought of *home* brings tears to my eyes. I blink furiously to chase them away, and Sean slows, falling in behind an eighteen-wheeler.

"Your dad *did* lose the house," he says. He glances in my direction, a strange expression on his face, before continuing. "But he never left, Courtney."

I stare at him. What he's saying doesn't make any sense.

"Your father's still alive," Sean tells me.

My entire universe comes to a screeching, crashing halt. My heart stops, my breath stops, and I feel my eyes grow as big as dinner plates. The only sound in my whole world is Sean's voice.

"Your father never stopped looking for you, Courtney. You were one of the faces on the milk cartons. Missing teen. The police never found a trace of you, and your father spent everything he had and then some hiring private detectives to find you. Every single one of them came back empty-handed."

There's no stopping the tears now. They flow out of my eyes in torrents. I think about all those wasted years and I want to scream out my rage.

"How could she tell me this?" I scream, my voice choked in my throat. *"Why?"*

"If you have nowhere to run *to*," he says, shaking his head sadly, "then you're less likely to run."

Yeah. It makes perfect sense. It was probably Satan's idea. Or maybe it was hers. I need to stop making excuses for her. She's manipulative enough to have come up with this scheme on her own.

"I know, it's sick," he says, hesitantly, "but if I had to guess? I'd say she did it because she loves you. She wanted to keep you by her side."

"And it worked," I admit. "If I had known he was still with us, I would have tried again and again until I got away." I ponder the depth of my mother's devotion to Father Emmanuel. How did he manage to get so much control over her? How did he make her blind to the sort of egotistic monster he really is? It's as if she had lost all free will. Sister Rebecca said my mother heard the voice of The Lord more clearly than anyone else. Was that a metaphor, or did she mean it literally?

Sean reaches out to me, and I take his hand, clutching at it like it's the only anchor I have to the real world, and in a way it is. His rough, callused touch gives me the strength to stop crying and brag a little.

"I'll be fine in a minute. Don't worry," I say with a wry grin. "They broke my leg but they never broke my spirit." Why did I say that? Why did I call attention to it? Out of the corner of my eyes, I see Sean's face darken with anger, and I look away in shame.

"It's hardly even noticeable," he says in a flat, even tone. I love that he cares, and I love that he cares *enough* to try and make me feel better with the lie.

Sean races south down Route 6 toward freedom. It's been so long since I've been anywhere bigger than Greenville. My first breaths of free air are heady. A horizon with no limits stretches before me, leaving me dizzy with hope for the future. All the little towns and communities we pass through, places I'd only heard of in snow day announcements on the radio as a little girl, had taken on an almost mythical status in my years of isolation.

Monson and Abbot, Guilford. Sangerville, where we turned onto Route 23. These places seemed as exotic to me as El Dorado or Atlantis. The quaint little mill town of Dexter, a virtual Camelot, where brave knights in shining armor and beautiful ladies in fine silk quested for-

"Oh, Sean! Look!" I grab his arm on the wheel, startling him, and the truck lurches to a halt on squealing tires.

"Huh? What? What's wrong?" He's not looking at me, but scanning the street around us. He shakes my hands off his arm, reaching for something behind my seat.

My breathless laughter calms him, and I take one of his big, callused hands in both of mine. "It's the Holy Grail," I whisper.

He looks at me as if I'd grown a third arm out of my forehead, and I have to laugh.

"No, not *really*. I'm sorry, I must sound like I've lost my mind. I didn't mean to startle you. It's just a Subway. I haven't seen a fast-food restaurant in so many years, Sean." I listen to my words, actually *hear* the things I'm saying, and suddenly my excitement turns to embarrassment, and I look away. "I'm sorry. I..." My voice trails off, and I shrink back into the vinyl seats, feeling small, silly. Dumb.

Sean's free hand clasps over mine for a long moment, and he won't let me pull away.

"Courtney." His voice is so gentle, so caring. It sends a thrill through me, in spite of myself.

I close my eyes, not wanting him to see the beginnings of tears.

"Courtney. It's okay. This is normal." Sean's voice is an anchor to steady me, his hands rocks to shelter me from the storm inside.

"Normal? There's nothing normal about this." I'm dizzy again.

Sean touches my cheek softly, turning my face to him, but I keep my eyes closed tight.

"Yes. *Normal.*" He's firm. Sure of himself. "Look at me, Courtney."

The turmoil inside me is gone, just as quickly as it started. The storm is over, and all that's left is a vast emptiness. I don't even have the energy to cry.

"It's totally normal," he continues. "This is what *happens*. We see it in troops coming home after long deployments, and you've been under continuous stress for, Christ, *years*. From some of the shit you've told me, you might as well have been in the field on constant combat operations for that whole time. But you're *home* now. You're in from the cold. You're back in The World."

The long sleeves of Sean's plaid flannel shirt are rolled up almost to the elbow, and through the colorful ink on his skin I can see lines of scarring. I trace a finger along one of the worst ones. His words now take on a whole different context.

"You-- have personal experience with this." It's not a question.

"Yeah." Now it's Sean's turn to look away.

"But how? You were in the Navy."

"The Navy's not all ships and submarines and Maverick and Goose and Iceman, Courtney. I was a SEAL. A Naval Special Warfare Operator."

"How long-- I mean, how much time..." I don't know what words to use, but he understands.

"Out of the last eight years, I spent five, five and a half, in-theater. Not a lot of down-time, because there's never enough SEALS to go around, and there's always some important *mission*, somewhere that some important *person* needs done."

"And when you came back home?" The emptiness I'd felt is filling in. I'm not alone.

"Yeah. Adjusting. Being back in The World, where nobody's shooting at me. Where I don't have to look behind every rock for an RPG team. Where a patched pothole in the road is just some new asphalt laid over a frost heave, and not camouflage for a bomb to kill me. Where a fluttering curtain just means someone wanted a breeze in their kitchen." He sighs. "It takes time, Courtney. You get through it, though. I promise. And talking, that can help."

"Will you be there? With me? I don't know if I can make it through this alone, Sean."

He doesn't answer in words, but instead reaches across the gap between the seats and hugs me. It's awkward, with seatbelts on and the center console in the way, but it's so comforting.

"Let's work on the first part of our recovery together, now," he says, putting the truck in gear after the embrace ends. At my questioning look, he just smiles and puts on his blinker, pulling into the Subway. "It's a little early for lunch, but we can save leftovers for later."

No sandwich has ever tasted so good to me.

"Warn me," I tell him, "before we see a McDonald's, okay? I haven't had chicken nuggets and french fries in *forever*."

We drive for another good hour before we reach the hunting camp. I gasp when we enter the cabin.

"I'm sorry about the place," Sean says. "It's not much, but we should be safe here."

"No, it's not that, not at all!" How do I explain to him that this place might as well be a palace, spacious and open, compared to what I've been used to? "It's beautiful, Sean. It's wonderful."

The cabin is really an old summer cottage on the lake. It's rickety and drafty with rattly antique glass windowpanes and a creaky floor. All the furniture is mismatched and mostly homemade, and yet it's so cozy and adorable. I love it. And there's plumbing! I squeal with delight at a sink where I don't have to carry water from a well, and *omigod*, no midnight trips to the outhouse! There's even a shower right here, and nobody to share it with! A wicked thought crosses my mind, and I turn my head to keep my grin to myself. Nobody to share it with... unless I want to.

Settling in is quick. I have brought nothing with me. Nothing but the clothes I'm wearing which I would gladly set on fire.

"Is that the bed?" I ask, pointing to a bare wooden platform in the corner, too low to be a table. "It looks about as comfortable as what I'm used to."

"I've got an air mattress in the back of the truck, and some sleeping bags." Sean laughs. "You'll be comfortable, believe me. I could dump out a whole bag of peas on that platform and you wouldn't feel a thing, princess."

There's a stand by the bed, with a book on it. While Sean brings in the last few things from the Blazer, I have a look at the book. Rather unexpectedly, it's poetry. *A Choice of Kipling's Verse*, edited and annotated by TS Eliot. It's quite old, well-worn and dog-eared, and has notes scrawled throughout. There is a reddish-brown stain on the cover, and along the edge of the pages as well.

"That's your father's," Sean says, putting down his load.

"Poetry?" I never remembered my father as a big reader, but when he did pull out a book it was Tom Clancy or something similar.

Sean smiles faintly at my question.

"Most people, when they think of Rudyard Kipling, only remember *The Jungle Book*, and the cartoon movie, or if they took some lit classes in college they might have read some of the more controversial stuff about colonialism, imperialism, that sort of thing. But he wrote a lot of poetry about war, about war in Afghanistan in particular, and about soldiers. There's a lot of military folks that read his work."

"He never talked about it. I never saw him with anything like this."

"He wouldn't have." Sean takes the book gently from my hands, handling it reverently, like a saint's relic. "This would be a very personal thing for him. These stains? He had this book with him that day. In Fallujah."

"How do you know?" I ask. "Has he talked about it with you?"

"No," Sean answers, shaking his head. "I'm making some guesses there, but I don't think I'm wrong. My father had the same book, carried it with him everywhere when he was at war. It came back to us with his personal effects, after he died. The medics wanted to destroy it as a biohazard, but Dad's platoon leader knew how important it had been to him, and he made sure it came home."

"Where is it now?"

"In my sea bag." Sean nods toward a green canvas bag, a fat sausage form with shoulder straps. "It's in pretty bad shape. The stains are worse than your father's. Some pages are almost unreadable, and... I've added a few stains of my own to it, too." Sean's eyes are far away, clouded by some memory of pain and blood, but he shakes it off, looking back at me with tender eyes. Caring eyes, so at odds with the brutal scars, I don't have the courage yet to ask about, or the vivid, brilliantly colored tattoos that wind around his arms and onto his shoulders.

"Tell me about my father?" I ask softly. "Please?"

Sean tells me all that he knows about the man that my father is today. How he's moved in with Sean's mother, married her even, and I'm so happy for them both. Unlike my mother, so obsessed with purity and sin, and who spent most of the time in an imaginary world of her own making, Sean's mom is a caring and down-to-earth woman. Even in the depths of grief for her own lost husband, she was still able to be kind to me.

Sean blows up an inflatable bed and we lay side by side as I tell him about my life in the community. Even though he tries to hide it, I see the rage boil inside him. His fists are tight and his shoulders tense up when I tell him about running.

About how the State Police found me, a sixteen-year-old runaway. There's no way I could have been telling the truth about the abuses that I'd seen and suffered, and returned me straight home. There's no way I could have been telling the truth, they said.

I tell him about the beating, the bruises that took weeks to fully fade, but which left no permanent damage, and about the week I spent in the penance box.

I fall silent after that, unwilling, perhaps unable, to tell more; to tell him about my *second* run. Sean's hand on my knee gives me strength. The warmth and caring in his eyes lends me courage.

"I ran on foot that time," I begin in a voice so flat and dead it could be coming from beyond the grave. "I left from the compound, in the middle of the night." I'm hardly even in my own body anymore as I recite the rest of the tale, or at least as much of it as I can force myself to remember.

Running away on foot in the middle of the night, fleeing through the woods toward the main road. Standing on the side of the road, thumb out to every passing vehicle and praying for one to stop, but cursing God when the truck that stopped was the wrong one. Sobbing as Brother Lucas and Jeremiah got out of it, trussing me up for the ride back to the compound.

The next day, when Father Emmanuel stood in judgement over me. When my own mother begged for harsher punishment, but in the end, even she blanched at his eventual decision.

I know, intellectually, what happened that sunny afternoon. I *know* that my own mother helped to hold me down for it. I remember the horror in her eyes, and how it changed to righteous rage when Father Emmanuel touched her shoulder and an engine sputtered to life. I *know* that something was driven over my leg to break it, but mercifully, my mind won't let me face the rest. There's only a vast, misty gray area after that.

What little I can remember is bad enough, though, and heaving, racking shuddering sobs take away my voice, but Sean's strong arms ground me and bring me back to Earth.

"And this," he says, in a voice as cold and implacable as an avalanche rolling downhill, "is how they taught you a *lesson?*"

"Yes," I reply in a tiny voice. "It *drove* the point home, don't you think?" It's the standard thing I say, bitter and cynical. It's a terrible joke. I know it's a terrible joke. I can't help it, though. I giggle, and I hate myself for it, but the giggling turns wild and I can't stop.

Sean's chest rises under my face as he takes a deep breath in preparation to say something.

"No," I say, cutting him off before he can speak. "No, no, *no*. Do *not* tell me that it's normal to laugh about that." I'm still breathlessly laughing about the terrible joke. Drove the point home! Hyuk-hyuk!

"It is, though." Sean's eyes are far away. "It *is* normal. The worst things in life? The hardest things to live with? Those are the things we *have* to laugh at. If we can't? They'll eat us alive. Destroy us."

After that, what else is there to say?

The hours tick away. I'm wrung out, completely. Adrenaline and emotion have left me absolutely drained.

Day fades to dusk, dusk to night, and through it all I stare at his face, studying every detail. Memorizing it. There are so many lines that weren't there before. Scars. Wrinkles. I wonder if I've aged as much but am unable to see it. Somehow time is always gentler with men, it makes them look mature.

It's been an intense day and despite all my efforts to stay awake and savor it just that little more, I feel myself drifting into sleep.

I don't fight it. I know I'm safe.

Sean is watching over me.

Chapter 12

Sean

Sunday Night, 14 August 2016

Lying in the shadowy cabin, watching the last pink glow of sunset fading, I know I'm not going to stay awake for long. I don't need to. I just need to stay awake until Courtney is completely asleep. It's been a long day for her, stressful, so she should be deeply gone before too much time passes.

I'm not too worried about any of the assholes from the compound finding us and kicking in the door. There shouldn't be any reason for them to suspect that I'm involved in this. They might go and have a look at home back in Portland, but there won't be any sign of Courtney there, and even if they talk to Bill he won't have any idea what's going on. Regardless, I sleep lightly enough, wake quickly enough, to deal with any threat that might come through the door, and the big Beretta is close at hand.

Behind me, between me and the wall, Courtney's breathing is slowly settling into the deeper rhythm of sleep. That's good. I'm going to be off again soon for my nightly visit with my brothers, and with any luck, I won't wake her.

The thin walls of the cabin don't filter out many of the sounds of nature. Crickets chirp, and the bullfrogs from Tilden Pond are particularly loud tonight. Trees whisper to each other, rubbing their leaves and branches together. An off-season spring peeper tries out its voice, heedless of the bats and owls that hunt by ear. A dog barks somewhere as I trudge along that empty street in Sadr City, and the nighttime Iraqi sun beats down on me.

Shit.

I'm not going to bother counting them this time. It doesn't do any good. Even if they vanish, they'll still be back just in time to get shot to pieces.

"Smart one, you are," Saggy approves. "You're learning."

When we turn into the alley, I'm point. The guys stack up behind me. I'll go first. Tinkerbell is behind me, then Mullet and Saggy. Meat follows last with the SAW. I don't bother with proper clearing procedures, sweeping from right to left while keeping as much cover as possible. Slicing the pie, it's called. I'm being sloppy. I know better, I know it's the sort of thing that gets you killed, but I've been in this alley so many fucking times that I know exactly where the threat is.

"Lock it up, asshole." Tinkerbell smacks me in the back of the head, and my boonie hat doesn't insulate the blow like the Kevlar helmet would. Saggy spits in disgust.

"Guys, just cover me, okay? I'll give her the target she wants. You guys light her the fuck up. Try not to let me get killed, okay? Stay back here where there's cover."

"Fuck it, whatever. Why not? We've tried it just about every other way." Meat is just as philosophical as always.

Once they've taken cover as well as they can, I start down the center of the alley. The butt of the M4 is pulled tightly against my shoulder, and as always, I've got the red dot centered on the rough-spun black curtain. The thought idly crosses my mind that I wish I had a grenade. Ah, well. Maybe next time I can put in a requisition. No point. It won't matter.

The curtain flutters again, and the muzzle of that fucking RPK pokes through. I know that when I pull the trigger nothing will happen, but I do anyway. The old Soviet-built machine gun barks and I'm on the ground again with the same two holes in my chest, right through the armor.

My brothers aren't in their cover anymore either – they're laying shattered and bleeding where they always are. The same half of Meat's head is missing, sprayed all over the dusty alleyway.

"C'mon, man," Meat says, then coughs wetly. Bubbles of blood form on his lips. "You know that nothing ever changes here. You can't change the past."

Fuck it. I don't even bother reaching for the SAW this time. Just let the insurgent girl with the machine gun take me. What the fuck does it even matter? She's shifting targets now, coming back to me. My brothers are all dead, and I'm the last living thing in this shithole.

My eyes are closed against the brutal sun, and I lie on my back, waiting for the bullets to hammer me into oblivion. It's no use, I can't change anything. Why bother trying anymore? When the machine gun fires, I tense in anticipation of the impacts that-- never come. I smell the acrid cordite over the blood and filth of the alley, but now there's a faint whiff of something else overlaying it – lavender, perhaps, and wildflowers.

The bullets I'm waiting for are deflected away from me. The *spang-ziiiiiip* is the sound of a ricochet off armor. What the hell? There's no cover here that could stop a BB, never mind bullets. Opening my eyes, the light around me has changed. It's not the harsh spotlighting of the nighttime sun anymore, leaving stark sharp-edged shadows everywhere. It's a soft light, filtered through translucent snow-white... feathers? Wings? The firing has stopped, finally.

"Sean?" It's an angel's voice. It has to be. Wings, protection. What else could it be?

"Sean, you're safe. It's okay." The wings retract, folding up, but her arms are around me and the angel's face comes clear. Sun-bleached hair, freckles, bright blue eyes huge with worry. She's shaking me. What the fuck? You're not supposed to shake someone with chest wounds. What if shattered ribs puncture a lung, or worse, the heart? "Sean, please wake up!"

The nighttime Iraqi sun winks out, and the bloody alleyway fades again into the darkness of the cabin. The barking dog is gone, and only the crickets and frogs remain.

The angel is still there, though, still with her arms around me.

"Sean? Are you there? Are you okay?"

Shit.

"Yeah. I'm fine. I'm sorry, Courtney. I...I'd hoped that it wouldn't wake you." I hate to leave the warm comfort of my sleeping bag. Of her arms around me. I need light, though. I unzip the bag and regretfully pull free of her. The Coleman lantern and matches are by the bed, and a couple pumps and a match bring an actinic white light. Sitting on the edge of the bed, I hear the zipper on her bag open, and the mattress shakes as she moves to sit next to me. Her hand is soft and warm on mine.

"Adjustments," I say in a shaky voice. "We both have them."

"Does this happen every night?" There's no pity in her voice. Only concern. Caring.

"No. Not every night. Most, though. Usually right when I fall asleep, then after that I'm okay." I scrub at crusty eyes, push a button on my phone to see the time. It's just past one in the morning.

Courtney squeezes my hand, then her arms are around me again. "When we were little, you were my hero, Sean, and later too, after my father came back from Iraq. After yours..." Her voice trails off, her eyes sad with the memories of those long-ago losses. "And you still are now. *Especially* now. Especially *today*."

I nod, but with her face pressed into my shoulder I know she can't see it.

"I'm not a hero, Courtney. I'm just doing what needs to be done."

"But you're doing it for *me*. Who else would?" She's looking at me, all earnest bright blue eyes. Serious eyes. I don't answer, just look away. She's seen the weakness now. I'm not supposed to have weakness, not like that. Hold fast indeed.

"Sean. Look at me." Her voice is forceful, and when I don't immediately obey her command, she forces compliance with strong fingers. "Do you remember when my dad was in the hospital and I'd stay with you guys? And there were monsters under my bed or in the closet?"

I can't help but smile at the memory of a much younger Courtney, terrified of monsters. On those long nights when her parents were at the VA hospital, I'd be exasperated at having to hunt monsters, but I did it for her. Every time.

"Yeah, I remember," I say with a grin. "I never missed one, either – you're living proof I used to be good at it, but--" My smile fades, I look away. "I don't think you can just jab a broomstick under my bed to get rid of mine." And you've got a whole new set of your own, too. What kind of asshole would I be to ignore that?

"Maybe not, but I can try. You quieted and stopped thrashing when I touched you. Lie down. Try to get some sleep." She scoots back to her side of the bed, tugs at my tee shirt to pull me down beside her, to make me the little spoon to her big spoon.

Courtney's breath is warm on the back of my neck, her arm strong and tight around my chest after she pulls one of the unzipped sleeping bags up over us as a blanket.

"Leave the lamp on. We can get more fuel tomorrow."

The rise and fall of Courtney's breasts against my back as she breathes drives home that the little girl I knew is a woman now, and reminds me of the fact that this is the first time I've been in bed with a woman for any reason in a very long time. I stuff those thoughts down: only danger lies on that path. Even if she does want to go there, we both have demons we need to deal with.

"Tell me about the monsters, Sean," she says. "If I'm going to hunt them down, I need to know what they look like."

I smile at the memory of our old game. She'd describe fearsome creatures with horns and glowing yellow eyes, fur of purple and gold with pink scales. Fangs the length of your arm. One night, she assured me with solemn and serious eyes that there was a monster with twelve mouths in her closet.

May God and Archangel Michael, patron saint of warriors, forgive me, but I tell her. My voice is rusty, hoarse as I speak for the first time to another living soul about the places I've been, things I've seen. Things I've *done*. Things that I'd never expected to talk about to anyone but a brother SEAL, but even then – why would we ever need to talk about it? If he'd been there he'd already know the story. But after the stories she's shared earlier? This is a strong, tough woman.

I tell her about boot camp at Great Lakes. About my first two years in the Navy as a deck seaman, earning my rate as a Bosun's Mate. The traditional Navy: knots, boats, the boring stuff like chipping away rust and then repainting, polishing brightwork. Two years of boredom before I got my dream shot: a spot at BUD/S, the US Navy's Basic Underwater Demolition School at Coronado, California. Basic training for SEALS.

My first tour with SEAL Team THREE as a NUB, a non-useful body. Combat in Iraq and Afghanistan. Kicking doors, never knowing whether there was a family eating dinner inside or a bomb-making factory rigged to explode. I tell her about the RPG explosion that seared my forearm and slashed my cheek, rocket attacks. Patrols. Hunting insurgent leaders in Iraq, and Taliban leaders in the tribal areas of Afghanistan and Pakistan. I tell her about five combat deployments in six years, about three Bronze Stars and a Silver Star. About the Purple Hearts. I tell her about that alley in Sadr City.

Does she understand? There's no way that she could possibly understand the jargon, the acronyms. She probably doesn't have a frame of reference for combat. But pain? Fear? Comfort? Courtney understands those things perfectly well, and lying there next to me she takes on as much of the old pain and fear as I can pour out and returns it to me as comfort.

As we go back to sleep, I'm still between her and the door, a physical barrier between her and any unexpected intrusion, any danger. Courtney's arms around me, her warm softness behind me, are a much more important protection, though. She's a barrier between me and my ghosts and demons.

When my eyes finally close I do dream, but for once it's not of the sun-drenched alleyway and my dead brothers. All I see is the bright angel with armored wings and the scent of lavender and wildflowers.

Chapter 13

Courtney

Monday Morning, 15 August 2016

As usual, I wake up at dawn, and I want to scream with joy when I realize it's not all been a dream. I'm not in my shack. I'm not in the dormitory... I'm in a cabin in the middle of nowhere and in Sean's arms.

Oh God! I'm in Sean's arms and my father is alive!

I wanted to call my dad yesterday, right away, but there's no signal here. Sean said if I really wanted, we could drive around today until we found a place where we could call home, but that our parents will be safer if they don't know anything yet. Even after so many years, though, if it's safer for us, I can wait just a few more days.

I watch Sean sleep. His handsome features are relaxed, he's peaceful now. I shudder remembering the tortured mask he wore earlier. I could almost feel his pain as he ground his teeth and fought his demons. For a moment, I thought he would never wake up.

He was so worried about my demons yesterday, and he doesn't want to spend the time to handle his own.

He doesn't want to lay any more burden on me. He'd probably just shrug it off, saying his pain is just a part of who he is. It's something that's just *there*. After all, that's what I say about my own pain, about the horrors in my memory. And again, just like all those years ago, Sean's arms had bled away my tears. Last night, I hope I was able to give back even the tenth part of the comfort and caring he gave me.

Yes, I'll let him sleep. He needs the rest and I want to savor this moment.

How many times I have dreamed about walking up next to Sean? More times than I can count. I snuggle against him, bury my head in his chest and breathe him in. He smells like home. He smells like safety. He smells like happiness.

I'm almost asleep again when he stirs. His embrace loosens and I take advantage of this to roll away and slide out from under the covers. I shiver as I sit up. An August afternoon in Maine might make it into the nineties, but the early mornings are still cold. It's chilly outside our sleeping bags but I'm parched and famished, and I could *really* use a bathroom.

In a corner of the room, I find a case of water bottles and something that looks like candy bars, but have a gritty texture and an odd, metallic flavor that makes me stop and take a second look at the packaging. Expiration date: June 2035. Huh. Tastes odd, but I'd rather eat these for the rest of my life than ever see another bowl of Sister Joanna's disgustingly lumpy gray porridge for breakfast!

When I come out of the bathroom, Sean's eyes are open and he smiles at me. I rush back into bed. My feet are frozen. I should have kept my socks on.

"My turn," Sean says as he sits up. "I'm counting on you to keep the bed warm."

"You bet," I say, smiling up at him as I curl up in a ball on his side before it cools down. The bed. *Our* bed. Those two words float around in my mind like two bright helium balloons.

When he returns, I have indeed kept our nest warm, and Sean slides back in next to me. His toes are as frozen as mine were a few minutes ago, and I wail in laughing protest as he puts those blocks of ice on my calves.

Sean opens his arms to me and I roll into them as if it were the most natural thing in the world. He hugs me and asks, "So what do you want to do on your first day of freedom?"

"I'm not sure." Actually that's not true: I know *precisely* what I want to do. Might as well just tell him. "What would you say about just staying *here* today?"

"You wanna spend the day in bed?" he asks ruffling my hair gently. His eyes are merry, but the scar on his jaw turns his smile into a smirk.

"I can't think of anything else I'd rather do," I confess. Yes, Sean, I know exactly what I just said.

"Hah! You need to be careful saying things like that to a guy like me." Okay, so maybe the smirk wasn't *just* the scar.

"You know what I meant," I laugh, slapping him gently on the chest. "What about you?" I hope you do know what I meant. What will you do about it?

"Sounds good to me." Despite the positive answer, I sense reluctance. I look up at him, my hand flat against his chest. When our eyes meet, I feel his heartbeat speed up under the thin, well-worn tee shirt.

"You still haven't learned how to lie properly," I say.

He acquiesces with a smile.

"So. Tell me what you'd rather do." I ask, then laugh as his smirk comes back. "*Besides* that!" But now I've got him thinking about *that* too, and we *are* still in bed, after all.

He looks away and shakes his head. "Actually there's nothing I'd rather do than spend the day with you like this--" He pauses and I sense a *but* coming. "But there are a few things we need to do today."

I hate that I'm right.

"Like what?" I ask.

"Well, for one, we need to get you new clothes." Sean does have a point. I ran away empty handed so I do need new clothes. Something clean to change into and moreover, something that's not threadbare, faded, and so out of date that it makes the Amish look like fashionistas.

"You're right." I nod and regretfully try to pull away, to sit up and give Sean space to get up again.

Holding me tightly, he whispers, "But that could wait for a while. If you want."

I laugh and rest my head on his chest again. One of his hands rubs my back and I purr like a kitten. His arms around me have only offered comfort, strength, and support, but his pulse races every time our eyes meet, his breath catches every time I touch him. I've wanted this, wanted *him*, for so long. I can tell he wants me too, but he's hiding it behind that polite, respectful mask. How long has that been there?

The sweet warmth I felt on waking in his arms is changing, morphing into something different. Something new, yet as old as time itself. Something I haven't felt since he left me, all those years ago.

Under his touch, my flesh heats. The sweetest burn, taking my breath as fuel. Our hearts beat in unison. Under the palm of my hand, I feel his, steady and strong, speeding up yet again as his touch gets more daring.

"Courtney," he whispers. His voice is strained, so choked up that it's almost frightening.

I lift my head and see a hunger in his eyes, and my own is growing to match it. He eases himself on one elbow and rolls me over to my back. The universe goes in slow motion as his face descends towards mine. My lips part in anticipation.

I'm so ready for this. I haven't wanted anyone's lips against mine since he left me, so long ago. How many years has it been? I don't want to count. I don't want to think.

I just want to feel.

Feel his minty, just-brushed breath on my face, feel his sweet lips as they brush against mine, his mouth taking possession of mine. Just *feel*, and bask in happiness.

Sean is here, he's kissing me, he's holding me and-- oh, *God help me*--he's setting me on fire.

I pull his tee shirt out of his pants and slide my hand under it. The barrier of our clothes has become unbearable.

I need to touch his skin. I need him to touch mine.

Sean's urgent fumbling with the buttons of my dress matches my awkward attack on his belt. Without breaking our kiss, he abandons those absurd buttons to help me relieve him of his pants. It's clumsy work inside the zipped-together sleeping bags, but when those are out of the way, he pulls at the hem of my dress, and I wiggle to help him slide it up my body. The bra flies away with the dress to the other side of the room with his tee shirt and my panties vanish beneath our feet.

My breath catches in my throat as he embraces me. At first I feel like we're a study in contrasts. His body, tanned skin and brightly-colored inks and horrible scars, stands out against the flesh of my own ever so pale body.

It's been years since anything but my arms and face were exposed to the sun. My soft skin molds against his firm muscles. But then I realize there's one thing we have in common. Scars.

He can't see mine, not yet, but all I see are his. My fingers trace their contour, I put my lips to the traces war has left on him and it's his turn to purr, but the sound deepens into a growling, predatory rumble in his chest as I explore.

The sound of it makes me bold, daring; more than I ever thought I would be. I reach out to the hardness pulsing against my thigh. The length of my hand delicately lands on steel covered in velvet and he hisses.

"Did I hurt you?" I ask.

He chuckles and whispers, "It's the sweetest kind of torture."

"You'll have to show me--" I can't finish my sentence. How do I ask? The words won't pass my lips. Can a woman tell a man that she wants to learn how to please him? I've been locked up in my warped world for so long, walking on eggshells that I struggle to revive my spontaneity. It's been systematically beaten out of me. "I've never-- I mean, I don't know what to do."

"Hush, Courtney," he says cutting me off. "We'll figure it out."

Sean's finger under my chin tilts my face up and we kiss again. He nibbles on my lips. We roll over until we fall off the inflatable bed, conjuring up memories of long ago happy times when we wrestled for the remote control on his parents' couch. We were so young then, so innocent. A lifetime away.

We untangle ourselves from the sleeping bags and climb back on the mattress. Somehow, I find myself flat on my back, Sean kneeling between my legs and looking at me with hooded eyes. "Do you trust me?"

"With my life." My answer is adamant.

"Then close your eyes and let me take care of you." I blink a few times and obey, shivering with anticipation behind my eyelids. The seconds tick away and the only sound in the room is our labored breathing. I feel him shifting to the side. Goose bumps rise on my arms, all my senses reaching out with new sensitivity, desperate for information denied by my closed eyes.

He leans over and wet lips latch on to my nipple. Oh. My. God. The sensation is too much! I can't breathe. My entire body tenses when he moves from one breast to the other and then peppers slow kisses down my tummy.

He spreads my legs and gasps at the sight of my thigh, at the tire tread scar, at the pockmarks where gravel had been ground in. The bent place, where the bones were broken and never properly set to heal straight.

Well, now he's seen my scars.

"It's nothing," I lie as I lift myself on my elbows to look at him.

Sean presses his lips gently against the marks of my long-ago lesson, then looks up at me.

"I didn't tell you to open your eyes," he scolds, and his growl sends a shiver through me, and the heat and anticipation in his eyes start a storm of flutters low in my belly.

I lay back and close my eyes obediently. I'm rewarded with the most extraordinary tingle as Sean's lips and tongue touch me. The tingle grows in intensity as his fingers explore parts of my body that only I have touched before. I bite my lower lip and whimper. My world tumbles. Sean makes it spin around on its axis.

Yesterday I was in hell; today I've reached the gates of heaven itself.

My hips take on a life of their own, lifting from the bed as the intensity of his kisses and caresses increases. Never have I felt anything like this. A few times, I think I've reached the peak but no—he takes me higher still with each touch of his lips, his tongue.

The sensations are all so new, so intense. With my eyes closed, my world is just a swirling mass of color and feeling and - *Oh, God* -it's incredible. Sean's tongue lashes hard over me, and every muscle in my abdomen clenches each time he touches my clitoris. Now there's something inside me! A finger?

I'm riding a tidal wave and terrified. I want the ride to last forever but I also need it to end soon or I will shatter into thousands of pieces. I want to cry for help, but am at a loss for words, calling out Sean's name over and over like a mantra until I can't speak anymore. The colors explode under my eyelids and I weep with joy.

Sean scoots up the bed and rests on his side next to me. I snuggle against him as he pulls the sleeping bags over us.

"That was--" I whisper into his chest, panting. "Wow. Just, wow."

He chuckles and I can hear the pride in his voice when he says, "You ain't seen *nothin'* yet." Since he's never been one to brag, I resist the urge to tease him. If *that* was nothing, I'll surely die of exhaustion and bliss before the day ends. But what a way to go!

"You *did* tell me to keep my eyes closed," I say.

Sean's hand on the small of my back has grown restless: apparently he thinks I've had enough time to catch my breath. He caresses slowly over the curve of my butt, and I press back against him, sighing happily at the touch.

His hand glides softly up over my hip, along the soft curve of my waist before he drags fingernails lightly up my side. I shiver when the nails graze the lower slope of my breast, and gasp when he tweaks one hardened nipple. My head rests against his broad chest, and it's not much of a reach for me to quickly nip at one of his in return.

"Oh, ho! Feeling frisky, are you?" Sean laughs, and suddenly I'm on my back, and he's on top of me. His movement was so quick, so fluid, I didn't realize it was happening until it was over. He stretches my arms above my head, crossed and pinned at the wrist with one of his strong hands. One of his feet is between my ankles, but he's left my legs together. "You've had enough of a breather, then?"

He has me thoroughly controlled. My hands are locked down, and he could force my legs open in a heartbeat. There's no way I could break free without his permission, his choice to allow it. In any other situation, with any other man, this would be a nightmare.

Here and now? With Sean? It's a dream come true.

"Yes," I say, spreading my feet and pulling my knees back. Opening to him, hiding nothing. Sharing everything.

Still restraining both my wrists tightly with one big hand, Sean reaches over to the emergency pack where I'd found the energy bar earlier, and comes back holding a foil packet. He tears it open with his teeth, and unrolls the condom over his shaft.

His-- his *cock* brushes against my belly and thighs as he kneels between my legs again, and I strain to lift my hips toward it. Sean laughs softly and pulls away, pulling my hands higher and tighter, pinning me to the mattress with a hand just above my mound.

"Please, Sean," I whimper. "I need you."

"I, uh, bought these for something else originally," he says wryly, shaking his head with a chuckle. "They're not lubricated. Have to make sure you're ready," he finishes, and his hand slips through my soft curls. I arch my hips up at him again, trying to make the right contact, and moan as his middle finger swirls a quick, hard circle around my clitoris. A shudder runs through my whole body at the contact, and before it's even subsided, his finger dips lower, pressing carefully inside me.

"I don't-" *gasp* "-think that-" *pant* "-will be a problem."

"Still," he says. "Best to make sure." He smirks at me again, slipping a second finger alongside the first.

I feel so full, so stretched, just from his fingers, but I'm so wet right now that he's able to slide them slowly in and out of me almost effortlessly. I know that his cock is much thicker than they are. He's going to split me in half, and *oh God I want him to!*

"Sean," I moan. "Please-" My voice is strangled to a gasp, my head spins, and a fresh new warm rush floods around his fingers as he curls them inside of me.

"You're right," he says, with a smug look on his face. "It's probably not going to be an issue." I almost want to sob with frustration and loss at the empty feeling when Sean takes his hand away, but now there's something else pressing against me. Something much bigger, and I can't wait for it any longer.

"Don't tease me like this," I tell him, crying out in frustration at the delay. He's right *there*. Just *push!*

"Courtney--" Sean's brow is furrowed in a look of sudden concern. "Is this really what you want? Are you really ready for this? I mean, in your heart?"

"Sean Patrick Pearse," I snarl. "This is the moment I've *wanted* with you, been *waiting* to have with you, ever since I was old enough to understand what it meant."

His eyes soften, and I take advantage of the moment to jerk my hands free.

"So, yes. This is what I want. And I'm ready for this." My arms go around his neck, pulling him down, close to me. Into me. "I love you, Sean."

"I love you, Courtney." His eyes never leave mine, not even for a moment, as his entire length enters me slowly. He's so careful, so gentle. This moment is perfect. It's everything I'd ever dreamed it could be. A steady rhythm of slow, easy strokes grows faster and harder as we find a pace that suits us, lost in a mindless animal passion. I've been holding this all inside for so long, never daring to hope this dream could come true.

It doesn't take long for him to push me to the brink. Sean's thrusts are short now, deep and fast. Every square inch of my skin is on fire, a roaring inferno of ecstasy, and if I try to hold this inside any longer, I'm going to be completely consumed. I scream his name, over and over, as I go over the edge, and Sean follows closely behind. He freezes at the end of a thrust, and I feel his muscles tense under the strain of his own release.

When it's over, when we're spent, both of us shattered and drained, I lay in his arms. I'm not naïve enough to believe he learned about all this in a book. So there's been another girl—or several girls—out there he practiced with, and I smile to myself thinking how odd it is that I don't feel any jealousy. If anything, I feel gratitude. He's mine now. I'm glad one of us knows what we're doing!

"Is it always like that?" I whisper the question.

"I hope so. I guess we'll find out, though." He pauses, and his eyes grow serious. "How are you?"

"I'm... good." I smile at him, softly kissing the edge of his jaw. "No, I'm better than good. I was serious before. Sean, I've wanted to have this with you for so long. I've loved you for as long as I remember, and I've been *in* love with you since I knew there was a difference." My vision is starting to go misty, and I turn my head away. I don't want him to see the tears forming in my eyes. How can I explain them to him? I don't even understand them myself!

"Hey! Hey, now! What's wrong, Courtney?" A callused finger ever so gently catches a droplet from my cheek, and all the years of pent up terror and sorrow and loss and anger and hatred pour out of me in heaving, racking, and above all *purifying* sobbing.

"Nothing's wrong, Sean," I tell him, through the tears. "There's nothing wrong at *all* anymore. You've come back to me. You've taken me away from that—*place.* We're here, together, and soon we're going to be home. But promise me, Sean. Don't run away again."

"I won't." Sean's lips are soft on my forehead, and then he kisses away a tear before it has a chance to fall. "I'm here, for as long as you want me to be." He squeezes me tightly, and long, lean muscles in his arms make a tanned skin and bright ink ripple around me.

There's an answering quiver in me, somewhere low and deep inside, and my crying turns to laughter instead.

"I love you," I tell him, nestling my head against his shoulder, lightly kissing the place where bullets had torn into his body in the ambush he relives in his dreams.

"I love you, too."

Perfect morning sun streams through the window of the cabin, and though we both had most of a full night's rest we drift lazily in and out of sleep in each other's arms. Twice more, I pull him on top of me, on fire with long-forgotten desire for him. The feel of him is glorious, the weight of him pushing down on me. Pushing into me. Setting me on fire wherever he touches me. The second time, he rolls us over and then I'm on top, clumsy and uncoordinated at first, but quickly finding a rhythm, reveling in the brazenness of it all, and collapsing in an exhausted heap after.

Sean lays a possessive hand on my belly, pulling me close again, and laughs when my stomach growls.

"We need to get some-- What time is it, anyway?" Sean pauses, looking around for a clock, then out the window at the sun. "Breakfast? Lunch? It's getting close to noon."

"You have those bar things," I say. "They're not too bad."

"Those are emergency supplies," he says. "They're not anything you'd want to live on, if you don't have to.

Trust me on that." He rolls away for a moment, lying on his stomach and rooting around in the bag. "There's another emergency supply that we're about out of, too." He grins ruefully, holding up the last two foil-wrapped condoms.

"Oh. Well, we don't want to run out of those," I say. "We've got lost time to make up for."

"Okay, then." Sean's voice is gentle, but decisive. "Get dressed, my love. It's about thirty minutes to Belfast. We can have some lunch and do some shopping."

"What'm I going to wear?" I nod at where my old dress and horrible undergarments lay. "Sean, I will *never* put that stuff on again. You took it off me, and it's going to *stay* off me. I want to burn it." I'm surprised at the adamancy in my voice, the venom, and Sean's eyebrows lift.

"Let's see," he says, digging in another bag. "A shirt, at least, that's no problem." He pulls out a well-worn dark blue T-shirt with a gold emblem on it, and hands it to me. Sean's much taller than me, and the shirt easily falls below my hips. "Pants, though, and shoes? Those might be a problem." He holds out a pair of jeans, but I'm skeptical.

"I, ah, don't think this is going to work," I tell him, after I try and fail to pull them on. The jeans simply won't make it over my hips.

"Hm. Well," he says, giving me a sly grin and running a hand over the curve of my hip where his pants won't quite make it past. "Myself, I think I like you without the pants, but I can see how it might be a bit of a problem in public." He pauses for a quick kiss. "So. What do we do?"

"Do you have any longer shirts? Anything that might work almost like a dress?"

"Let me look. I don't think I do," Sean says, digging in his sea bag. "No, doesn't look like I do." He straightens, frowning. "What if you just stay in the truck while I run in, get you something? Nobody would know you were only wearing a shirt," he offers.

"Sean?" I laugh. "Two words for you: *vinyl seats in August* and *my bare legs and ass*. Okay, fine, it's more than two words," I finish, and now it's Sean's turn to chuckle.

"Yeah, I see your point, there," he says. "Not the most comfortable thing."

"Just go. Be quick. Bring food, and some sweatpants and sandals for me. Flip-flops, or something. We can find something nicer later."

"What size? I've never, um, bought women's clothes before." Sean looks nervous at the prospect.

"Oh, big tough Navy SEAL? Scared to go into the women's part of the store?" I laugh.

Sean just shakes his head ruefully, but it's a good question: the last time I had store-bought clothes I was only fifteen. Since then I haven't worn anything new, anything with a size printed on a tag. Anything that hadn't been hand-made, not to mention handed down through at least two or three previous owners.

"Just do your best," I tell him. "Something stretchy, maybe, so if the size isn't quite right, I can at least wear it to pick out something that *does* fit."

"Okay. I can do that. Stretchy pants, food, and some more... emergency supplies."

"And Sean? Come back home to me soon," I tell him. "I don't want to be away from you any longer than I absolutely have to be."

After the rumbling sound of the truck fades into the distance, I have a look around the small cabin. It may be small and spare by Sean's standards, even after his time in temporary barracks and tents in Iraq and Afghanistan, but to me, it's a palace after the hovel I shared with Daniel on the farm. And it's dusty, too. If we're spending a couple days here, then I'm going to make good use of my time while Sean's away. Finding a rag and some cleaning supplies in the small bathroom, I set to work.

I catch a glimpse of my reflection in the mirror over the sink, and I stop to have a longer look at myself. There weren't many mirrors back *there*, and even when I found myself in front of one, I hated to look in them. I couldn't stand to see the haunted look in my own eyes, but that's all over now. The girl who stares back at me from the mirror is a much different version of me: free, happy. Full of hope.

Sean's shirt is big on me in most places, but it's stretched tightly over my chest, emphasizing the gold logo. It's an eagle perched on a crossed trident, pistol and anchor, with a big number 3 behind. There's a motto on it:

"I KNOW I'M GOING TO HEAVEN BECAUSE I'VE SPENT MY TIME IN HELL" in blocky letters.

I'm not going to Heaven. I'm already here.

I lose myself in cleaning, lose all track of time, but I'm getting the cabin into some sort of order. The small shower is cleaned, the dust is mostly gone from the flat surfaces, and I've set wildflowers gathered outside in a vase on the small table where we'll eat.

I smile to myself at the familiar rumbling sound of a truck pulling into the driveway, and tuck away the rag I've been using. After a quick look in the mirror, I wipe away a smudge of dust or fireplace soot from my nose and cheek, and tie my hair back in a ponytail with a ribbon I found in a drawer in the small kitchen, and rush to the door to meet Sean.

My hand has already turned the knob, and the door is already open just a crack when I realize why the truck sounded so familiar.

It's not Sean.

Chapter 14

Sean

Monday Afternoon, 15 August 2016

Holy shit.

What a weekend.

Just a few days ago, I was bored, wondering what I'd do with my life now that Uncle Sam had decided I was too broken to keep on killing people for him, and now here I am on my way to buy lunch and clothes for the girl of my dreams. And of course, more condoms, also for the girl of my dreams.

Life is looking up. Just add a job and a place of our own, and it'll be perfect.

So, clothing first. There's not a Walmart or K-Mart or a Sears or anything within a reasonable distance of the camp in Belmont, but Belfast is close. When my grandpa was young, Belfast was referred to as the "Big City" by folks who lived in the small communities of Waldo County. I suppose that a city of less than seven thousand people is pretty huge when you have to walk a mile and a half to find your nearest neighbor, but it feels tiny these days.

Still, there's shopping there. The tourist boutiques are a non-starter. I don't know enough about women's sizes to even think about shopping at one of them. Ah! That's perfect, a Reny's, that pillar of the Maine retail industry. Selection might be a little hit-or-miss there, but I'm sure there's something that will fit Courtney.

They say it's always best to buy a woman clothes that are too small rather than too large, so I buy a few copies of each thing in different sizes. I'll give them to her smallest first, and stop when we get the right fit. A couple pairs of stretchy pants, some panties. Sandals. I don't even bother with bras-- I might not know much about women's clothing, but I know that a guy picking *those* out without knowing the right size is just begging for a disaster.

Just down the street there's a Walgreen's, and item number two on my list. There's a good selection, and-- what the hell, let's be adventurous. I'm definitely looking forward to trying out some of these with Courtney. How did I get this lucky? There's some basic food stuff here, too-- junk food, mostly, but we've only got to hide out for a short while. We can start eating healthily when we get back to civilization.

Speaking of eating healthily! There's the McDonald's. She'd mentioned missing it on the drive south yesterday. The fries won't be exactly *hot* anymore by the time I get them home to her, but it's been so long since she's had a french fry that I don't think she'll mind too much. And there's a Dunkin' Donuts behind it, so that's breakfast tomorrow taken care of as well, and I could certainly use a cup of coffee, right now, anyway.

Shopping is over as quickly as I can manage, and I set out on the drive back Route 3 and down the Lincolnville Road. It's a good time to think, to take stock of where I'm at.

All those daydreams I'd had, imagining a life with Courtney while I was at war? I'd never expected to see them come true, but here I am driving home with her waiting for me. Sure, it's only just her waiting for me, but a family can come in time. It'd be nice to have time to ourselves, too. Just for a while.

A family. I think back to the other night, watching over Courtney through the binoculars at the compound. Watching her playing with that little girl. She's good with kids. Every movement she made spoke of a deep caring for that child. Back in the war zone, I'd never dared to even think too loudly about the idea of a family, but now? I look forward to having serious conversations on that subject with the woman I love, and soon.

It's impulsive, sure, but I have to talk to my mom about this. I know Courtney and I had agreed that we'd wait and surprise Bill when we went back to Portland, but I want to give my mom a little time to prepare. She's got a flair for the appropriate, and she deserves some advance warning.

I've only got a few miles before cell coverage runs out—it's insane, to me, that there's perfect coverage at

Moosehead, but it's so spotty here within a few miles of civilization, but I guess, that's what happens when you have a paper company that's willing to spend money in order to stay in touch with their logging crews. She picks up on the third ring.

"Sean! I was just talking about you to one of the other nurses. How are you?" She's bright, cheerful. Happy to hear from me.

"I'm fine, Mom. Listen, I only have a minute, I'm on my way back to the camp, and you know how the reception is there."

"Sure do. Bill uses that as an excuse whenever he goes up there," she says, laughter in her voice. "I know your father- God rest his soul- would have, if he'd had a cell phone." There's genuine warmth and care in her voice when she speaks of Courtney's father, but there's still plenty of sorrow for my father, too. I'm glad she found someone, though, and Dad would be as well. "So how'd your wild goose chase go? Did you find anything up there to Greenville?" Mom has no expectation that I've found anything. She's just making conversation.

"Yeah, listen, Mom. About that." I pause, take a deep breath. "I've got something for Bill. A surprise package, so to speak. Special delivery."

"No way!" Mom's excited, now. "No kidding? That really was them in that picture?"

"Yeah," I tell her. "It was really them, and Courtney's with me at the camp now--"

"When are you guys coming home?"

"Not for a couple days. There's... safety concerns. Pretty serious ones, in my opinion." No way I'm telling her just *how* serious I think they are. "Look, I don't have much time. I can't really tell you any more, right now. I just wanted you to be ready. Keep it to yourself, though. Don't tell Bill yet. What he doesn't know can't hurt him. Or you."

"Mum's the word, Sean. I won't tell him anything at all." At least, I think that's what she said: her voice is statical now, cutting in and out.

"Okay. Good, thanks. Look, Mom? Signal's getting lost now. We'll talk to you again soon, okay?"

Dead air is the only answer. I'm out of the coverage area. Maybe we ought to invite the paper companies to do work out here, just so they can put up more cell towers.

There's still another five minutes' drive left after losing the signal. It feels like an eternity before the turnoff for Camp Road comes up, and at least three more ice ages could have come and gone in the mile or so from there until I pull into the driveway.

A cardboard drink carrier full of coffee in my left hand, donuts, McDonald's and clothing in my right, I kick the Blazer's door shut and fumble the cabin door open.

"Hi, honey, I'm ho-"

My sixth sense urges me to duck and something heavy flies over my head. There's movement to the right, and instinctively I pivot toward it. The shopping is dropped, forgotten, and the coffee in my left hand is an impromptu weapon swinging up. *What the fuck is going on here?*

Even before the coffee – hopefully still hot enough to hurt – takes the first target in the face. I see, at least, three more sources of movement. *Sploosh!* The coffee is still apparently hot enough. The guy to my right screams. Two quick punches to the gut, duck to avoid something behind me, elbow to the balls to keep him out of the fight. Pivot. New target.

Whenever I'm in combat, time seems to slow. It's like watching the world go by in slow motion. I have plenty of time to recognize the stringy, greasy black hair, patchy beard and acne scars on the face of the young man I labeled Target Alpha just a couple days before. Jeremiah, Courtney called him. He's the asshole they intend to marry her off to. He's off balance now, reeling, having unexpectedly missed my head with a baseball bat.

Alpha starts his backswing, but he doesn't really know what he's doing. In half a heartbeat, I've taken the bat from him and given him a couple sharp love taps in the stomach, and a quick – but very hard – shot to the nuts. I spin again, checking the first guy – I recognize him now. Brother Lucas, the wife-beating cocksucker. I watch for any sign of threat, while digging in the small of my back for the Beretta. He's still down, but there are other people here, too. I'll come back to him in a moment, finish the job, but first I need to scan the room for other danger.

And find Courtney.

It only takes a moment.

Three other people are in the room. Courtney, dressed again in the threadbare dress she'd worn when she ran away from them, stands between that old prick Emmanuel and her mother. Courtney stands unnaturally straight, her head back, as if someone's pulling on her long hair from behind. Her face is streaked with tears, her lip is split and swollen, and she has the start of a truly spectacular black eye. Emmanuel has a rusty revolver pressed hard into her right breast.

Someone's going to pay for that. In blood.

I hold the big Italian pistol in a two-handed grip, the front sight blade centered between his eyes, below the saintly halo of frizzy white hair. What a load of bullshit that image is.

"I strongly suggest you let go of her," I say. My voice is calm, even. He has to know this is a no-win situation for him. He watched me plow through the toughs he brought along.

"I'm sorry, my son," he says. "But I'm afraid that's just not possible. You see, Sister Courtney belongs to God, and he has called upon us to bring her home."

"Called upon you?" I ask. "Personally?"

The old man's only reply is a half-smile and a small shrug. He's amused.

"I think you should request a verification of your orders. I can arrange for you to speak to God, one-on-one, if you'd like?"

"Oh, that won't be necessary," the old man says. "The New Revelation is quite specific about many things, and I've never yet been wrong about The Lord's Will." The good cheer drains from his face, and there's iron in his voice when he continues speaking. "Now, my son, you need to submit to The Lord's will, or it will go very hard on the young woman here. Put. Down. The. Gun."

"Right," I say. "About that." My pistol doesn't waver from his face. "The way I figure this, you fucks didn't drive all the way down here from your little let's-drink-Kool-Aid-and-play-farmer bullshit just to *kill* her. She's valuable to you for some reason. You want her alive."

"I do want her alive," Emmanuel says, nodding. "Very much so. But, I'm afraid that her life is less important to the success of The Lord's plan than is my own." He jabs harder with the muzzle of the revolver, and Courtney gasps with pain.

"If you want to live to keep on carrying out your plan, then you need to let her go and get the fuck out of here." My voice is cold, and utterly sincere. "And I think you're rational enough to understand what's going to happen to you. And that means that you're not going to kill her."

"You know what?" He smiles thinly, nodding again. "You're right, my son. I absolutely couldn't kill this beloved girl. She's going to be my daughter-in-law, after all. She'll be mother to my grandsons."

"Oh, right. Of course. You'll have to wait a while for grandchildren. Your boy's not going to be doing much with his dick for a while." Okay, what's his play now? He's not giving in, not this easily.

"You do certainly have quite the talent for digging to the heart of things, don't you, Mister Pearse?" He pulls the gun away from Courtney's breast, holding it upside down by the trigger guard. "You're right. I won't kill her." He sets the gun on the floor.

"Courtney, come away from them." There's the briefest flash of hope in her eyes, and she takes a hesitant step toward me, but Courtney is hauled up short by her long hair, held tightly by her mother, a straight razor in her hand. Heather yanks on Courtney's hair, jerking the girl's head back, and lays the blade against her daughter's throat.

"Whore!" Heather's voice is shrill. "You're not going anywhere." I shift targets.

"You see, Mister Pearse?" The old man is smug, satisfied. "You're right. I am rational. You and I both know that were I to kill the girl, I'd never be able to continue The Lord's Work on this sinful, fallen Earth. But Heather?" He shrugs eloquently, gesturing to the woman. "You are, I believe, fond of Kipling? I saw his book on your nightstand. 'The female of the species--'"

"Is more deadly than the male," I interrupt, finishing the line. "Yeah. I get the reference."

Until now, I hadn't paid a lot of attention to Heather, but now that I have a reason to look at her I see that the old son of a bitch is right. Heather Dwyer – or whatever her last name is now – has lost weight. Never a heavy woman, now her skin is stretched grotesquely tight over her skull, and a fey light shines from her eyes.

"You can't have her, Pearse!" Heather spits my name as if it's the vilest curse in the English language. "Her father's sin cannot touch her! *Your* father's sin cannot have her! I won't allow it!"

Oh, fuck.

"Heather?" I've never been good at the whole soothing thing, but I'm trying my best. "Please, put the blade down, let her go. You don't want to hurt your own daughter, do you?"

Heather's eyes go wide and she howls wordlessly. I can't take my eyes off the glittering edge of the razor in her trembling hands. There's a faint red line beneath the blade now.

"Look, I get that you don't like your ex-husband, and I'm sure you have some perfectly good reasons." Reasons that make sense in your fucked up reality. "But I don't know what my father ever did to you, and Courtney? She's a good person. She's..." I trail off.

I have no idea what to say here. My normal method of dealing with armed crazy fucks isn't going to work here. I could easily disassemble her head with a bullet, but the way she's holding that knife? Gravity would take over, and Courtney would be just as dead.

"You see, my son?" The asshole's voice is gentle, his hands spread in a gesture of peace. "We will be leaving here, with Courtney, and you will remain here. Alone." He smiles now. "Unless you'd prefer that we all remain here, together."

For a moment, I consider it. God help me, but I consider it. There's no good outcome here. Either she goes back with them to a life of hell, and I'll be the one that allowed it to happen, or she dies. And I'll be the one that allowed it to happen. *Fuck.*

"You see, Mister Pearse, now we're in a much different position." Emmanuel slowly approaches me, step by deliberate step. "I hope you understand the severity of your situation. Of her peril?"

I'm willing to die for what I believe in, but am I willing to let the woman I love die for what I believe in? A drop of blood slides down the edge of the blade, hanging near the tip. If I'm going to do it, it's got to be now.

Emmanuel steps between me and the mother-daughter pair, and places his hand on my gun. A slight pressure pushes the barrel down and to the side. My decision is made. I can't allow her to be killed in front of me. I'd survive, guaranteed. I'd be the only motherfucker walking away from this place, but I wouldn't want to, not with the woman I love lying dead with her throat slit by her own mother. The female of the species, indeed.

"There, you see, Sister Courtney?" The old bastard beams triumphantly, and turns away from me. He doesn't even bother to disarm me first. He took my measure, and knows I won't do anything to get Courtney killed. God forgive me. No, fuck that. It's Courtney's forgiveness I'll need, not God's. "Is there anything that you'd like to say to

Mister Pearse, Sister Courtney? Or, no, I'm sorry-
Daughter Courtney. Perhaps I'm a little ahead of schedule,
but I've always thought of you as a daughter. And soon
you will be."

"Don't hurt him!" Courtney's voice is frantic.
"Please," she begs. "Please! I'll do anything. I'll be the best
wife Jeremiah could ever want, I'll have his babies, I'll
cook, I'll clean--" Her voice breaks, cracks, as her mother
jerks her head to the side by the hair, using leverage and
pain to force my love to her knees on the floor. It breaks
my heart to hear her plead like this. She doesn't get it. Yet.

"You'll do your duty to your husband and your
sons," Heather shrieks at her daughter. "You'll do it
because it's your duty! Because it's your punishment! For
Eve's sin! I've fought my whole life to overcome the
temptation of Eve's sin, and I'll help your husband as he
does his duty to purge the sin from *you*, whore! The
Scarlet One, the Whore of Babylon, will have no part in
my household!"

Where there's breath, there's hope. She'll be alive, at
least. So long as she lives, she can fight. She can escape.
Even if I'm dead, she can live to fight another day.

"You wish me to give him mercy, my daughter?"
Emmanuel shakes his head sadly. "I'm sorry, child. There
are some things beyond my power to grant. Mister Pearse
has committed a great wrong in the eyes of The Lord."
Courtney's eyes go huge as she understands.

My father's pistol is dead weight by my side, useless
to me. I could save myself, but Courtney's life is more

precious to me than my own. Anything I do to save myself will doom her. Out of the corner of my eye, I can pick up movement. Lucas and Jeremiah are on their feet again. Jeremiah has the bat again; Lucas has a sawed off double-barrel shotgun. My window of opportunity has closed.

Emmanuel pulls a radio out of his pocket and makes a quick call, ordering a truck to be brought around. While issuing his orders, he waves idly at me, and Jeremiah takes the pistol away from me.

"You're finished," he whispers in my ear. His voice is fuzzy, he's lisping. *Finissed.* I must have broken some teeth.

I'm oddly pleased by this. I hope his balls are in worse condition.

Through it all, Courtney and I do not break eye contact. The red line on her throat stands out in stark contrast to her tanned neck, droplets welling up along the length of the cut.

"Sister Heather? If you would, please escort my future daughter-in-law to the truck." Emmanuel stoops to pick up the revolver, and points it at me. "Jeremiah?"

Jeremiah's look of triumph is spoiled a bit by the swollen lip and rapidly blackening eye. I know he's missing some teeth. I hope I broke his jaw. He's hunched over a bit, too. Maybe I didn't get him in the balls quite as hard as I'd thought. Heather and Jeremiah each grab one of Courtney's arms, and Heather still has a hand tangled in her hair, but my love drags her heels and twists to keep her eyes locked to mine. I think she understands, now.

"I love you," Courtney says. My heart breaks. It's the last thing I can say to her. The last memory she'll ever have of me. What the fuck do I say?

"I know" is all I can come up with, and then she's gone, whisked out the door and away from me. Forever.

With my love out of the cabin, I'm alone with Emmanuel and Lucas.

"All right, asshole." My voice is steady. "Let's get this over with."

"Hm?" The bushy white brows furrow in a question, then he laughs. "Oh, Mister Pearse. You misunderstand me. I'm not going to kill you."

"You're going to have wife beater here do it?" All the scorn I can muster is layered into those words. I'll never have the chance to kill Lucas myself. It's not the biggest regret of my life, but it's definitely on the list of things I wish I'd managed to accomplish.

"Ah, you saw that?" Emmanuel nods sagely. "In a way, that will make this simpler. It provides a framework, if you will, through which you may reach understanding."

"Right. Because understanding is so important now." I shake my head. "You gotta be shitting me. Is this the part, seriously, where you explain your evil plan before you kill me?"

"You mistake me, Mister Pearse. Sean, if I may." He's smiling at me, but it's a 'more in sorrow than in anger' kind of thing. "Let me be clear: I do not intend, desire, or expect for you to die here today."

"So, what, you're going to just let me go?" Are you fucking serious?

"Your fate will be in the hands of The Lord." Emmanuel steeples his fingers, bowing his head slightly. Beady eyes glitter underneath bushy white brows. "You have done great wrong in His eyes, Mister Pearse. You have stolen His property. But it is not for me to take your life today."

"Why? 'Thou shalt not kill?'" I should just shut the fuck up, but in spite of myself I'm curious.

"The Lord's Commandment actually does not say 'thou shalt not kill,' it says 'thou shalt not commit *murder*,' if you read the original wording. It's a fine distinction, but I'm sure you understand. The Lord himself commands killing, from time to time." He looks at me expectantly.

"Oh, of course. It makes perfect sense." No, no it doesn't. You're insane.

"You are no threat to me, to *us*, my son. Should you attempt to intervene, to stop The Lord's Work and spirit her away again, it will not go so easily on you. You believed yourself hidden away securely, yet we found you in just barely twenty-four hours. You cannot hide from His eyes, my son. Even as Adam and Eve tried to hide their sin from The Lord in the Garden, you will *always* be found."

"Yeah," I say. "I was a little curious about that."

"Sister Heather has not been well, of late," Emmanuel says. "She has not, shall we say, been herself.

She made a remarkable recovery, though, at my son's description of a blue four-wheel drive Chevrolet with rather a loud engine. We did, at first, assume that it was her former husband driving it, though. When the truck was not found at her father's place of residence, Sister Heather remembered this place. You, however, were a bit of a surprise. The Lord suggested a cautious approach to me, that we not confront you until we had something in the way of a lever with which to control you."

"A hostage. Courtney."

"The young lady's life was my surety of your good behavior today, and she will remain so in the future. You care deeply for her, as she so obviously does for you. She will believe you to be dead, and she will mourn you, and then she will live out her life as the mother of the next prophet. I have foreseen it." The crazy old bastard smiles benevolently at me, as if this explains everything.

"So, you're going to murder her if I get out of line in the future?"

"No. If a death is caused in defense of myself, or of my flock, or of The Lord's Work, then it cannot be considered murder." His eyes go flinty, his voice cold. "And if you become a threat, Mister Pearse, even then I won't kill her. Her mother will." The engine idling outside revs twice, and Emmanuel looks at his wristwatch. "This has been a pleasant diversion, my son, but my flock grows impatient. We have an important matter to take care of at home. Brother Lucas, if you would please?" He points to his revolver on the floor, and Lucas wordlessly hands him the rusty weapon.

"Now, my son, we need to finalize today's lesson. You need a couple days to think about this, and to understand that it truly *is* for the best. We don't need you doing anything rash in the heat of the moment, you understand. Give me your phone, please?"

I pull it from my pocket, toss it to him wordlessly. The throw is intentionally short, and the old man is forced to stoop on creaking knees to pick it up.

"That was beneath you, my son."

"I will not steal from you, and I despise the necessity of damaging your property, but, I'm sure you understand that you must have solitude to consider things. You will be as Our Lord in the wilderness, though I doubt you'll remain here for forty days and nights."

The gunshot is loud in the cabin, and turns my brand new phone into scattered wreckage of glass and aluminum. Even over the ringing in my ears and the truck outside, I hear Courtney screaming in grief and horror.

"Brother Lucas? If you will conduct the lesson?"

The big man slaps his palm with Jeremiah's bat, stepping silently toward me.

"This gives me no pleasure, Mister Pearse," the old man says. "None at all. I want you to remember this lesson and learn it well. I need you to remember that her life is surety for your good behavior. Repent of your sin, and never become a threat to us who do The Lord's Work."

Lucas is a big man, strong, and he swings the bat with authority. The first strike takes me in the gut, and after only a few blows I feel ribs crack. He's untrained, used to beating people who can't fight back. I could take the bat away from him in a heartbeat, but if I walk out of this building and these two fucks don't, then Courtney's dead and it will have all been for nothing.

"I believe the young man has learned his lesson now, Brother Lucas. We need to be on the road for home." Emmanuel looks at his watch again, and pauses by the door. "Goodbye, Mister Pearse. I trust you'll keep this lesson in mind?"

Never interrupt your enemy when he's busy making a mistake. It's a mistake to leave me alive, but if that's what they want to do, then I'm certainly not going to argue the point. I'll absolutely make them regret it later, though.

"Believe me. I'll never forget it," I say, gritting my teeth against the pain.

"Lights out, sinner," Lucas whispers in my ear. They're the first words he's spoken since I arrived. He steps back, the floor creaking under his bulk as he winds up for a final swing of the bat.

Hold on, Courtney. I'll come for you. Just hold on. I'll come fo-

Chapter 15

Courtney

Monday Late Afternoon, 15 August 2016

The stench in the truck is horrible. The acrid reek of bile seeps into everything. My only consolation is that I'm not the only one who has to suffer through it. Yet, no one else seems to notice. Not Jeremiah because he can't breathe through his nose. Not *her* because she's in Never-Never land. I lost my love.

I lost my mother.

I lost my future.

I lost everything today.

The woman sitting next to me is not my mother. She's just the shell in which my mother used to live, hollowed out and refilled by Father Emmanuel. By Satan.

A childhood memory burns through my mind with absolute clarity. It's one of those moments when an adult's statement, something that didn't make any sense at the time, comes back to light after being tucked away in a dark memory corner for years. I remember my dad coming back from the nursing home one day and telling my mother that the hardest thing to do was to mourn someone who was still alive.

I get it now. I finally understand what he meant. Dementia had stolen my grandmother's identity just as surely as Satan has broken my mother's.

So today, I'm mourning the woman sitting next to me. My mother is gone. Strange how it doesn't hurt as much as I thought it would.

I've known for a long time where this was going. Is that why?

Or is it because the pain of losing Sean is so overwhelming?

My heart stopped at the instant I heard the sound of the gunshot inside the cabin. Of course, it started beating again, but I may as well be dead inside. As empty as my mother's husk. The most precious part of me is gone.

Other girls dreamed of meeting Prince Charming, but not me. I always knew who my handsome prince was. Sean was always a part of my life, and even when he ran away, he still visited me in my dreams. The fantasy of a future life with him kept me going.

Satan has stolen everything from me. But I will get even.

Maybe I already did?

I was blessed to have had one night with Sean. Just one night, and that one glorious morning. It's more than I imagined I would ever have, and not nearly enough.

The minutes tick away and time takes on a strange quality. The ride lasts forever and yet it seems so much faster than driving the opposite direction with Sean. It makes no sense.

Then again, what *does* make sense in my twisted little corner of hell?

It's dusk by the time Satan parks the truck in the compound. The lights are out in the refectory already. We've missed dinner, but I don't care. I don't think I'll ever be hungry again.

Jeremiah opens the door and slides out of the truck very slowly. He looks like he's in pain. Good! There's no kindness in me, not a caring bone left in my body. My own pain helps me hide the pleasure I feel watching him hobble away, but my exit from the truck is just as pitiful as his.

Heather – I can't think of her as my mother, not anymore - is right behind me, catching me before I stumble. She's so thin now, so wasted away, yet her strength amazes me. She props me up and pulls me in direction of the penance box. I don't have it in me to resist anymore. Even if I did, what good could it possibly do me? Sean's dead. Because of me.

But I get a reprieve from hell, issued by Satan himself.

"My dear, Sister Heather," he coos. "We shall attend to your daughter's ... *correction* in just a moment. There's a much more urgent matter that requires my attention first, and since it concerns her, she should be present." His tone is so sweet that I fear the worst. Over the years, I've learned that the honey dripping from his lips is always the prelude to the bitterest taste. "Please take her to the chapel."

My mother pulls on my arm, and in obedient silence I follow and enter our most well maintained building. The hard benches and uncomfortable pews have been moved around so the elders of the community can sit in one long line in front of the pulpit, facing an empty space where the congregation would normally be seated. Empty, but for two folding metal chairs.

They're seated as judges, but Satan had said my punishment would wait? Who are the chairs for?

A sense of foreboding comes over me, breaking through even the numb emptiness that's—oh God, I can't think about that. I shiver involuntarily. Last spring, the elders sat in judgement on an adulterous woman. She was stoned to death. Because that's what the Bible says to do. But the Bible also says "let he who is without sin cast the first stone," and when that horrible old man repeated Jesus' words of mercy, every single one of those hypocritical bastards stepped forward with a rock in his hands.

Elders? More like apprentice demons, twisting anything good and right about Jesus and turning it into horror. Thugs, Sean called them. *Oh, Sean!*

It was not supposed to have been a public execution, but it happened so close to one of my hives that I heard everything. Her screams will be etched in my memory forever.

The thugs end their hushed conversation when Satan walks in behind us. Surprisingly, he doesn't join the elders but stops right beside my mother and me.

"Have you reached a decision?" he asks to the silent assembly.

"Yes, Father Emmanuel. We have," says the eldest member of our community. "They were caught. They were witnessed in their unnatural act by your sons, Brother Jeremiah and Brother Nathan. There can be no defense of this... *abomination*." He sneers at me. Why would he be looking at me? What do I have to do with anything here?

"I see," Emmanuel says. He doesn't seem affected or surprised. He knew all along what was going to happen. "The Lord is very clear on the matter. The Book of Leviticus," he intones. His voice is deep, projecting. He's on a stage, acting. It's a performance. "The twentieth chapter, the thirteenth verse."

I didn't think my day could get any worse. I've been shattered already, destroyed. On top of everything that's already happened today, there's nothing that could break me further. Except that verse. I know it by heart, from a thousand sermons – rants, really, more than preaching – on sin, and how God will destroy America, and why God will destroy America, and it always comes back to this verse. I'm ready to vomit again when Satan continues.

"If a man also lie with mankind, as he lieth with a woman," he recites, "both of them have committed an abomination: they shall surely be put to death; their blood shall be upon them." There is an ecstatic glee painted on his face.

And that's why I'm here. That's why there are two chairs: Daniel and Joshua. I've been so wrapped up in my own pain, I couldn't see what was plainly in front of me.

Despite my mother's deadly grip on my arm, I turn around to face Emmanuel.

"No!" I scream, heedless of the danger to myself. "No, Father Emmanuel! You can't do this! He's your brother!"

He looks back at me and, just for an instant, sadness replaces the ecstasy in his eyes. He shakes his head, "Courtney, my child, I *must*. The Lord commands, and it is not for us to disobey. How could I face my flock if I showed weakness where my own flesh and blood is concerned? The Lord detests sin."

This is twisted, this is evil! He's going to execute his own brother!

My marriage to Daniel may have been a fraud, nothing but a convenient fiction to keep us both safe, but over the past five years, I've grown to care about him very much. He's kind, sweet. He's a good man. And now his own brother is going to murder him, simply because of who he loves.

"And yet, though The Lord's commands must be followed, we may show some mercy," Emmanuel continues. "I will *not* stone my brother."

I let out a sigh of relief but tense again quickly as the silence grows heavy. "What will you do to my husband?" I ask. Daniel isn't my husband, not anymore, if he ever even was, but I don't want this to happen to him. He's a good person, a gentle and loving man.

"The Lord's Word tells us that these abominations must be put to death, but it does not say we must be cruel about it. My brother will be granted a quick death." Emmanuel keeps on speaking but the buzzing in my ear is so loud I can't make out what he's saying. The words "merciful bullet" echo in the room but I refuse to hear them.

This can't be happening. This is not real. This is just a dream, like one of Sean's nightmares.

In full denial mode, led by my mother and Emmanuel, I follow the elders to a clearing in the forest, where a small backhoe sits next to a pit. Daniel and Joshua stand next to the hole, blindfolded, hands tied behind their backs.

"Daniel!" I scream out, and his blindfolded head turns, looking for my voice, but then his head droops, his shoulders slumped. I'd meant to offer him comfort, let him know I cared, but all I'd done was let him know I'd been found and brought back. He'd had such hope for me, for my future. For my happiness. Now he'll spend his last moments without even that slight consolation.

I've only made things worse.

Jeremiah, standing behind them, roughly shoves both men to the very edge of the pit. Their hands are tied, but their shoulders brush together, and Joshua's mouth moves as he says something I cannot hear. Daniel nods his head, and the two men lean against each other, looking for one last touch, one last moment together. Heather takes my hand, and for just a moment, I think – I hope – that she's trying to offer me comfort, but when I glance at her, my mother's teeth are bared in anticipation.

When Jeremiah raises the gun, I close my eyes. I can't watch this. This is evil! These are good men! They've never hurt anyone!

I flinch at each of the gunshots, and I don't open my eyes again until I hear the backhoe's rumbling engine and whining hydraulics. I can't even cry yet. My tears have all been shed. I have none left for the kind man, that sweet, gentle, and naïve man that pretended to be my mate. I try to find solace in the fact that he and Joshua are now together for eternity.

Lucas pushes the dirt into the hole with the backhoe, covering the last two pieces of goodness in my life, but I manage to hold it together until Jeremiah comes to stand behind me, placing a hand on the small of my back.

"Now don't be sad, my darling." Jeremiah's breath is hot, wet in my ear. "You'll get to be with a *real* man soon enough. You didn't need that *faggot*." He spits the word in my ear, and the disgusting hand on my back slides down to my backside, cupping and squeezing.

"I've *already* been with a real man," I whisper back to him. "And I'll be with him again before I'll *ever* be with you." The emptiness inside me, the void created by the loss of everything that mattered to me in the world, is suddenly less empty. I'm filling with a white-hot rage.

"If you want to be a bitch," Jeremiah hisses through lips swollen and cracked from my lost love's fists, "then I'll treat you like one. You can live on all fours like a dog, eat off the floor like a dog whenever I feel like throwing you some scraps." He reaches around, grabbing my chin, and yanks my head around to look at him. "And I'm going to fuck you just like a dog." I can smell the acrid reek of burnt gunpowder on his hand.

"Is that what you like?" I ask. I know that taunting him is dangerous, but I just don't care. What more can he do to me? "Is that what gets you off? Do you like that? Fucking a dog?" The fury in his eyes gives me some satisfaction.

"You'll pay for that," he whispers, groping harder, deeper. He's reminding me that I'm property, not a person. *His* property. "I'm going to enjoy our wedding night. Much, *much* more than you will." Groping me has left him excited and hard, and my stomach turns again as he presses himself against my backside. *Sean must not have hurt him as badly as it looked.*

"No, you won't," I tell him, surreptitiously making a claw of my hand and holding it straight down, hidden in my long skirt. Jeremiah leers at me, keeping eye contact, holding my chin steady. He doesn't want me to look away when his other hand reaches its goal, touching me through the skirt. He wants to see in my eyes that I'm beaten, that I recognize his triumph.

Not. Gonna. Happen.

I quickly jerk my hips forward, away from him, and dig my hooked fingers into the softest bits of Jeremiah's body, squeezing his balls, twisting them as hard as I can through his jeans, and I smile viciously at the gasp of shock and pain as his eyes go wide in breathless agony. You're the one that wanted me to look in your eyes, you filthy monster!

For the first time in my life, I become a wild thing, giving in to every violent impulse. I jump on him, catching a fistful of greasy hair and clawing at his face with the other as I drag him to the ground. My nails are short and ragged, but I'm out for blood. Jeremiah's fluttering hands bat at mine, blocking me while I try to gouge out his eyes with hooked thumbs. Even surprised and in pain, he's stronger than I am, and he's starting to catch his breath. Can't let him recover yet!

I lift a knee and drive it squarely into his balls and fresh pain deflates him like a popped balloon, and his hands go limp for a moment. That moment is all I'm going to need. Snarling, I reach for his eyes again but never quite make it. My advantage ends when I feel fingers knotted in my hair, dragging me off him, leaving me sprawled on my back on the ground. The break is all

Jeremiah needs, and he scrambles to his feet awkwardly, hunching over from the pain between his legs.

My mot- no, not my mother. Heather! -and Father Emmanuel pull me to my feet, and Heather slaps me squarely, her face red with fury. She takes a deep breath, getting ready to scream, but Satan stops her with a raised hand.

"Now, now, Sister Heather," he says. "It's no longer your place to discipline her."

"But--" she sputters, but Emmanuel interrupts coldly.

"It is *not. Your. Place!*" Satan turns to Jeremiah – could anyone ever by more accurately called 'the spawn of Satan?' - holding out his hand. "My son will provide correction for her. After all, she will be *his* wife."

"Not yet!" I spit the words defiantly at him.

"A mere technicality," he says with a shrug. "Which will be corrected soon enough."

"I will *never* be his wife!" With effort, I regain my calm, forcing my face to relax into an expression of serenity. "I'd sooner spend eternity in that hole with Daniel and Joshua than spend a single *moment* as wife to your son."

"Oh, my dear child." Emmanuel seems amused by my defiance. "You have a *much* grander destiny than that. You will come to accept your place in The Lord's Plan. In time."

I open my mouth to make a hot retort, but Jeremiah has recovered enough to silence me with a hard fist on top of the already black eye my mother had given me at the camp. He's cocking his fist back for a second blow when his father stops him.

"You should perhaps go easy for now," Emmanuel tells his son in a deceptively mild voice. "After all, if my dear daughter Courtney is unconscious, she may not absorb the full impact of today's lesson."

"Yes, father," Jeremiah says, with a venomous glare at me.

Emmanuel looks at me, folding his hands as if in prayer. "You should pay attention, my daughter. My brother, your husband – your *late* husband, I should say – violated The Lord's commands. I did not wish to see him come to this end, but Daniel's unnatural acts doomed him. As The Lord's word says: 'their blood shall be upon their own heads.'"

"You're a murderer," I say. My cheeks may be swollen and bruised, wet with involuntary tears, and I feel a trickle of blood again from a re-split lip, but I won't give him the satisfaction of crying. Never again.

"Hardly, my child. Hardly. Man's law may say so, but we do not recognize the laws of Man. The Lord has commanded that sodomites be put to death, and the faithful must follow his commands." Emmanuel turns to look at the now-filled pit where his brother is buried, and his face shows regret, maybe even grief, but he hardens again before meeting my eyes. "Those who flout The

Lord's commands must pay for their sins, and those who try to thwart His plans? They must learn obedience to His laws, submission to His will. As your young Mister Pearse learned this afternoon."

I lunge again, this time at the father instead of the son, but even my adrenaline-fueled strength is fading fast, and my mother is able to easily hold me back.

"Fuck you!" I shout at him, and with the last shreds of my defiance, spit at him. It's more blood than saliva. Focused on my triumph – small, but the most I can manage, right now – I don't see Jeremiah's fist until it's too late to avoid it. My head rocks to the side from the blow, bright lights flashing in my eyes and a strange sour metallic taste in my mouth. I fall back and my head hits something hard. My last thought is a wish for death.

My wish is not granted. I'm still alive. I know because I'm wet, cold and my head hurts. I slowly prop myself up on my elbows and look up. I can't make sense of my mother's triumphant expression until she starts speaking, "I understand your frustration, Brother Jeremiah," she says with her false-patient schoolteacher tone, "but you have to see the good side of this. Her uncleanliness is a blessing in disguise." The frown on Jeremiah's face shows he's also clueless about what she means. "Can't you see? It means there will be no doubts, the child she will carry will be yours."

I don't need to look at my dress to understand. The wetness I feel is of my own body's making, and I could almost laugh. Emmanuel searches the Bible for all the insanity and hatred he can find, and Leviticus 20:13 may have sentenced his brother to death, but the *eighteenth* verse has given me a reprieve. For once, I agree with my mother. This is a blessing. I've never been so happy to see that time of the month. Four days of safety. Maybe five. It's not much, but it's all I've got. It's something, at least.

Heather helps me stand and silently walks me to the outhouse and then to the penance box. Was Andrea let out early? No, today was her third day.

Huddled on the dirt floor in the corner of the box, I clean myself up the best I can with some of the pile of rags that Heather threw in here after me. It's a pitifully small pile, and I'll have to use them carefully if it's going to last. I don't see them giving me fresh ones soon. However, with luck and planning I won't need more than this: the fresh light of morning will help me gather my thoughts and figure out a way out of here.

I may have lost Sean, but – thanks to him – I now know someone waits for me outside this hell. I was wrong, before: there *is* still one bright spot in all the darkness around me. I do have one thing left in my life, one thing good and pure and clean, one thing that's not spoiled by the hate and festering evil of this... *cult.*

I will find a way out. I will run and find my father.

Chapter 16

Sean

Monday Night, 15 August 2016

Voices. I hear voices.

My face is wet. And that smell. I think a cat pissed on my face.

When did we get a cat?

My head hurts.

Fucking *everything* hurts.

I grit my teeth and open my eyes, breathing only shallowly. I know there's at least cracked ribs, but I don't know how badly.

"He's awake!" My mother's voice. She's relieved. "Sean, honey, can you hear me?"

"Yeah. I can hear you just fine. But I've got the devil's own headache. Can you turn down the volume just a bit?" I start to move, try to roll over so I can push to my knees, but my mother stops me.

"No, sir. You lay *right* there." Nurse-mode now, all brusque and business-like. "You've got one hell of a head injury, and I don't need you moving. There might be some spinal problems."

"Fine, okay, but can you at least wipe the cat piss off my face?"

"The what?" She's confused, and I hear a man's laughter. Bill's here, too.

"Water and smelling salts, Sean," he says. "That's all that is."

"Oh, good," I say. "I had a pretty shitty day, and that would have just been the last straw." It's a weak attempt at humor. What the fuck happened to me? "Why am I laying on the floor?"

"We were hoping you'd tell us," Bill says.

"Not now, Bill," Mom shushes him, and puts a small, but very bright flashlight in face. "You know the drill, boyo. Follow the light."

Light. A blinding flash of light. Pain in the back of my head. Something hit me in the back of the head. What? Why?

"Yep," she says. "You've got a concussion there. Wiggle your fingers and toes for me." I comply, and grudgingly my mother gives me permission to sit up slowly.

Bits and pieces are coming back to me. There's something missing.

"I talked to you this afternoon, Mom. I told you... something, and you weren't supposed to tell Bill about... whatever it was. But here you both are."

"I didn't tell him anything," she says. "I told him I wanted to get away for a couple days, come up to the camp and lay out on the dock and work on my tan, and he got a couple days off approved at the last minute to come with me."

"Your mother can be pretty convincing when she tries, Sean," Bill says. "Now will someone *please* tell me what the *fuck* is going on here?"

I'm almost up and into a chair now, and a wave of dizziness catches me, and nausea with it. My mother gets a trash can in front of my face just in the nick of time to catch the flood of bile.

My shirt. The SEAL Team THREE shirt. It's laying on the table. Courtney was wearing it earlier.

Where did she go? Wait, when the hell was this? I haven't seen her in years.

Oh, fuck.

I remember everything.

"Mom," I say. "You remember I mentioned about security concerns? It's a good thing you didn't get here a little earlier."

"And it's a *damn* good thing we didn't get here much later! How long were you out?"

"I dunno. Since maybe a half-hour after we talked. What time is it now?"

"*Christ*, Sean. You were out for six hours, almost seven. You need a hospital. An MRI."

"No," I snarl. "What I need is the keys to my truck and some weapons."

"Not. Happening." Her voice is flat, definite.

"Will someone *please* tell me what in the name of *hell* is going on here?" Bill is confused, and he's getting pissed off.

"Bill..." I don't even know what to say. How to say it. "I'm sorry, man." Christ. The emptiness. "I found her. And then I lost her again."

"You found—no, no." His face lights up. "My daughter? Courtney's alive? How is she?"

"When I went down for my nap," I say, "she was alive." I have to close my eyes and fight down another wave of nausea. "But I don't think she's okay. I need to get back there. Get her out. Permanently, this time."

"You're not going *anywhere*, mister!" Mom is emphatic. "You need to let the cops handle this one."

"No, Mom. That's not going to work." Shaking my head is pure torture, but I fight through it. What was it they said in boot camp and at BUD/S? Pain is weakness leaving the body. I'm going to be made out of solid titanium after this.

"What about Heather? Did you see her?" Bill asks.

"Yeah. I saw her," I say. "Bill, she's lost it. She's completely around the bend. She had a razor blade to Courtney's throat, and I truly believe she was willing to do it. To kill her own daughter, to save her from sin."

Bill's jaw drops.

I'm unsteady on my feet still, but with help, I make it into the passenger seat of Mom's car. I give Bill the keys to my Blazer, but he comes back with bad news. My tires are slashed.

"Motherfuckers." It's one last bit of insult on top of everything else. "They really didn't want me following them."

"I think you need to start from the beginning," my mother says. "Keep talking, anyway. I don't want you falling asleep for a while yet. We need to get you looked at."

"It's a long story," I warn them.

"Then you'd best get started," Bill tells me. "I need to hear it. Everything."

"We've got plenty of time on the ride," my mom says. "We'll go straight to Maine Med. Further away, but I can get you straight in there, and I don't think Waldo County even has a twenty-four-hour emergency room anymore."

It's almost a two-hour drive to Portland, and I tell them everything. Well, *almost* everything. My mom is wheeling me in through the automatic doors of the emergency room by the time I finish.

"I can't hardly believe this, Sean," she says. "I mean, I believe *you*, but how does a group like this just not get noticed? I mean, how do they stay unknown?"

"It makes sense," Bill says thoughtfully. "Nobody ever heard of David Koresh until the very end, and then *everyone* heard about how Waco ended. The idiots with their comet and purple Nikes, same thing. Jonestown."

"Bill, those guys were amateurs," I say. "This asshole Emmanuel, or whatever his real name is. He's the real deal. He's one-hundred-percent pure, USDA grade-A batshit crazy. And he's got these other fucks locked down tight under his thumb." I pause while an orderly walks past us in the hallway, continuing only once he's clear. "That's how they do it, though. The public image, it's just harmless eccentricity. They don't let anyone else see the truth, see what's on the inside. Whenever that comes out, things always unravel."

"Once we get finished up in here, Sean," my mother says, "we're going straight to the State Police barracks and you're telling this whole story all over again."

"No, Mom." It's my turn to be firm, now. "That's exactly what we're *not* going to do."

"And why not?" My mother rounds on me, fists balled up on her hips. "Why in God's name *wouldn't* you get the police involved?"

"Oh, I don't know," I say with just a touch of sarcasm. "Calling the cops has always worked *so* well in the past. Ask the poor bastards that got the building burned down around them by the cops in Waco. See how they feel about it. Besides, the first hint of police asking questions? Heather gets off the leash." I drag a thumb across my throat.

"So what do we do about it?" she asks. Bill and I lock eyes. He reads my intentions clearly, and after a long moment, he nods.

"You probably don't want to know," I tell her.

"Oh, God. Sean--"

"Mom. Don't bother. It's happening." I speak calmly, softly, and her face blanches. She opens her mouth to speak, but I raise a hand to stop her. "No."

"I... I'm going to find the X-ray tech," she says, blinking rapidly, and flees the small room. I sigh as the door closes behind her, and the deep breath shifts damaged ribs.

"*Fuck*, that hurts," I say, wincing. "In the grand scheme of things, this is about the least serious thing that's ever sent me to the body shop, but there's just something about ribs, y'know?"

"Yeah." Bill nods sagely. "They don't break out the good drugs for the minor stuff, and so you feel *all* of it." He looks at me again, thoughtfully. "So. It's like that, is it? For you?"

"Sorry, I'm not tracking."

"You and my daughter." For the second time today, I'm being weighed and measured. His face is an unreadable mask.

"Oh." How do I answer this? What the fuck do I say to him? Yeah, I'm in love with your daughter, and oh by the way I'm sorry I fucked this all up and I promise to do better next time?

"Yeah. I figured as much." Bill breaks what has become an uncomfortable silence, then leans back in his chair and runs his fingers through his hair. "What a mess. But she *does* want to see me? You're sure?"

"Yes. Yes, *sir*," I say. "She's believed you were dead all these years. She tried to get away from them twice before, and it went... hard on her." The scarring on her thigh is vivid in my mind, and the memory of the moment of fiery passion when I saw those marks burns even hotter now with the added fuel of rage. "*Very* hard."

"And she feels the same way? About you? As you do about her?"

"Yes, sir," I say. "She does." Bill smiles at this, eyes distant, lost in memory.

"Tell me more," he says. "Not just what happened, you've already gone over that. Tell me about *her*. What's she like now?"

"She's warm, and kind. Caring. Brave. And strong. So strong." I close my eyes, lean my head back against the cool cinderblock wall. "And she's beautiful," I whisper. "So very, *very* beautiful." When I open them again I watch Bill's own eyes get misty, and he swallows hard.

"We're going to see her again, Sean."

"Yes, sir. We will. I just got her back, and I'm not losing her again. Not like this. Not ever."

"If there's anything I can do to help? Anything at all," he says. "I'm probably not much for a ruck march or a firefight anymore, not with the peg leg, but I'll be there if you need me." He's sincere, and there's a grim purpose on his face that mirrors the one in my own heart. "I want my little girl back, Sean."

"So do I, sir. More than anything in the world."

"For what it's worth, son, you have my blessing. I wish you both joy of each other, and many happy years together."

"But first, we've got some obstacles to get thro-" I cut off sharply as my mother returns with a doctor. "We'll talk about that later."

"Sean, Sean, *Sean*. What have you gone and gotten yourself into?" I do a double take at the sound of his voice, and my head protests the sudden movement with waves of agony. I know Portland's a small place, but seriously-Jimmy Moloney? He's a doctor now? He'd been two years ahead of me in high school, we'd played football together in the fall, lacrosse in the spring.

"Oh, Jesus," I groan. "Mom, couldn't you have found someone around here that didn't get their M.D. out of a Cracker Jack box?"

"Show some respect, boyo! *Doctor* Moloney is a bright young resident here, and I have absolute faith in his ability to look you over." Mom gets an impish gleam in her eyes, and continues: "But yeah, *Jimmy* was a little punk."

"You wound me, Ms. Pear- sorry, Ms. *Dwyer*." He laughs, and my mom pats him affectionately on the arm. "Still not used to that, yet. Now, let's have a look at you, buddy." Jimmy puts the X-rays up on a light box on the wall, and hums tunelessly while studying them, tracing details of the images with the tip of a finger, then consults the notes from the initial intake nurse.

"Somebody worked you over pretty good," he says, raising his eyebrows and whistling. "And this isn't the first time, by the look of the films. You've got enough metal in you that I don't dare put you in an MRI."

"Yeah, it's been an interesting few years."

"Looks like it," he says. "So what happened tonight?"

"Shaving accident," I lie.

"Right, of course. What were you shaving? A silverback gorilla?"

"Nah, it was your mom," I say, and Jimmy laughs. "Her beard's pretty thick, and all that back hair?"

"Well good! That's less work for the yard guy to handle," my friend says. "He charges by the square mile, after all." I laugh, and then instantly groan from the stabbing pain in my chest and the blinding headache.

"Oh," Mom breaks in, "it hurts to laugh, does it? Good!" She turns on Jimmy, and he holds up his hands placatingly, his face contrite. "Your mother's an angel, Jimmy Moloney, and you know it!"

"You're right, Ms. Dwyer. You're right." Mom turns away from him in disgust, and Jimmy flips me off over her shoulder. It's a struggle not to laugh, never mind the pain. I don't want to piss off Mom.

"Give it to me straight, Doc," I tell him, and Jimmy shifts back to professional mode.

"Sean, you've got two broken ribs, well and truly broken, and six more are cracked. The shape of the bruising, location of the cracks, it looks to me like you must have been standing right in front of the plate at Fenway during batting practice, and someone was swinging for the fences. You've got a solid concussion, and if it came from a baseball bat then you've got the world's hardest head, because you somehow managed *not* to get a skull fracture."

"Oh. Well, if that's all, then no problem," I say. "I'll just be on my way, then."

Mom rolls her eyes at me.

"Sean, no bullshit here--sorry, Ms. Dwyer--dead serious, Sean, you need to stay off your feet for a bit. The ribs aren't going to do much but hurt. They're not going to shift and puncture a lung, or rip the pericardium or aorta or anything, but you've got a lot of pain ahead of you during the recovery. Ribs aren't serious, but your head? That's a whole different matter."

"Let's assume that weeks of bed rest are not an option," I say. "How long?"

"I want you off your feet for five days, minimum, and I'd really prefer ten," he tells me, and he's serious. "Doctor's orders. No shit, Sean. You were unconscious for a *long* time. Waking up after that and just carrying on with your day? That's Hollywood shit. It doesn't happen in the real world. Most people out that long don't wake up afterwards. Ever."

Jimmy stares at me, waiting for me to say something. I stare back, silent. He shakes his head and continues.

"Your brain, Sean? If it gets worse, if it starts swelling out of control? You jostle your head around too much, it could happen. And it won't end well. Persistent vegetative state. Coma. Bed sores. Nurses changing your diaper twice a day, need it or not, and maybe wiping a layer of dust off you every couple months."

"I'll take it easy, then. Scout's honor."

I will, too. At least, until I figure out my next course of action. Courtney doesn't have much time. She may be out of time already.

Chapter 17
Courtney

Tuesday, 16 August 2016

Sleep is my solace, but there is little solace to be found here in the penance box.

When I can sleep, I can dream, and my dreams are a refuge from this waking nightmare, but I don't think I managed more than an hour or two last night, at most. My grief is still too fresh, my pain too raw.

I haven't eaten or drank anything since yesterday morning, the bottle of water and an energy bar while I watched Sean sleep, but somehow I still have to pee. So kind of them to leave me a bucket in the corner of the box, at least. Once I've relieved myself I sit back in the opposite corner, tightly hugging my knees to my chest, and close my eyes.

Even if I can't sleep, though, there are other kinds of dreams that can take me away from this waking nightmare. I was an accomplished daydreamer even as a little girl, but in the years since my mother brought us to this little corner of Hell on Earth, I have achieved absolute mastery. Huddled in the corner of the outhouse-sized penance box, my supply of tears is exhausted for the moment.

I escape into happier worlds of my own making, wonderful worlds where Sean and I escape, get married, and live happily ever after. Worlds where he never left. Even worlds where he left, but never came to find me would be happier, because he'd still be alive. It's a way to pass the time until I have more tears ready.

I'd been shattered, destroyed when Sean left eight years ago. It broke my heart. The day he left for boot camp I told him I loved him.

I thought he knew. How could he have missed it?

It wasn't enough to make him stay. I grabbed him by the front of his shirt, kissing him fiercely under the chipped paint of the Greyhound station's sign. A real kiss, one that burned my lips, fueled by the all my years of unspoken feelings and wants and desires for him. All the love that I'd felt, but of which I'd never dared be the first to speak.

"I love you, Sean," I told him, when I let go of him. "Don't leave."

Sean looked at me as if he was seeing me for the first time, as if he'd never even seen me before. His eyes were opened, finally, and I watched a whole lifetime's worth of feelings cross his face: confusion, joy, grief, lust, and each change was a hot needle, burning the memory of that moment into my soul.

He glanced over his shoulder at the bus, ready to leave, and when Sean turned back to me there was sorrow written in his eyes and I knew I'd waited too long to tell him. I'd lost him.

I couldn't bear to hear him speak, to apologize. I burst into tears and then I did my own running, up the long, gentle slope of Congress Street, stopping in front of the hospital where Sean's mother worked. I couldn't make out their figures standing there, but I imagined him giving his mother one last hug before he got on the bus and left. Even the bus itself was an indistinct blur of red, blue, and silver as it pulled out of the station, carrying the boy I loved from me.

Melissa Pearse came for me. She left the car parked at the bus station and walked, giving me time for the worst of the tears to fall and fade, and found me sitting on the sidewalk, face buried against knees hugged tightly to my chest.

"Is this what it was like for my mother?" I asked her. "For you? With Sean's dad?"

"Yes," she answered, eyes bright with her own tears. "Always. But you can't stop them. You just—all you can do is wait, honey. And you pray for them to come back."

No prayers can bring him back to me. Not this time.

A full day passes without anyone coming to check on me.

There are no clocks in here, but there are cracks in the high, sloped roof of the small shed where sinners are sent to contemplate and repent. Pale, misty light filters through the cracks in the morning, with blinding spears that highlight every floating mote of dust at noon. The light dims slowly toward evening until the floodlights come on, striping the walls with the yellowish fire of the halogen bulbs.

My stomach growls but I'm too numb to feel hunger or pain in my body. The only pain that matters are the gaping, ragged-edged holes in my heart where Sean and Daniel were both ripped away from me in one bloody afternoon. I turn my back to the light and will myself to go to sleep on the dirt floor, in spite of the filth and blood. My blood. It hadn't saved me from Jeremiah, but only granted me a few days' delay of my fate.

I've almost faded out when the noise of pebbles bouncing off the wall draws me back to reality, denying me the solace of sleep and the refuge of dreams that I've been futilely seeking for... thirty hours? Thirty-six? I don't even know anymore. I don't even care. What's the point?

"Courtney?" A small voice intrudes softly into my misery. "Courtney? Are you okay?" It's Jennie. Rising to my hands and knees, I crawl to the side closest to her voice and sit slumped against it. Through the cracks in the wall, I can barely make out her silhouette in the penumbra.

"Yes, honey," I whisper back to her. "I'm fine, don't you worry about me."

"You're sure? 'Cuz Matthew, he told me your Mama, she locked you up. And he said no one came to see you since last night." Oh, you sweet baby. You could be a spy or a detective out there. You could be any damn thing you wanted to be. But you're here instead.

"I'm okay, Jennie. I promise," I tell her. It hurts to lie to her, but it's hardly any extra burden on top of everything else.

"Have you been bad?" Jennie's voice is plaintive, mixing equal parts of suspicion and disbelief. I can't help but chuckle at her question: this is a little girl's logic at work. If my mother is punishing me, it means I must have been bad. It doesn't matter that I'm an adult.

"I don't even know anymore, Jennie," I say. An adult? Physically and legally perhaps, but I've been acting like a clingy child, hoping my mother would someday snap out of it. Though now that I think of it, I didn't behave like one. I was a clingy kid who wouldn't let go of her mother.

"Well, I don't know what you did, but I don't think you can have been bad enough to not have water," she adds. Her tone is dead serious. "Come on, take it."

There's the smallest gap imaginable underneath the wall of the box, and with a moment's effort I've enlarged it and my tiny angel slips a plastic bottle through the hole. My heart swells with gratitude as I unscrew the cap. The whole bottle is gone in three long swallows. I hadn't realized how parched I was.

"Thank you, honey," I tell her, returning the bottle to her. "I really needed that." I wish I could hug you, Jennie. "You need to go, Jennie. Get back to the dorm, into your bed, before you get into trouble."

"Goodnight Courtney," she says.

"Goodnight, my sweet, be careful now!"

The soft crunching sounds of her bare feet in the gravel fades as she runs away, and I have a sudden new reason to cry. I may not have carried her, given birth to her, but I couldn't love Jennie any more if I had. My baby girl, my small angel of mercy, gives me back some of my faith in humanity. What if she was mine, though? What if she were mine, though? What if Sean were your father, Jennie?

A new little world builds in my mind, full of bright lights and pain, and I'm screaming because it hurts, but I'm so happy too, and Sean's voice is telling me to push but he's so calm and quiet, even when I yell *THIS IS YOUR FAULT! YOU DID THIS TO ME!* and my mom is holding my hand and I love her so much, we're so close, and I'm so glad she's here with me today it means so much but she laughs at me because she did the same thing yelling at my dad when I was born, and then my dad and Sean's father too, they're at the door, and the nurses are yelling at them to get those filthy cigars out of the building, but they're smiling anyway, and then it's over and one of the nurses is my mother-in-law and she gives me my baby and it's a girl and her name's Jennie, and Sean and I take her to her first day of school and there's birthday parties and oh, my God, how did our daughter get to be sixteen already? You're growing up so fast and your father and I love you so much and—

"Courtney! Courtney, wake *up!* I have to talk to you!" A shrill voice jolts me out of my sleep, jerking me away from my too-short rest and my too-fragile refuge.

My eyes come open slowly, crusts in my eyelashes sticking them together, and my beautiful dream turns into the living hell I thought I'd left behind forever. My mother stands in the doorway, backlit by bright sunlight. Still groggy from too long awake and not long enough asleep, I'm too slow at getting up for my moth- *Heather*, dammit! *Heather*'s tastes, and she prods me with a toe.

"Wake up you lazy whore!" she hisses.

"Mom!" I protest, sitting up and leaning against the corner of the box.

Quicker than I thought possible, my mother's hand flies at my face. Her strength is incredible. My cheek is on fire, and I don't need to touch my mouth to know my lower lip is split. Again. I try to remain as still as I can. When she's like this, absolutely anything can send her deeper into her madness. Eyes riveted on her hands, ready to parry the next blow, I listen to her ranting.

"Don't you call me that! You are no daughter of mine. You're a disgrace, you're a filthy sinner, Courtney. You turned away from The Lord!" She clasps her hands and looks heavenward, as if she could talk directly to Him through the crack-filled roof. "What did I do to deserve this?"

Oh, I have a few answers for you, Heather. Let me count your sins! You abandoned your husband when he most needed your support. You stole me away from my father and never gave us a chance to see each other again. You lied to me and made me believe my father was dead. You gave the order to mutilate my body, and you held me down while it happened!

I keep my answers to myself. Silence is safer, and besides, the way she stands with her head cocked to the side, I'm not sure she isn't already getting answers from someone else. Her head tilts occasionally, in the barest hint of a nod, and once in a while her lips move but no sound comes out. On Saturday night when I visited her in Rebecca's infirmary, she'd talked about *His* voice, and the more I watch her, the less I think she meant Father Emmanuel. How did I never notice before?

After a moment, her eyes open and mouth curves in a smile that would be sweet and loving, but the ecstatic fire lighting her eyes turns it terrifying instead. I brace for the worst.

"You don't realize how lucky you are," she purrs, and her words push me to the very brink of laughter. If I were even a little stronger, a tiny bit braver, I'd be wetting myself over how stupid that idea is. If I were even the least fraction weaker, it would be nervous laughter, the escaping squeals of my brain gibbering in fear. It's a delicate balancing act, and I'm barely keeping it all together.

"*You* have been chosen!" Heather says, and her voice rises a full octave while she says it. "*He* has chosen *you* to carry out the prophet's bloodline. It's your sacred duty, Courtney. Your *duty* in this life is to bring new heirs of

Father Emmanuel's bloodline, so that *His Work* may continue!" I stay quiet, but that doesn't matter. The woman that bore me waves her hand to chase away the excuses that I'm not even making.

"Father Emmanuel has accepted it was not entirely your fault. He knows you're weak, that you could not resist the temptation, and The Lord has inspired him to mercy!" Her voice is calmer now, more rational, and the fires burning in her eyes are only glowing embers of madness. "And in that mercy, Courtney, *He* has commanded forgiveness. Do you realize how fortunate you are? You're going to marry his son! Once Father Emmanuel is called to glory, *Brother* Jeremiah will be *Father* Jeremiah." Her voice is pleading. She's begging me to understand, and the start of a tear glistens in the corner of one eye. "Just submit. *Please*, Courtney. For me," she finishes.

"Mom?" I cringe away from the blow that doesn't come. "I'm sorry, you told me not to... What do you want me to call you?"

"Oh, honey!" She falls to her knees in the bloody dirt, wrapping her arms around me. "I'll always be your mother. I'll always love you. No matter the sin."

"You, you..." I'm at a loss for words. The constantly changing mental state of the woman that kneels here before me, telling me how much she loves me, is too much for me to process. "Mom, they *crippled* me. You *let* them drive a tractor over my leg."

"It was the only way," she tells me, tears running freely down her cheeks. "Courtney, it was the *only* way. You were so close to sin. I couldn't let you backslide; I couldn't let you go back to *that* life."

"What life, Mom?" I yell, but my voice is hoarse already. My grief for Sean and Daniel has ravaged my vocal cords. "*What* life? Back then, I went to school, I came home, I did my homework. I didn't do *anything!*"

"Honey, you are not *submitting*. He has *revealed* His Plan to Father Emmanuel. You *must* submit!"

"Mom," I say, taking a deep breath, drawing up all the dignity I can manage while smeared with dirt and my blood. "I will *never* submit to that sick bastard."

"'Rebelliousness,'" my mother says, softly and earnestly, "'is as the sin of witchcraft.' The prophet Samuel tells us this. It is the Word of The Lord. And Samuel *also* teaches us that 'thou shalt not suffer a witch to live!' Courtney, I *love* you. I *love* you enough to *disobey Him*. This is *mercy*, Courtney. Because I *love* you. I'm endangering *myself* by disobeying *Him*. Why can't you just be grateful?" Tears fall freely from her eyes, and the fires of madness are empty, sad, and broken. "But there will come a time when I can't disobey *Him* anymore. No matter how much I love you. And it's going to come soon." My mother sighs, mopping at the tears on her cheeks.

"All I've ever wanted was to be *free*, Mom." She flinches when I say it.

"You're weak, Courtney," she says. "You always were. It's from your father. He couldn't ever turn aside from temptation either."

"*What* temptation, Mom? I have no idea what you're talking about!"

"The temptations of the flesh. He- your father- *Bill*... he could never resist. He- *wanted* me. I tempted him. And he succumbed to his lusts, dragging me down with him." My mother's eyes flare again, and the hands she's using to rub my back become claws. "And you were going to throw it all away for, what? Sean Pearse?" She snorts as if Sean was a lower life form and it takes all my willpower not to shout back at her that Sean was worth a thousand of that piece of shit Jeremiah. What has Jeremiah done with his life so far? Nothing! Nothing, that is, but be his father's son.

Sean? He was a hero. A hero who fought for his country. A hero who fought for me. If I can't escape, then I will fight for him as well, and I will make sure I join him before Jeremiah can ever claim me as his wife.

"Listen to me, you stupid little harlot," my mother snarls. "You think I don't notice when you get lost inside your own head?" And that she does; she always has. It started when I was a very young child, she could always spot it, the very instant my attention waned and I started drifting away. Now that she's made sure she has my attention, her crazy smile returns.

"Good. I want you to understand," she tells me, "*this* is your last chance." I can't help myself: I roll my eyes. Oh shit, I should have known better, it's all that she needed to snap! Her hands come down again, but this time I'm ready and move fast enough for her to miss my face.

"How dare you?" she asks catching a fistful of my hair and pulling me up. "Kindness and mercy are wasted on you!" She pulls away from me, the sadness in her eyes at odds with the sneer on her face.

I don't have the strength to fight any longer. I just want to go back to sleep where I can forget this nightmare, and go back to the world where my husband Sean and my beautiful daughter Jennie live. Please, let me escape this hell!

Escape.

Of all the things I've done of late that have been called sin, I can't think of a single thing that would be more sinful than sitting here. God gave me a few days' reprieve from my appointment with a sadist, and so far I've been wasting it.

What would Sean think of me?

Chapter 18

Sean

Wednesday Evening, 17 August 2016

After two days, the dizziness and that fucking headache are both – finally -- starting to subside. My ribs are still agony, though, and it's hard to breathe with all the layers of Ace bandages wrapped around my chest to support healing ribs. Individually they may be soft and stretchy, but if you put enough layers together, the bandages might as well be bands of steel.

I need help. The gear I bought at Cabela's the other day is okay stuff by civilian standards, but if I'm going in to get Courtney by myself, it's not enough. I need every advantage I can beg, borrow or steal. Fortunately, I have plenty of old friends who might listen to me beg, let me borrow, or look the other way while I steal.

My phone call is answered before the second ring.

"Naval Special Warfare Development Group Quarterdeck, PS2 Larkin speaking, how may I help you, sir or ma'am?" Larkin, a Personnel Specialist, is the one that processed my retirement paperwork, and he sounds somewhere between bored and annoyed. DEVGRU, popularly known as SEAL Team SIX, gets phone calls every day of the week from journalists, cranks, and conspiracy theorists around the country, and even the world. Thank Christ, though, it's someone I know.

"Hey, Larkin," I say.

"Pearse!" His voice brightens. "How the hell are you?"

"Better than you," I say. "I don't have to stand duty anymore. I'm all comfy up here at home, wrapped up in my DD-214 blanket," I laugh, pulling out the old joke about discharge papers.

"Yeah, yeah. It's warm and soft and insulates you from all the bullshit." Larkin sighs ruefully. "I've filled out enough 214s for you guys, I'm starting to look forward to my own. But, yeah, Sean! Good to hear from you, man. What can I do for you?"

"Angela should have the duty today, right?" I keep the question casual. PS2 knows he shouldn't be talking about scheduling of any sort, but after a momentary hesitation, he answers me.

"Yeah," he says. "Angela's the CDO." CDO. Command Duty Officer. The poor bastard that has to stay overnight in charge of the duty section in case of an emergency.

"Great, thanks," I say, feeling a definite sense of relief. If there's anyone I'd rather talk to about this problem than Angela, I can't think who it might be. "Lemme talk to the CDO then? Actually, no—can you get me a call back? We need to talk offline." I really don't want this conversation recorded anywhere. Better for Angela, better for me.

"Offline, aye." Larkin pauses again. "Everything okay, Sean?" he asks, his voice full of concern.

"Yeah, yeah. Nothing to worry about," I tell him, and he's off to find Angela for me.

It takes less than a minute for my phone to ring, and caller ID says it's a 757 area code. Virginia Beach. It's an off-base number.

"How they hangin,' Angie?" I say, answering the phone.

"Still one below the other, punk," says a man with a deep, gruff voice. Chief Special Warfare Operator Max Anghelescu, Angela, to those of us who have fought and bled alongside him. "What's your malfunction, Pearse?"

"You know how it is, Chief. I think some shrapnel's shifting around in my shoulder. Hurts like a son of a bitch." It's an oblique way of reminding Angela that he owes me his life. He'd been dazed from a near miss in a rocket attack on the air base in Kandahar, and I caught a piece of the next wave while dragging him to safety. "More immediately, though? Bunch of broken ribs and a concussion from hell." I play the honesty card here. He's calling me from a cell phone, so we're probably safe to talk.

"What's the other guy look like?" Angela grunts in surprise. My reputation in the Teams is *not* as the guy that loses a fistfight.

"Guys. Plural. And they look a lot better than me." I take a deep breath before continuing. "I need a favor, Angie."

"Sounds like," Anghelescu says. "Why don't we just take a step back here, and you can tell me what the actual fuck this goat rope is that you've gotten yourself into?" A brief recap takes only a few moments, and Angela whistles. "You don't need a favor, shipwreck. You need a *miracle*."

"Yeah, I sort of figured that part out for myself. You got any up your sleeve? Or maybe in the Lucky Bag?"

Historically, the Lucky Bag was a sort of naval lost and found for unclaimed items owned by sailors who transferred or who died at sea. Today, it's a *very* unofficial repository for the high-dollar / low-inventory equipment reported as 'lost in combat' rather than turned in at the end of deployment for re-issue to another unit. Does it suck for the other guy that doesn't get the gear he wanted for deployment? Of course it does, but since *his* unit's got its own Lucky Bag, there's a lot of trading going on. In the end, everyone deploys with the equipment set *they* think is necessary, rather than the list of items the *Navy* thinks they need.

"What do you have in mind?" He seems skeptical.

"Night vision, that's the big one. I've got a shitty little Cabela's toy, but I'm going to need the good stuff. I'd like to borrow a set of the 18s, if you can swing it. Armor. Threaded barrel and a suppressor for the Beretta. Blue backing me up?" Blue is one of the four *officially* acknowledged squadrons of the Development Group, alongside Gold, Silver, and Red. I know I'm not going to get any company on this trip, but if you don't give them the opportunity to say *no* then they also don't have the opportunity to say *yes*.

"It ain't *Blue* you need here, Pearse. You want *Black*," he says, referring to DEVGRU's semi-mythical fifth squadron, the Keyser Soze of the Special Operations community. Angie sighs on the phone, and I can picture him running a big, callused hand through a high and tight crew cut. "Pearse. Is this gonna be clean? In accordance with the creed?"

"It's righteous, yeah. 'Always ready to defend those who are unable to defend themselves,'" I say, quoting part of the SEAL creed. "'I serve with honor on and off the battlefield,' Angie. 'Uncompromising integrity is my standard. My character and honor are steadfast. My wo-'"

"'My word is my bond,'" he interrupts, finishing the line. "Yeah. You've never given me reason to question you before, so... let me see what I can come up with, okay? This a good contact number for you?"

"Yeah. And, Angela? I need to go hot on this, and fucking *soon*, man. I don't have a lot of time to waste. *She* doesn't have a lot of time to waste. And you fucking *owe* me for Kandahar."

"I get that, Sean." His voice is full of sympathy, and it gives me hope that he's going to come through for me. "I really do. But, you rush a miracle man, you get rotten miracles. Hold fast, shipmate. I'll get back to you."

"I appreciate it, man. I really do."

"Yeah, yeah," he says. "Whatever. I *do* owe you for Kandahar. I'll be in touch."

I feel a profound sense of relief when I put the phone down. Chief Anghelescu says he's going to do something, he fucking *does* it. He might not be able to deliver everything I *need*, and *definitely* won't be able to get me everything I'd *want*, but he'll get me everything that he *can*.

"You're still set on doing things this way, are you?" My mom leans against the frame of my bedroom door. Oh Christ. How much of that did you hear?

"We've been through this, Mom," I say, rubbing at my temples. "You *know* why I have to do this, *and* why I have to do it myself."

"Yeah, you've talked a lot about the danger to *her*, Sean, but what about the danger to *you*?" My mother sits next to me on the narrow bed and takes my hand. "Look, I don't want to see anything bad happen to Courtney, God knows I don't. I've been lighting candles for her, saying a rosary every day, but you *heard* what Jimmy told you. *Doctor* Moloney."

"Yeah," I say. "I was there, remember?"

"And is that what you want?" The beginnings of tears glisten in the corner of my mother's eyes. She's really worried about me. "If you don't take the time to heal properly, you could *die*, Sean! I don't want to lose you. Not now that I've just finally got you back."

"Then you understand how I feel about Courtney," I tell her. "I *found* her, Mom. All these years I've spent thinking about her, imagining what my life would be like if I hadn't walked away from her when I was a kid. If I'd just had the balls to tell her how I felt before it was too late."

"Is it worth the *risk*, though? I *can't* lose you, Sean."

"Mom, I don't *want* to die. I don't *want* to spend the rest of my life as a vegetable. I'd rather kill myself than live as a fucking *turnip*."

My mother blanches at the harshness of my tone, as much as the words themselves.

"But every minute *I* spend here healing? That's more time *she's* getting put through hell. *My* comfort and safety? They're not worth a single second of *her* pain and danger."

"So, either I lose you, or Bill loses Courtney. Again." The tears that threatened to fall have begun to track down my mother's cheeks, and she wipes them away angrily with the back of her hand, sniffling. "There's no good answer here, is there?"

"I'd say we're at an impasse," I say, and fold her into my arms. "Mom. You're only looking at the worst case. I'm *good* at my job. You're not going to lose me, and Bill's not going to lose her. Courtney and I will both be back here, and we'll both be perfectly safe."

"*Good at your job?*" Her voice is almost a wail, and she roughly grabs my wrist, pulling my forearm up to eye level, pointing out jagged white lines through the tattoos. "You didn't get these from being *good at your job!*" My mother drops my arm, poking me hard in the side of my chest. "*That* didn't happen because you were good at your job!"

"The ribs? Yeah," I say, gritting my teeth from the pain. "Yeah. I slipped up. I underestimated my enemy. But in Iraq? Afghanistan? There were a lot of guys there who were pretty good at *their* jobs, too, after a while. You kill the stupid ones, and all you're left with are the ones smart enough to learn and survive. It's Darwin in action. But these pricks? I'm not going to give them a decade and a half to evolve and figure out how to fight me."

My mother moves to poke at a broken rib again, but I snatch her hand mid-jab.

"I'm not interested in playing that game anymore, Mom. It hurts. And yeah, I'll be fine. You'll see."

"I'm sorry, Sean. That was awful of me. But you promise?" My mother pulls back, red-rimmed eyes meeting mine. She really is scared. Intellectually she knows I'm tough, knows I've survived worse things than what happened to me Sunday, but she's never seen me wounded before. I hope she never will again.

"Yeah, Mom," I say with a kiss on the very top of her head. "I promise."

"Bill's not going to lose what?" His voice comes from the hallway, along with the step-thump, step-thump of his prosthetic. "Everything okay?"

"Yeah," I tell him. "Everything's just fi-"

"Like hell it is!" Mom interrupts, and turns to her husband. "Bill, can't you talk him out of this? Talk some sense into him?" Dammit! I thought I was making progress here.

Bill looks from my mother to me, then back to my mother, before his steady gaze settles back on me.

"Melissa, if there were any other way that made sense, I'd tell Sean to scrap his plan and just get the cops in there," Bill tells her. "But he's right. It'll take the police days, weeks even, to watch and figure out what the fuck's going on, never mind actually getting an operation together and getting my daughter out of there, throwing this Emmanuel character in prison, and putting Heather out to pasture on the funny farm. There are no good options, and Sean's the best of all the bad choices."

Bill turns to walk away, but stops, looking back over his shoulder to add one more final—and brutally practical—thought. "Sean's way is more likely to get my daughter out alive. And it's probably going to wind up being cheaper than a trial."

"Men!" Mom's tears have started in earnest now. "Can you *really* not think of *any way* to do things that doesn't involve violence? When has that ever solved anything?"

"You should ask King George about that one, Melissa," Bill says, in a voice like rocks grinding together. "Or the Confederacy. Maybe the Tsar would have some thoughts to share on the subject. Check with Hitler, see what his opinion is." My mother's husband turns back to me, clearly finished discussing other options with her. "Sean, I've got your old wheels out of the garage. You want to go over with me to get new tires for the Blazer? Maybe tomorrow we can take them up to the camp and put 'em on the truck? If you're up to it?"

"Yeah," I say, untangling myself from Mom's carefully fierce hug and standing carefully. "It's gotta get done some time." My vision blurs momentarily, and there's a brief flash of dizziness. Not too bad, all things considered. Better than yesterday, for sure. "Let's get it over with."

Chapter 19

Courtney

Friday, 19 August 2016

Five days in the penance box should have broken me. I am starting to see cracks around the edges of my resolve, but my tiny flesh and blood guardian angel has been there for me. Jennie has slipped water bottles under the wall of my prison every chance she can, and has brought me every scrap of food her clever little hands can hide away.

No slice of bread ever tasted so good as the stale, dry piece she brought me last night, but I'm even hungrier now that it's gone than I was before I started eating it. How much worse would I feel if Jennie *hadn't* been here for me?

It's hard to get comfortable, to find a position to relieve the stiffness and aching in my leg. Sitting on a hard dirt floor for five days would be unpleasant for anyone, but the inability to stretch out or just to walk around a little leaves me with a constant, throbbing pain. I sit back in my corner of the box and try to work the muscles as best I can, but nothing seems to help.

My daydreams still take me away from this miserable hellhole, but they're no longer escapist fantasies about a life that will never happen. Now they're fantasies of simply escaping, and finding some sort of life I can actually have, but I have to figure out a way to make the fantasy a reality.

The first step is getting out of the penance box. There's no lock, but I haven't figured out a way yet to pop the simple latch that holds the door closed. All I need is a flat piece of metal or wood. Even a stiff piece of wire should work. But I don't have any!

There's no foundation under the box, only the dirt floor. I could dig my way out, just like I dug the small hole to let Jennie pass me water and food, but with no tools it will take far too long, and never mind how obvious it would be to anyone watching. I can't even flip the thing over-- the heavy square beams in each corner are set in concrete, like fence posts.

I've gone through every possible scenario, everything I could try. There's only one thing left, and it's the course of absolute last resort: I have to ask my little guardian angel for a different and more dangerous kind of help. If there were any other way, I'd have done it already.

Tonight. It has to be tonight. The longer the delay, the weaker I get. But strength and weakness hardly matter, because I'm out of time anyway. I've always hated their obsession with ritual purity, the constant reminders that women's bodies are unclean things just filled with sin, but right now it's the only thing that's keeping me out of Jeremiah's bed. My period has already run almost a full day longer than normal, but it's almost over. Today will certainly be the last day.

The door opens and I'm blinded by the midday sun. Squinting and shading my eyes with a hand, I can barely make out my mother's bony silhouette against a sky so bright, it washes out my vision. Another shape stands next to her, and as my eyes adjust I recognize Jeremiah. They exchange a conspiratorial glance and my mother shrugs. They've come to check on the goods. I've jinxed myself, thinking about how to get out of here.

"Get your lazy ass up," Jeremiah says. There's no anger in his voice, no specific intent to be more cruel than usual. This is simply his baseline of sadism. I move slowly, exaggerating my weakness, and manage to get to a kneeling position, then 'try' to stand, using the wall for support.

They smile as I drop back to my knees, panting with false effort. That's right, that's exactly right. You haven't fed me for five days, and you've barely allowed me any water. I'll be just as weak and helpless, just as pliable, as you want. Of course, I will be.

Jeremiah's face twists in disgust. I can't tell if it's the smell of the bucket or the sight of the used rags, evidence of my sinful impurity. He reaches out to grab at me, drags me to my feet, but his hand stops when he takes in my filthy dress.

"You get her," he tells my mother. Asshole. And my mother wonders why I'm not delighted at the prospect of being your wife?

"Let's get you cleaned up," my mother says taking one of my arms. Her voice is gentle, but even she grimaces at the smell. She and Jeremiah flank me as I stumble my way to the showers. "Thank you, Brother Jeremiah, I'll take it from there," she says once we're next to a stall. When Jeremiah hesitates, she shoos him away with her best schoolteacher's voice. "I can handle her. Look at her, she can hardly stand on her own."

I lean against the wall and remain silent. Good. That's what I want you to think.

"Fine," he grumbles. "I'm going, but I'll be right outside."

"Just be patient. Your wait is almost over," my mother tells him. She's soothing a petulant child, not talking to a grown man.

You'll have to be patient another day, you bastard. I'm not done with being unclean. Not yet.

As soon as he's out of sight, my mother shakes me by the shoulder and orders me to undress. After laying for so long in the combination of dirt and my own bloody filth, this shower is going to be *such* a treat. It won't be as long or as hot as I want, nor as private as I could wish, but I'm past caring. I want it so badly, need the feeling of the water streaming over me, I want to strip my clothes off in an instant. I fight the impulse, forcing my hands to tremble as I undo the buttons one by one, and step under the lukewarm stream once my stinking, dirty clothes fall to the floor.

It's glorious, even if it's not particularly hot. My mother narrows her eyes as she notices me swallow water collected in my open mouth, but she doesn't say anything. I start with my hair and work my way down, ignoring my observer kneeling on the lip of the shower floor, carefully scrutinizing the color of the water running down my legs and swirling toward the drain. It's still undeniably sullied.

"Two more minutes," she says and walks out of the room leaving the door open. I'd best make the most of it.

Once my time is up and I'm drying off with a thin towel, I hear voices outside the shower room. From inside the stall I can't make out the voices, but there's no mistaking the angry tones. I only catch the end of the conversation when my mother opens the door

"*No*," she says adamantly. "I *told* you yesterday that it might not be over yet. You're simply going to have to wait another day."

"So, it's settled then?" Satan is on the other side of the door as well. "Sister Heather was right. The decorations and preparations can stay up for another day. The wedding will happen tomorrow, instead of today."

I lean against the wall again, allowing my head to wobble in pretend weakness. Have to stay in character. Don't break the scene. I stare blankly at the fresh clothes and rags my mother has laid out for me until she prods me into action.

"Come on! Hurry up, Courtney! I don't have all day to waste taking care of you."

"You never do," I mumble, intentionally skipping a button and doing another up crooked.

"What'd you say?" She glares at me, then bats my hands away the dress and fixes them herself, *tsk*ing at me. "Oh, *you*. Can't leave you alone for even a minute. C'mon, Courtney! There are things to do! We have to have your dress fitted, you have to see the flowers!" The angry zeal is gone from her eyes and voice, and she's... happy? Is that what happiness looks like on her face? Is that the expression that another woman would wear when putting together her daughter's wedding? "It's going to be so beautiful. But we have to be quick, I have something else important to take care of this evening."

"We, you want *me* to- what, *approve* things? For my wedding to *him?*"

Mom, even for you, this is insane.

Her eyes widen in shock, and she covers her mouth with both hands. "Oh no! No, no, no, no, *no!* Not to *Him*, silly! To Brother Jeremiah!" She laughs at what she thinks is an obvious and silly misinterpretation by me. "You couldn't marry *Him*," she whispers.

Wait, who did you think I was talking about?

"Right. Of course not. How silly of me," I say, as she ties my hair back into a ponytail. The wide, coarsely woven ribbon started life white, but age and repeated washing have made it a faded grayish-yellow. "What preparations do you need me to look at?"

"Well, first off, we have to go and witness the purification," she says and continues rattling on about food and embroidery, but I'm not listening.

What the hell does she mean by 'purification'?

My question is answered soon enough, when my mother escorts me out of the shower and over to the pathetic little garden shed that I shared with Daniel. It's being torn to the ground by half a dozen men, under the supervision of Brother Lucas. All of my things are still inside, all of Daniel's things. Jeremiah is part of the wrecking crew, and he's going at it with a vengeance.

It wasn't enough for you to get the obstacle out of the way, was it? You couldn't be satisfied with having me, or even with killing your uncle. You need to destroy his home, erase his memory.

"All right, that should be enough," Lucas says when he deems the destruction sufficient. They've piled everything up in the middle of the small plot of land, and everyone standing around holds a bucket of water. A rototiller and a bag of road salt stand a short distance off.

The final piece of the puzzle falls into place when he pours the contents of a small red plastic gas can over the heap. Everyone takes a respectful – and cautious – step back as Brother Lucas turns and scans the crowd.

"Sister Heather, would you do the honor of cleansing the abomination from our community?" he asks.

"Oh, absolutely!" My mother lets go of my arm and beams like a giddy schoolgirl as she joins Lucas, who entrusts her with a large box of wooden matches. Handling the box like a sacred relic, she strikes the match and throws it on the splintered rubble. It sputters for a moment before a large drop of gasoline falls on it, and with a *whoooosh* the pile is engulfed in an instant.

"And he broke down the houses of the Sodomites that were by the house of The Lord!" Brother Lucas screams out at the gathered community. "His Word tells us this! The Second Book of Kings!" Lucas preaches to the crowd, ranting about sin and abomination, and how some High Priest named Hilk-something-or-other purged the wickedness from the Children of Israel.

He seems as crazed as my mother, but he doesn't lose himself in his zeal. Lucas keeps a shrewd spark of awareness in his eyes, adjusting his tone and direction to bring the crowd to a frenzy.

I don't pay any attention to his words. I'm watching the people instead. All around me, every rapt eye is focused on him, standing in front of the flaming mass of my former home, and nobody is paying attention to me. Even as I edge away from my mother, jostling through the crowd, nobody looks at me twice. Well, this is as good a time as any, and someone was careless enough to leave a truck in front of the main house.

I continue to move away, slowly, pausing between each step, until I reach the corner of the main house. As soon as I'm in its shadow, I turn and head for the truck, going just as close to a run as my leg will allow. Just a few more steps and I'll be there. Just... a little... I've made it!

My heart sinks as I find an empty ignition. Where are the keys? There's nothing in the center console, nothing over the visor. Nobody ever takes the keys out of the trucks! Why now?

I keep searching, frantically, for the literal keys to my freedom, silently pleading and begging the heavens for some help when I see him.

Nathan. He's standing in front of the truck, leaning against the wall. Holding up a set of keys in his hand, dangling them by the ring.

The little boy stares at me, expressionless for a moment before a smile forms on his lips, impenetrable, inscrutable, betraying no hint of what he thinks. He walks around to the side of the truck and I roll down the window.

"Please, Nathan," I beg. "Please. Give me the keys. Let me be free."

Nathan's smile fades, his eyebrows scrunching together, and he raises the keys toward me. Please God, please God. Please dear God in Heaven! But God's not listening to me, not today. At the last second, with the keys less than a half inch from my outstretched hand, he yanks them back.

"Courtney's running away," he screams at the top of his lungs.

There's no point to fleeing on foot, not now. If you can't run, then you can't run away.

I lean my head against the padded rest, and await the inevitable with my eyes closed.

Jeremiah and Lucas are the first to reach me, of course, and I'm clean enough that the men don't have any purity-based concerns about dragging me out of the truck by force.

"Disrespect. Utter and *complete* disrespect," Lucas says, as the two of them drag me back to the penance box. "You're going to have to learn, Sister Courtney. You *will* learn submission to your husband and to The Lord."

"And the lessons will start tomorrow afternoon," Jeremiah says as he opens the door to the box and pushes me inside. I bounce off the wall, and wind up on my knees in the filth again.

"Aren't you going to do something *now* to teach her some respect?" Lucas asks, a look of surprise on his face.

"Like what?" Jeremiah answers, looking down at me. "She already has a black eye and a split lip. Lenience today is a gift. My wedding present, let's call it." He turns to Lucas as he continues. "But don't worry about *her*. Once I am her husband, she *will* know her place. Besides, I've got something I have to take care of today. I don't have time to deal with her. Starting tomorrow, I'll have all the time in the world."

I don't flip him off as they close the door. I *so* badly want to, but I wait until the door is fully closed and I've heard the latch click. A show of bravado could make him change his mind and for once he's being *generous*, so I don't want to tempt fate.

I don't want despair to get to me, either, but somehow I feel it creeping up my spine.

I'm right back where I started. Well, almost. I'm somewhat cleaner, at least. It would have been stupid not to try to take advantage of that opportunity. If not for the little shithead, it would have worked!

It doesn't matter. I will try again tonight as I had planned originally. Yes. In a few hours, after dark, when all is quiet, and Jennie comes to bring me water and whatever food she's managed to squirrel away. It doesn't matter.

I repeat it, crying out the mantra in my mind, until I fall asleep in my corner, resting up for my next try. It seems like I've barely closed my eyes when pebbles against the wooden walls of the box jolt me back to awareness. It's dark already, but they haven't turned on the floodlights yet and only the silvery light of an almost full moon streams through the cracks in the roof and walls.

"Courtney! Courtney!" Jennie whispers. I peer through the cracks and smile at her. "I'm sorry, Courtney," she whines. "I couldn't get you any food tonight."

"It's okay, baby." I tell her. "Don't worry. I'm going to be just fine." She sounds so forlorn, and it hurts not to be able to take her into my arms and bring a smile back on her face.

"It's because of Nathan. He was watching me all the time." The poor thing is almost in tears.

Yes, that makes sense. Nathan is anything but an idiot. He knows Jennie and I are close, and he's seen enough people stagger out of the penance box to know what a *truly* starving and dehydrated woman should look like. If someone has been feeding me, she'd be the obvious suspect. And that means she's in danger. He's probably going to try and prove it, try to score points with his father.

"Be careful of him, Jennie!" I warn her. "He's dangerous. If he catches you helping me, you could get hurt!"

"Oh, I know *that*," she says, in a tone of disgust. I laugh softly, almost able to see her eyes rolling at the stupidity of grownups who warn children about something so obvious, but she's so sweet and trusting that I felt like I needed to warn her. *So* sweet and trusting that I hesitate to ask her for one last favor, but I have to. She's my last hope.

"Would you do something for me, Jen?" I ask.

"Of course, Courtney, anything!"

"Okay, do you think you could bring me back something I could use to open the latch?" It kills me to think of Jennie putting herself in danger to sneak back up here again, but I can't think of any other way to get that latch open. "Something, I dunno- something flat, thin, something I can use to lift the bar from in here?"

"I don't think that would be a good idea," she says. "The lights are off right now. Brother Jonathan couldn't get the generator started tonight, but he's fixing it. I don't know if I could come back later."

"Jennie, please," I beg. "There's nothing in here I can use to lift the latch, and unless you help me I'll never get away."

"That's just stupid," she snorts in a very grown-up whisper. "Don't be stupid."

"What? What do you mean?" I'm utterly in shock. Stupid? You have a better idea, kid?

"Why would I go and find something for you to try to open it yourself?" she asks, as if I should be able to figure this out all on my own. "I'm right *here*, Courtney, I could just open it for you."

Out of the mouths of babes comes wisdom. I've wasted so much time. Five. Whole. Days.

Jennie easily slips the latch on the door in an instant and crouches back down in the darkness against the wall.

"Anything else?" she asks.

"No, that's it. That's everything I could ever ask for," I tell her, my eyes filling with tears. "I want you to go now, go back to the dorm and hide. Make sure you don't stay alone."

"You're going to try to run away again?" she asks. "I'm going to miss you, Courtney."

"Yes, honey," I tell her. "And when I do, I don't want anyone suspecting that you helped me. I don't want you to get in trouble." She shrugs as if being punished for helping me wouldn't matter at all.

"So I'll never see you again?" she whispers. I know there are tears rolling from her eyes. I can't hold back my own, either.

"I'm going to miss you so much, Jennie." My voice is choked with emotion. This little child has shown me more kindness and generosity than my mother ever did. "Go, honey. Go and don't look back." Watching her leave through the cracks of the shack, I feel my heart crumble a little more. I thought I was done feeling after Sean's death. I was wrong. There's still enough left of me to feel fresh pain.

I give my tiny savior several minutes to get clear before I open the door and begin hobbling away, crouched as low as I can. Even with the floodlights off, there are still no shadows in which I can hide in the open area around the penance box. My dress glows almost ghost-like in the light of the full moon, but no voices call out in alarm. Once I get to the cover of the small buildings, I can steal a dark shawl or something off a clothesline, then make my way into the woods. Halfway there.

I only make it a few more steps, though, before I hear the rumble of the big generator coming to life, and the floodlights begin to glow, their intensity slowly increasing as the generator spins up. I'm so close, though, only a few more steps until I'm out of the ring of light.

Sighing in relief, I slump against the wall of the barn, out of the glow of the lights, and start looking around for something, anything, to cover my light-colored clothes, and almost immediately spot a clothesline swinging nearby, still heavy with laundry. Oh, Sister Ruth! You lazy, lazy creature. You were so busy preparing for my wedding, you didn't get your laundry done in time. Thank you so much!

The shawl is wet, but it's long enough to cover me. It'll work very nicely.

As I reach for the first clothespin, I hear shouts of alarm starting.

"The door's open!" Brother Lucas yells. "Find her!" The door! Oh, I'm stupid. Did I forget to latch close the door shut? Did the latch just not catch? Did I leave it ajar? No matter. Just the clothespins left, then I can head for the woods. Please, please, please, pleeeeease, let this work.

And for the second time in one day, God ignores me.

The clothesline shifts ever so slightly, but it's fastened into the thin sheet metal sides of the hovel in which Sister Ruth lives with her husband. The slight change in the pressure of the line causes the wall to flex, popping like the vacuum seal on a jar lid. Just as the wall is bigger, so is the sound, and alert ears are already looking for me in the silent darkness.

Wrapped in the wet shawl, I make for the darkness outside the compound, but all my efforts are in vain: after only a moment I hear gravel crunching behind me, and when I turn around, Nathan stands there, Brother Lucas behind him, looming like a terrible shadow.

"I told you she'd try again!" Nathan sneers, but this tone of voice doesn't reach his eyes. He's curious. He's thinking. Does he wonder why I still try to run, after everything they've done to me? Does he try to understand? Will he ever?

"You were right," the older man says. "I told your brother he should not have given such a generous wedding present, but... it's not my place to interfere between a man and his- almost wife." Lucas shakes his head sadly, but the moonlight shows his eyes are eager. "Your lessons tomorrow," he continues, "will simply be far, *far* more intense."

Chapter 20
Sean

Friday Night, 19 August 2016

The T-shirt Courtney wore, a relic of my years with SEAL Team THREE is still a blue-and-gold heap on the small table, and deep rusty-brown stains on the floor bear mute witness to the fighting on Monday. *Has it been so long already?*

Memories of the wonder and beauty of Monday morning, turned to pain and fury by evening, fill my mind. On the one hand, a few hours from now I'm going to need every scrap of that rage as fuel, but on the other? Sitting here staring at the bed I shared with her and getting maudlin isn't going to get me in the right frame of mind, so I go back outside to wait.

Bill went home to Portland as soon as my Blazer was off the jack, with brand new tires mounted on the spare set of wheels from the garage. The camp is dark, quiet. I'm alone. But not for long: the heavy rumble of a big diesel engine thundering up Camp Road from the south is attenuated by distance and dense forest, but I recognize the sound of Angela's crew cab Ford. Moments later, the big vehicle sits next to mine, the last dying summer twilight glinting dully off its deep red paint.

Time to see what sort of miracles Max Anghelescu has been able to gin up for me.

"Thanks for coming up, Angie," I grunt under my friend's bear hug but still manage to reach up and tweak his bare chin. "What happened to the beard? Last time I saw you, it was magnificent! Glorious! How's anyone gonna know you're an *operator* without the tactical beard?"

"Last time you saw me was in Trashcanistan when I was loading your ass into the meat wagon. We're not on deployment anymore, and they're being assholes about grooming standards. So, yeah." He runs his fingers glumly through the imaginary mass of hair from his memory.

"How's school going? You still working on that?"

"School. *Fuck* school, man," he rumbles angrily. "I've got exams on Monday, and I should be studying about ancient near-eastern trade routes, the socio-sexual-political implications of priestesses in the Hittite empire, and how conflict between the Hittites and the Egyptians has had lasting implications for the Middle East thirty-*fucking*-five centuries later." Angie's eyes have glazed over, and he shakes his head as if to clear it. "Gotta have an advanced degree to get promoted, though, and if I want to make master chief, it would help to have a PhD," he says with a hint of glum whining. "I'm supposed to be a hootin,' lootin,' parachutin,' door-kickin' *killin'* machine, not some ivory tower academic."

"*Doctor* Angie, two-fisted history major!" It's funny, though, in a way. SpecOps troops are selected for high intelligence, in addition to physical prowess, and tend to be very well educated men. And these days? The only path to promotion *is* education. You don't make chief petty officer without a degree, and to get senior chief or master chief, you'd better have a masters or a PhD. "I've only got a few credits to go for my bachelor's. Maybe I'll get around to finishing that up, just in time to never use it again."

"Yeah, yeah. Indiana Jones, but without the stupid whip. But seriously, Sean. You okay?" He stares straight into my eyes, looking for pupil dilation and tracking. "You had enough down time to be ready for this?"

"Enough?" I shrug. "Depends on your point of view, I suppose. Not enough according to the medical profession. Possibly too much, depending on what I find up north. And speaking of finding things?"

"Yeah. I managed to liberate a few things for you, temporarily. Deniably." Angie pauses to open the back door of the truck. "And speaking of deniability? I have no interest in spending the rest of my life in Leavenworth, okay? So, I'm not going in with you. *I'm* here to make sure this gear makes it back home safe and sound to DEVGRU, where it goes back into its invisible hidey-hole."

"Roger that. I hadn't really expected anyone to go into the compound with me anyway."

"You're not listening, tadpole," Angie says, opening the back door of his truck.

"Tadpole?" I shake my head sadly. "Angela, what'd I ever do to you to make you call me a thing like that? I'm a full-fledged *Frogman*, not some fucking new-meat *tadpole*."

"Frogmen are smart, and retirement's done somethin' to your brain." Anghelescu's voice is muffled as he digs around inside the cab. "Or maybe it's just the head injury. Ah! There we go!" He hands me a gray metal case. "You're not *listening*," he says. "Tadpole."

The case is heavy, and I've handled one just like it a thousand times. I don't need to look at the data plaque to know what it contains. My heart races as I open it to find the finest night vision instrument known to man: the GPNVG-18, the four-lensed, vaguely insectoid headgear that let American SpecOps troops utterly fucking *rule* the nighttime battlefield.

"I'm here to make sure this gear gets back to base without anyone having the opportunity to look at serial numbers and question how they wound up in the middle of the woods in East Bumfuck, Maine. If those NVGs are attached to your head, then anything I do to bring *them* back is probably going to be of some minor and purely incidental assistance to *you* as well."

"Overwatch, then?" Having the Eye of Sauron looking down on me is almost better than having boots on the ground behind me. I can go on a sneak-and-peek, and anything out there that's not Courtney is an enemy.

"Yeah. I've got a suppressed Mark Twelve. I'll scratch your back if you need it, but, Jesus fuckin' Christ, *please* try not to need it, okay? When we're done up there, I want to put all this shit back into the truck and melt away into the darkness like I was never there."

"Right. Hey, Angie?" I say, opening the box running an adoring finger over the night vision goggles in their foam-padded case with as nearly as much pleasure and anticipation as I'd touched Courtney's body. *Fuck, yeah!* "I ever tell you how much I love you?"

"Hey, now, I told you—we're not on deployment." The chief laughs. "I've got the armor you wanted. The heavy shit. It'll stop an AK round, but these backwoods fucks probably have deer rifles. You take one of those straight on, it'll blow in through the front plate and out the back plate, and take a lot of your insides with it."

"No kidding?" My voice is earnest, serious. Certainly no hint of sarcasm. "All those years in the Teams, how'd I miss learning about that?"

"Yeah, yeah. Whatever. Just want to make sure you remember. You're retarded, sorry, *retired* now." Angie holds out a meaty paw to me. "Gimme the Beretta, I'll swap out the barrel, get you ready for the silencer while you get suited up."

Once I'm dressed ready to go, we load the coordinates into Angela's GPS.

"Rendezvous point here," I tell him. "We'll keep some separation between the vehicles on the way up. And Christ. Gotta keep my foot off the gas. Five over, no more."

"Yeah," Angie agrees. "Probably don't want to get pulled over."

"Leavenworth's got a good volleyball team, I hear."

Fort Leavenworth, Kansas is home to the US Army's Command and General Staff College, but the part that *we* worry about is the *other* half of the base. Leavenworth is *also* home to the Department of Defense's only maximum-security prison. If we get pulled over with this load of illegal weapons and carefully-prepared improvised explosive devices, we're both going to spend a lot of time there.

"Yeah, well, leave volleyball for the fighter pilots," Angie says, his voice dripping with scorn. It's an article of faith in the SEALs that the rest of the Navy is made up of the prissy weaklings who couldn't hack it at BUD/S. Fighter pilots? They're the worst of the worst. Vain creatures, unable to form a deep and meaningful relationship with anything other than a mirror. "You ready to roll, killer?"

"Let's get it on."

Insertion has always been the worst part of any mission for me. The interminable waiting. In the back of a C-130, waiting for the ramp to drop and the jumpmaster to give the order. In the back of a truck or personnel carrier, jostling over cratered roads or spine-shatteringly rough off-road terrain, waiting to get somewhere.

Time doesn't pass any faster, no matter how often you look at the clock, no matter how often you look at the pipper on a moving map screen showing your route.

Waiting.

Music is an important part of gearing up for a mission. Gotta be in the right mindset. I *need* my hate, my rage. I *need* the love, with it. It's a weapon, in and of itself. I *need* all of it, heated and forged into a blade, tempered and ground down and honed to the barest razor's edge, and insertion is the time for that preparation. In the back of a C-130, I'd be listening to my phone on earbuds, barely audible over the sounds of the airplane itself. The sound system in my truck? *Much* better than cheap earbuds.

Slayer and The Deftones, Faith No More and Anthrax bring the base material of emotion to a white heat, ready to forge; Metallica's precise rhythms and blindingly fast guitar riffs are a steam hammer, pounding me into the right shape. The heavy brutality of Type O Negative, Nine Inch Nails and Rob Zombie grind the raw forging into a blade. It's a long drive, but I need it to be: by the time I pull in to the rendezvous point, sparks fly in my soul as Megadeth's *Symphony of Destruction* puts the finishing touches on my cutting edge.

I'm ready.

We separate at the rendezvous, after Angie pulls one more miracle from his backseat.

"Thought this might come in handy for you," he says, handing it over. My eyes go wide when I recognize what it is: an MP5-SD. The German-made 9mm submachinegun, long obsolete, and replaced years ago by the newer MP7, is perfect for tonight's mission. Lightweight and easy to carry, it features a built-in suppressor so effective that the mechanical *click* of the trigger is audible over the shot. *Much* better for my purposes than a full size – and above all *noisy* – rifle, and a good adjunct to my suppressed pistol.

There's no long goodbyes here, no need for them. We're both in the zone, and it's time for action. A quick radio check to verify comms, and I'm off on foot while Angie creeps my Blazer along as quietly as he can toward my observation post on Trout Mountain.

It's a twenty-minute hike to the edge of the compound, studying my objective through the green filter of the panoramic NVGs, when the bone-conduction radio headset crackles to life like an itch inside my skull.

"In position," Angie says.

"Roger that," I reply. The subvocalized whisper, barely enough to trigger my matching microphone, is inaudible from more than a yard away. "Moving in."

Only one area is brightly lit up: the penance box, standing alone in the empty area in the middle of the compound. This late at night, there's nobody visible outside, and few of the windows show lights inside the buildings. There's a flickering light--a candle?--in an upper story window of the main house, but it grows faint and vanishes.

Someone's moving around up there. Late night piss call maybe. Stay alert.

The main house is my first stop of the night anyway. I'm not loaded any lighter than I would be on a recon patrol, but I don't have any need for a sleeping bag or other snivel gear, and I don't have to hump ammo for the squad's machine gunner. All the extra weight I'm packing tonight? Just like me, it's here for a single reason--one way or another, Courtney is leaving this place with me. The things I've brought with me on this mission will be used to noisily break as much shit as possible to create distractions, and quietly kill anyone who refuses to be distracted.

I really, *really* hope that Lucas, Jeremiah and that son of a bitch Emmanuel refuse to be distracted.

Slipping from shadow to shadow, I easily make it to the propane tank by the main house, and the first distraction comes out of my rucksack. The number 1 written with an infrared-reflective marker, glows bright green in the goggles, and a strong magnet sticks it to the bottom of the steel tank. I hope you assholes paid your gas bill and got this fucker filled up.

Next stop is their motor pool. They don't want anyone to grab a car and drive away, so there's only one locked and chained gate in the metal fence surrounding the vehicles. I don't want anyone driving away tonight either, so it looks like we agree on something, at least. Distractions two through five are tossed over the fence, and at least a couple of them roll underneath one or another of the ramshackle vehicles. Just in case, though, a couple drops of a fast-setting epoxy in the padlock ensures nobody will be opening the gate easily, either to rescue a car or to use one in pursuit while we make our escape. More of my distractions wind up attached to electrical panels, and the last one goes on the big tank of kerosene for the generator.

A quick sweep through the inside of the chapel reveals it to be empty, but it's been decorated. Streamers and bunting made of bleach-whitened sheets and scraps of cloth hang over the door and throughout the inside of the small building. Great bundles of flowers fill the air with their scent.

It looks like a wedding. Has it already happened, then? Or is this set up for tomorrow?

Movement catches my eye, phosphorescent green, and a sudden flare of light washes out the sensitive night vision for an instant before the optics adjust automatically. Someone's sitting on the front stoop of one of the shacks, a tiny glowing spark in front of their face.

A cigarette.

The flare was probably a lighter.

Go ahead: destroy your night vision along with your lungs.

Stupid enemies make my job easier. I can't identify who it is – even high-end NVGs don't like too much light when it's otherwise dark – but it's not as if I've got a chart of all the faces and names here anyway.

The pin that Courtney dropped on my phone's map said her hovel should be right about ... here, but there's just empty space between two other shacks. The ground's been turned recently. A new garden? Odd place for it. Doesn't matter right now. Where is she? Where else could she be? Heather's place? The women's dormitory?

Crouched low, the submachine gun pulled tightly against my shoulder, I glide silently through the night, searching for my love. Heather's shanty, little more than a plywood garden shed, sits empty. The bed is made, with no sign that anyone has been inside tonight. Where the fuck are you, Heather? One more mystery. Next stop, women's dorm.

"Heads up, Pearse," Angie says in that buzzy voice inside my head. "Two assholes. Ten meters ahead, left around the corner, then three meters. Looks like they're just standing around talking."

"Roger that," I answer. "Is one of them smoking?" I smell the cigarette, but that doesn't mean he's close.

"Affirmative."

I close the distance to the corner, but remain crouched in the shadows without closing it. It's too early to start the party – I still haven't located Courtney – but perhaps I can gain useful intel by eavesdropping. Two low voices carry on the still air.

"It was your own fault, you know." A man's voice. It's Lucas. I've only heard him say a few words, but I'd recognize that son of a bitch anywhere. "And you're lucky Jeremiah's whore needed some time to repent of her sins."

The penance box.

Is she still there? Or did they marry her off to that greasy-haired prick already?

"I know." A woman. Andrea, then? "I'm sorry, Lucas. You're my husband, and it's your place to discipline Matthew. I should never have interfered."

"It's okay," Lucas says, his voice gentle. "I know you only did it because you love him, and so do I. And I love *you*, too. That's why I have to discipline you both. If you sin and do not come to repentance, you cannot be saved."

"And you have to set an example for the flock," she says, sniffling. "And I have to set an example for the other women, and Matthew for the children." More sniffling, verging on crying. "We failed you, Lucas. I'm so sorry."

"It's not *me* that you failed, Andrea. It's The Lord."

Are you fucking kidding me? You're going to stand here and tell me that a mother trying to protect her child was somehow going against God's will? That ain't my God, you sorry piece of shit.

"I know," Andrea sobs quietly. "I'm sorry. I'll do better."

"I know you will. Pray for the strength to do right, and The Lord will give it to you. You'll see." I hear rustling, and Andrea's soft crying stops after the sound of a kiss. "I love you, Andrea."

"I love you too, Lucas," she says, then sighs. "Tomorrow is going to be beautiful. The chapel is so pretty."

Tomorrow?

The wedding hasn't happened yet.

A wave of relief rushes through me. Tension I hadn't even recognized evaporates into thin air.

"You women did a fine job on it," Lucas agrees. "Better'n *she* deserves, for sure."

"And Sister Courtney, she's going to be so beautiful! I did some of the stitching on the dress!" Andrea's pride in her work is clear in her voice. "I wish they'd wait a few days, though, and let that black eye heal up a bit more."

"The Lord's plan does not wait for man's pleasure," Lucas tells her. "And you'd best remember that."

"Yes. I'm sorry, husband. I forgot myself." Andrea pauses. "I'm going to cry tomorrow. I always cry at weddings," she says, her voice brightening.

"You might cry *at* the wedding," Lucas says. "But the whore's going to be doing a lot of crying *after* the wedding, unless she learns to submit. Honestly, I don't know what Jeremiah sees in her," he finishes.

"Brother Jeremiah will be a prophet of The Lord, his father's successor, if The Lord takes Father Emmanuel to Glory before the End arrives," she says fervently. "And did not The Lord command His prophet Hosea to marry a prostitute? Perhaps this is part of Brother Jeremiah's witness to us? Have we fallen, Lucas? Like the Israelites had, in Hosea's time?"

My jaw drops in shock at her words. She's not just a battered wife, she's a willing and eager participant. Stockholm Syndrome? It'd take an army of shrinks a lifetime of work to fix this woman's head.

"Maybe so, maybe so." Lucas considers. "It's not my place to question the prophets, nor yours. The Lord will reveal all to us in his own time." He heaves a heavy sigh, then continues. "But speaking of Brother Jeremiah's reluctant bride, I'd best go check in with Brother Jonathan. I'm sure he'd like to get some sleep, and after last night? We can't leave the harlot unattended. I still haven't figured out how she managed to unlatch the door."

Oh, really? You're still fighting, Courtney! Stay strong. I love you, and I'll be there soon. Guess I don't have to check the women's quarters for you now.

"Go, husband." Another kissing sound. "Do your duty to The Lord and his prophets. I'm going back to sleep now."

"Goodnight, love," Lucas says, and then his heavy footsteps crunch gravel as he walks away.

I need to follow him, but I can't move until Andrea goes inside. The squealing of ungreased hinges is almost deafening in the otherwise silent night, and I wait for a count of ten heartbeats after the latch clicks before I move.

"Gimme some direction here, Angie," I mutter into the throat mic. I know where the penance box is, but I still don't know for sure that's where Courtney is.

"Twenty meters, west-northwest. Moving slow," he replies. "Target's fat, dumb and happy. It'll be just like that one asshat in Drosh." I can hear the grin in his voice, and there's a matching one on my own face. Drosh had been a good op.

"Not entirely," I say, remembering stalking the oblivious local politician through the marketplace, and the look of utter shock when a black hood went over his face before he was tossed into the back of a van. He'd been funneling money to Taliban leaders across the virtually meaningless border in the remote areas where Pakistan and Afghanistan are neighbors. "That guy was a body *snatch*. Lucas? He's just going to be a *body*."

"You really don't like this guy, do you?"

"I'll like him just fine once he and his baseball bat are both in the ground," I say, moving out in the direction where Lucas had vanished. Where Lucas's footsteps had been noisy on the rocky path, my own steps are virtually silent. Stealth is a survival skill, and I'm good enough at it to have survived this long. My feet instinctively find the soft places, grass with no dried leaves or sticks to break, no gravel to grind, and I make up the distance easily.

"Ah. That explains a lot," Angie says. "Don't lose your head, though. Stay frosty."

My target is almost certainly heading for the penance box. Even with Lucas being completely unaware of me, it's not going to be the easiest thing in the world to approach the only brightly-lit area of the compound undetected, particularly not with two men there.

Patience. Lucas said he was going to relieve this Jonathan guy on watch. That means in a minute, there'll be one guy there, and he can't watch the other side of the box, even if he's alert and expecting danger.

Lucas chats with Jonathan for a moment, laughing at the other man when Jonathan yawns hugely, covering his mouth with a forearm. What the fuck am I supposed to do with Jonathan? I don't want even a slightly-awake threat possibly behind me. Does he fit the ROE? My own personal rules of engagement for this mission are flexible, and I don't lose a single second of sleep over a righteous kill, but killing is not always the best option.

The question is answered a moment later, as Jonathan walks away from the box and approaches close enough to make out his features in the green light of the NVGs. He's the motherfucker who grabbed Andrea by her braid, held her still for Lucas's correction. Yeah, you meet the ROE, asshole. Killing isn't always the best option, but sometimes it's the right one.

Jonathan passes right by me without noticing I'm there, tucked away in the shadows behind the propane tank.

"Brother Jonathan!" I stage-whisper, urgently. "Brother Jonathan!"

He pulls up short, looking around in confusion. "Who's there? Where are you?" He's whispering too.

I almost have to laugh. Answering a whisper *with* a whisper is a strong survival instinct in humans, but it's backfired this time. If he'd spoken loudly enough for

Lucas to hear, the outcome might have changed, but Jonathan has run out of luck. He dies almost silently, with my stiletto in the side of his neck, and I lower the body behind the cylinder. It's a messy, bloody way to kill, but it's quiet, and if you're good, you can stay clean while doing it. And I'm *very* good.

Now it's your turn, Lucas.

The big man is leaning against the box, his back to the door, and I hear a thumping sound as he taps the baseball bat against the door. Poor Courtney. It must be like the inside of a drum inside there. Is he doing it on purpose to keep her exhausted and awake?

Stupid question. Of course, he is.

Standing in the middle the floodlights, there's no way Lucas can see anything outside the ring of illumination around him, and I'm getting impatient. A few careful moments of near-silent sprinting and I'm on the opposite side of the box from him.

Stay stupid, motherfucker. Stay stupid.

Around the first corner, my own back against the wall.

The goggles have adjusted to the available light, and the world is visible in color instead of shades of green. They're usable in all light conditions, and I can leave them down, but I flip them up out of the way of my face.

I want you to see me, Lucas. I want you to know at the end.

In an instant, I'm around the final corner, and the long blade is buried to the hilt in the side of Lucas's neck, and that's when everything goes to shit. I'm pleased to see recognition in his eyes while the light begins to fade from them, but he's tougher than I expected. His life is draining away swiftly, but he still has enough energy to try and scream, flailing his arms.

The high-pitched squeal of agony and alarm is easy to silence. A quick twist-and-tug and sound is changed to a rattling gurgle as the blade slices forward through cartilage and flesh, opening him the rest of the way forward. But I would have been happy to let him scream for hours if it would have prevented the *big* sound the asshole had caused while he died. Lucas's dying hands had reached for a shotgun leaning against the side of the building. He no longer had the fine motor control to aim it and fire it at me, but as he died, Lucas did something almost worse. He knocked it over, and the ancient weapon fired both barrels when it clattered to the ground.

I didn't want a half-awake enemy behind me, but now I'm going to have all the enemies behind me, and they'll all be awake.

"Think you used enough dynamite there, Butch?" Angie's voice is somewhere between amusement and anger.

"That was *not* part of the plan," I shoot back.

"Didn't figure it was. Get a move on. We need to di-di the fuck right outta here, good buddy, and make it number-one-most-rikki-tik."

The compound around me quickly comes alive with lights. I pull a burner phone from a utility pocket on my chest, ready to send the text message that will trigger my distractions.

Time is running out. I feel the itch of watching eyes behind me as I reach for the latch securing the door.

Chapter 21

Courtney

Friday Night, 19 August 2016

Tap. Tap. Tap.

It's Lucas out there now. It has to be him.

Tap. Tap. Tap.

Brother Jonathan isn't this cruel. He'd let me sleep.

Tap. Tap. Tap.

This is driving me mad.

Tap. Tap. Tap.

What'm I resting up for? Today was my last chance. All I'm doing is making sure I'll be healthy and alert for tomorrow. For my wedding. To a monster.

Tap. Tap. Tap.

I swore to Jeremiah that I'd die before I let him touch me, and I'm rapidly running out of time to make good on my vow. As soon as the sun is up tomorrow, the women will begin getting me ready to be delivered to the waiting demon, and I won't have a moment by myself. Even if I was alone for a moment, nobody would be stupid enough to leave a sharp object within my reach, and I wouldn't have time for anything slower than opening a vein.

Tap. Tap. Tap.

Do I even have the courage to do it?

Can I kill myself?

I know what Jeremiah wants, what he plans to do with me. Is a quick death now truly better than a – very short - lifetime of torture at the hands of that sadist? Better than most likely dying in childbirth before age thirty, screaming away the last moments of my life as I give these twisted, evil assholes another generation of 'prophets'?

Tap. Tap. Tap.

If I make it, what then? Is Hell a real place? When I was a little girl, the priests always said that suicide was a mortal sin, and that you'd go straight to Hell. The God I knew was kind and loving. Merciful. Surely, he will forgive me. Surely, he will understand. Won't he?

Tap. Tap. Tap.

The wooden walls of the penance box are smooth, with no splinters or jagged edges I could use. There's no lights in here, no electricity that could stop my heart.

Tap. Tap. Tap.

There it is! A hook, at the peak of the low roof. It's meant to hang a lamp, but it should be able to hang something else. It only needs to support me for a few minutes. It won't take long, will it? I don't want it to hurt.

Tap. Tap. Tap.

The rags that Heather left for me are not long enough to make a rope, but the long skirt of my dress provides extra fabric. Torn into strips, braided together, there should be plenty. If Lucas even hears me ripping my clothes, he won't care anyway, and I've braided my own hair for years now, so it goes quickly.

Tap. Tap. Tap.

I'm so scared. But I'll be with you again, Sean, and you, too, Daniel. I hope you're at peace, with Joshua. I'll see you all soon.

Tap. Tap. Tap.

"Hail Mary, full of grace," I begin. I haven't said the old prayers in years, but I was raised Catholic, just like Sean. The words are comforting, so different from what they preach here. "Our Lord is with thee. Blessed art thou among women, and blessed is the fruit of thy womb, Jesus. Holy Mary, Mother of God, pray for us sinners, now and..." I laugh softly, bitterly, before finishing. "Now and at the hour of our death, which will be in just a few minutes. *Amen.*"

Tap. Tap. Tap.

My bucket, upside down, gets me to the right height. When I kick it away, my toes won't touch the ground. I loop the end of the makeshift rope over the hook, and settle the noose around my neck, carefully getting the knot clear of my hair. I don't want it to pull, after all. I'm going to die, but I don't need to be uncomfortable while I'm doing it.

Tap. Tap. Tap.

A deep peace settles over me, a serene calm. One more Hail Mary, and it's time. I panic a little at the first bite of the rope, but Sean's face in my mind calms me again. He's smiling at me, holding his hands out to me. I'm coming, my love. I'll be with you again in just a moment.

Tap. Tap. Shriek!

What's that? It doesn't matter now. I don't care what it was. It doesn't affect me. I'm going to be at peace in a moment, with my love.

My vision is starting to narrow, now, a ring of blackness surrounding the faint light that leaks in through cracks in the roof. The screaming stops as abruptly as it started, ending in a wheezing, choking sound. My hearing is going wrong, too. A lamb makes that sound when they cut its throat. It's not time to slaughter the lambs yet, is it? Doesn't matter. Why do I care? I'm never going to have lamb again. That shouldn't be important but somehow it is.

Light. Bright white light, in the distance. A pinpoint of it, and I'm falling.

Falling? No! I can't be falling. I need to go up, toward the light. Toward Sean!

My feet hit first, slipping, and I land hard. Something's shaking me. I hear a voice.

"Courtney! Courtney! No, *no*, honey!" It's Sean's voice. *"Fuck!* Gimme a minute here! *Yes,* I fucking *realize* we need to egress! Shit just went *seriously fucking FUBAR on my end, okay?* Yeah, yeah. Distraction in five... four... three..."

"I couldn't stand to be without you, Sean. I came to be with you." I smile up at him. He's covered in blood. "They must have been awful to you before they killed you. I didn't realize I'd have to fall to get to Heaven, but here I am?"

Why is that even a question? Of course this is Heaven. It must be. Sean's here.

"Close your eyes, honey. Keep your mouth open!" His hands cover my ears, and he lays on top of me.

"This is a strange way to--" The ground rumbles and shakes, and a blast of heat washes over us as the light changes from pure white to an angry reddish-orange.

We're not in Heaven. We're in the other place, and the gates just opened to let us in. The priests were right about suicide.

"Courtney, can you get up? Are you okay?"

"I'm with you, Sean. I love you, and I couldn't stand to be without you, so here I am." I reach up to his face, run a hand over his beard, still wet with blood. "I'm so sorry. It's my fault we're here."

"No, that's fine. Don't worry about that," he says, looking over his shoulder at the flames. "None of the blood's mine. Can you walk? We need to get the *fuck* out of here, like ten minutes ago."

"I think so," I tell him, and he helps me to my feet. "But, Sean? This is *Hell*. We can't get out of here."

"Hell? Hell on *Earth*, sure, but..." Sean looks at me quizzically, then laughs. "Oh, Christ! Courtney, honey. You're not dead. I cut the rope in time. You're *alive*."

Alive. The concept is a difficult one to wrap my head around.

"But *you're* dead. Sean, you're *dead!*"

"Death cannot stop true love," he says, a twinkle in his eye. "It can only delay it a little while." He laughs uproariously, and beats the heel of his hand against the wooden wall. "God*damn* but I have always wanted to use that line! But yeah, I wasn't dead. I was only *mostly* dead, because that shithead Lucas swings a mean bat."

Not dead. You're not dead. We're both alive? Mary, you were with me then by delaying the hour of my death. You gave me back my life, and you gave me back my love.

"If that's not hell outside, then what's going on?" Nothing makes sense right now, and I don't care. Sean's alive!

"Oh. My, uh, *distractions* were very successful." He looks sheepish. "A little too successful, maybe. I blew up the propane tank, and the fuel tank for the generator. And all the electrical panels. I think this place is going to be attracting a lot of attention, and *really* soon. A big propane tank like that? It's a good bet they heard that blast all the way to Greenville." Sean pauses, cocking his head to the side, listening to something I can't hear.

"Yeah. Roger that. On the way." Sean puts a hand on my cheek, and I squeeze the rough, callused fingers tightly against my face. "Courtney, we need to get out of here, *right* now. Can you walk?"

"Walk? Sean, you're *alive!* If you want me to, I can *fly!*"

"Let's get out of here," he says, kissing my forehead and running a black-gloved hand through my tangled, dirty hair. "Keep behind me, and stay low."

Sean takes shelter by the doorframe, peeking around it through the sights of a compact black gun, and I gasp at the sight of the body just outside the door.

"Sean?" I tap him on the shoulder. "Who is that?"

"Mm? Oh. Lucas," he says absently.

"Did it hurt?" My voice is raspy, hoarse from the rope. "Please tell me he was scared and in pain."

"Yeah. It hurt. It hurt a *lot*. Okay, so the plan. Our ride is going to meet us on the other side of the chapel. It's not the closest spot to us here, but it's the easiest place for him to get to and still be able to get us out of here without running into complications."

"Complications?"

"That boom," Sean chuckles. "There's going to be game wardens coming down on this place *any* minute, from the air too, and we do *not* want to get stopped on our way out of here. Fire trucks too, but the Warden Service will get here first."

"Let's go, then," I say, and follow Sean. Just outside the door, I freeze, transfixed by the sight of Lucas. With Sean's cut, and the angle his head's sitting at, he looks almost like a Pez dispenser! My train of thought is interrupted by a gunshot and a spray of gravel as something hits the ground a few feet away from me. Oh no, I've gotten too far behind!

"Move! Move! Move!" Sean's yelling at me, and it looks like he's shooting back at something. I see flashes in front of the black gun at his shoulder, but there's only a clicking sound, and a metal-on-metal rasp. "Yeah, I see it. *Shit!* I should have brought the rifle." Who is he talking to?

In a moment, I'm behind Sean again, following him into the shadows. In temporary safety, we can stop for a breath, and I have a moment for my first look around. I've lived here for years, yet the layout is completely different now. When the propane tank went up, it must have leveled half the-- my God! Look at the flames! A billowing column reaches skyward, swirling sheets of red and orange.

"I was right," Sean says, with a laugh so full of wonder and delight, I can't help but smile with him.

"About what?" I ask.

"It really *does* look better on fire." Sean's face grows serious again. "We can't take the shortest path. Seems like they can't decide whether they're more interested in putting out the fires or making sure you and I don't get out of here. We need to get around to the back of the chapel. You know the terrain here, what's your suggestion?"

"Go right here, behind these houses," I point at the plywood-and-tarpaper shacks, sheltered from the explosion by the now-burning main house. "There's a fence on the other side of them, but there's a space we can walk down, and we'll turn right again at the corner of the fence. We can make almost all the way to the chapel there. At the end, we go through the barn, then through the chapel and out the back door."

Sean glances around the corner of the shack. The shadows in the narrow space are deeper, blacker than normal, after staring up at the pillar of fire. I don't care about shadows or fire! I'll go anywhere with you, and I won't be afraid ever again.

"Works for me. Let's go."

I follow Sean through the gap, then down the path between buildings. He's pulled the night vision goggles down over his face again, and has no problem finding sure footing around the mess of broken children's toys, garden tools and other stuff littering the small back yards. I can't see nearly as well, but by staying close enough to touch Sean and walk where he does, I avoid the worst of it.

When we reach the corner of the fence, Sean flattens himself against the post, reaching back to touch me in the darkness, wordlessly telling me to hold up.

"What's wrong?" I whisper.

"Nothing," he says. "Yet. Let me clear it first."

Sean's training takes over, and he sweeps the barrel of the gun around the corner, his body following with fluid grace and blinding speed, but then he freezes, silhouetted by the flames above. His lips move, but I can't make out a thing that he's saying over the roaring flames and the barking of panicked dogs.

He's staring at something.

What does he see?

The muzzle of the gun at his shoulder dips, and I frantically go through my memory to try to understand. There's just twenty, thirty feet there. The rectory at the end, the kitchen door. Back door to the barn on the left. What else? I creep up to the corner.

"What is it, Sean? What do you see?"

"Do you *hear* them?" Sean's voice is hoarse with-what? Fear? That makes no sense. He cut a path through this place to get to me, and he hasn't shown the slightest sign of panic. What's wrong now?

"Hear what?" I ask. With another shift in the flames, the area around us is almost as bright as the noon sun.

"The dog," he says. "A dog, barking. The sun at midnight." Sean reaches up to flip the four-eyed goggles back on his helmet, then steadies the gun again, pointing at something I can't see. His eyes are wide, and he's breathing hard. *"The black curtain."*

A dog? The sun at midnight? The black...

"...curtain," I finish aloud, understanding finally and risking a peek around the corner to see if my suspicion is right.

Sure enough: Sister Joanna left the window in the rectory kitchen open, and the curtain is fluttering in the breeze.

"Sean," I say, stepping out from around the sheltering fence. "The curtain is *blue*. It's made of homespun wool, some of the most beautiful cloth we've ever made here."

Sean's eyes flick toward me, away from the open window, and the barrel dips again.

"I spun some of the thread for it myself, Sean," I say, stepping close enough to touch his arm. "Last winter. It's okay. This..." What do I say? That there's no danger? They were shooting at us back there! Of course there's danger. How do I bring him back? "Sean, love, this isn't your dream."

"I know that," he grates. "I'm completely fucking awake, and I'm *there*. Again. And she's back there, behind the curtain. *Just. Fucking. Waiting.*"

"We need to go, Sean. Remember?" I tug at his sleeve, but I might as well be pulling at a cloth-covered statue. "That's the door, right up there. Through there, out the front of the barn, and then we're safe."

"She already took my brothers, Courtney! I won't let her have you, too."

"Look," I say, backing slowly away from him toward the window. "It's safe."

"No," he insists. "It's not. Come back."

I stop when I feel the rough-hewn timber wall of the rectory at my back, the curtain against my hair.

"See? Now, come on, Sean," I urge. "Let's go. Through the door." The gun droops again, and he takes a hesitant step toward me, then another. "Good! Just a few more, then we can leave here forever. We can go home. Together."

The wind shifts again, and the curtain brushes against my shoulders and-- that's not the wind. Someone's there.

"*SEAN!*" I scream, but whatever it is, he's already seen it.

"*Get down, get down! Down, down, down!*" I drop, curling into a ball at the base of the wall and cover my head with my arms. The silenced gun is up again, steady on the window, and Sean pulls the trigger as soon as I'm clear of the window.

Click.

Sean's face falls, eyes huge again, and now he's truly panicking.

Why? What happened? What's wrong?

The weapon is so quiet anyway that it takes me a moment to understand that it didn't fire, and by then I see a shape sticking out of the window directly above me.

It's long, black, and narrow and the tip of it is less than ten feet away from the man who's risked his life to rescue me. Sean drops the submachine gun and reaches for a pistol with a fat black can on the end of the barrel. He's fast – the pistol is clear of the holster by the time gravity drags the first weapon to the end of its strap.

He's fast, but not fast enough. He'll never make it in time. Nobody could miss him at this distance!

I reach up to the gun barrel sticking out of the window, grabbing and tugging as hard as I can. Whoever is holding it tries desperately to pull it back, and of course they pull the trigger, but it's not pointed at my love anymore. The shot is deafening, and I know I'll have blisters on my hands from the heat of the barrel, but I don't care.

It's a tug-of-war now, with whoever holds the other end of it, and tug-of-war tricks work. I relax for a moment, bracing my legs against the wall and then pull as hard as I can. Not only does the gun come out the window, but a squirming body follows it out to land on top of me.

"*Get clear, Courtney! Get clear!*" Sean orders, but I'm still struggling, pinned underneath whoever it was that fell on me. The *small* person that fell on top of me. Short hair. It's not a woman. It's just a boy.

"*Nathan!*" I yell, with as much authority as I can manage. "Get off me, *right now!*" All the fight goes out of him in an instant, and he falls to the ground beside me, shaking with silent tears.

He's not scary. He's just... scared.

"Why are you doing this, Courtney?" I kneel, taking the little boy's hands and pulling him up to his own knees in front of me. Nathan looks over at me with tears streaking his soot-covered face. "Why did you bring him here to kill us?"

"Because you had her locked in a fucking box," Sean says, standing behind him. Nathan flinches as the muzzle of Sean's pistol touches the back of his neck. "Because you were going to marry her off to some greasy, sadistic piece of shit."

"My brother's a good man!" Nathan yells, turning to face Sean with a face screwed up in hatred, but freezes after a sharp rap on the head from the pistol barrel.

"Your brother?" Sean asks, suddenly full of courteous curiosity. "Jeremiah is your brother?"

"Yes," Nathan whimpers. "He's a *good* man. He'll be a prophet, one day, when our father ascends to Heaven. A holy man." The tears fall in earnest now, and his shoulders quiver. He's trying so hard to be brave.

"Oh, Nathan," I sigh, and hug him. "Sweetheart, your brother is a monster. He *hurt* me, Nathan. And he was going to keep on *hurting* me. Until it finally killed me."

"But if you submit..." The boy looks up at me with confused eyes. "Courtney, you *have* to submit. It's The Lord's *Will* that you submit. You're a *woman*. You *have* to be punished for Eve's sin, for causing the fall of Adam!"

"Sweetie? I'm not going to submit, not to *anyone*. I'm never going to be *property* again. *Ever again*." Another tight hug, then I release him and stand. "And the only sins I'll be punished for will be my own. It was never *The Lord's* Will. It's your *father's* will. But, you see, I love Sean. And Sean loves me."

"My father is The Lord's prophet?" It should have been a statement, but the boy's inflection makes it a question instead. Maybe I've accomplished something with him after all. "A holy man?"

"Speaking of your father," Sean says, tapping Nathan on the head again. "Shut the fuck *up!* I *know* time's a factor here. Look, we're working on it, but I think there's one more piece of unfinished business."

"But I didn't say anything," Nathan whines.

"I know, sweetie. He's not talking to you."

"Right," Sean says, his attention back on Nathan. "Sorry, where was I? Right. Your father. Holy man. I'd like to meet this *hole*-ly man. See if I can help him become even *hole*-lier."

"He's, he's..." Nathan stammers, hiccupping from the tears. "He's in the chapel. He went there to pray for our deliverance from Satan's evil power. Who were you talking to just now?"

"Sauron," Sean says with a truly vicious grin, but Nathan just looks confused. "Courtney, my love? Let's take a moment to visit the chapel. See if we can't help answer the old bastard's prayers."

"Nathan," I say. "Sweetheart? Be safe, okay? We're going now. When the policemen come, when the firemen come tonight? Go with them. They'll take you somewhere safe and warm, and you can have a bath and something to eat, okay?"

"I'll be okay," he says, numbly.

The little boy stays on his knees, back to us, as we disappear through the door into the barn. He never even looks at the shotgun in the dirt next to him.

"That kid's a piece of work," Sean says. "He was in the running to be just as bad as his father and brother."

"It's how he was raised," I tell him. "He's never known anything different."

"He didn't even know who Sauron was. Can he read? We gotta send him a copy of *Lord of the Rings* for Christmas or something, if we can find out which juvie he winds up in."

"Sean, I'm worried about the kids," I say. "Jennie. Matthew. All the others. What's going to happen to them?"

"Pretty much what you told little killer back there," he answers. "They'll go into the system, probably. If that's what they're turning out here, I don't see any of these nutjobs getting to keep their kids." He sighs, shaking his head. "I mean, Child Services... it's not great, but it'll be better than anything they've known here. They'll be able to get counseling, at least. Try and undo some of..." Sean trails off, gesturing with the barrel of the pistol, encompassing not just the barn but also the entire compound.

"I wish we could just take them away right now. Take them with us."

"Yeah," he agrees. "Me too. I saw how you were with that little girl. You love her. You're probably more of a mom to her than her *actual* mother is. But we can't," he says gently. "We just can't. We need to get *you* to safety first. *Then* we can see about getting Child Services in here, if the Warden Service and the fire fighters don't do it for us tonight."

Flames lick at the edges of the barn, and sparks blow through the front door. Any moment, it will become an inferno when the straw on the floor catches.

"We'd better get out of here," I say.

"Yes," Sean agrees. "First, though, the chapel." His face is hard, his mouth a narrow, grim slash.

The chapel is on fire. It's not fully involved, not yet, but the roof is already burning and it's only a matter of time before it's completely gone. My heart soars as I watch one of the bleached-white streamers bursts into flame.

It's the best news ever. My wedding is cancelled.

I look up at Sean's face, impassive and pitiless, and squeeze his hand. His face does not change, but he squeezes back.

There's a small crowd gathered there now, men and women, some of the children. I don't see Jennie or

Matthew. Most of the men still have rifles or shotguns, some have hammers or axes, but leaderless, nobody raises a hand against us. The crowd parts silently, the Red Sea before a grim latter-day Moses covered in armor and blood. Sean releases my hand and removes his helmet as we climb the few steps up to the already-opened double doors.

The heat inside the chapel is intense. Flames lick at the base of one wall, and the flowers gathered around the altar have wilted and browned. Father Emmanuel kneels in prayer before the altar, under a cracked plaster ceiling. Charred black spots grow, moment by moment.

Sean's heavy boots are drumbeats on the wooden floor as we approach Emmanuel, stopping between the first row of pews. The old man does not look back.

"I'll be with you in a moment," he says in a weary voice.

"Take your time," Sean answers equably, and after a handful of seconds the old man rises to his feet, brushing off his knees. It's a reflex: his hands, black with soot, leave more of a mess than they cleaned off.

"I see I was wrong about you, Mister Pearse," he says finally. "You *were* a threat after all."

"No," Sean replies, softly. "I'm not a threat. I'm vengeance."

"'Vengeance is mine, I will--'" Emmanuel begins, but Sean interrupts him.

"'The Lord is a man of war,'" he quotes. "The Book of Exodus. And as for vengeance? *I. Will. Re. Pay.*"

"You dare blaspheme in this, the house of The Lord? You blaspheme with the very words of The Lord himself?" Emmanuel throws up his hands, his hair an insane white halo. Smoke is gathering near the ceiling, and now a second wall is starting to burn as well.

"This is not God's house, Emmanuel," I say. "Or whatever your name actually is. In fact, I really don't know what your name is. Even a last name, for your sons." I snort, shaking my head at the realization.

How stupid are these people? Following someone when they genuinely don't know a thing about him?

Emmanuel looks daggers at me, cocking his arm back to slap me, but stays his hand, relaxing it and slowly letting it fall when Sean raises the big pistol.

"Isn't it amazing how our perception of size changes?" Sean muses. "I mean, nine millimeters? That's not very big. But right now? To you? It looks as big as the deepest, darkest gateway to hell."

The flowers around the altar are burning now, the altar itself wreathed in flame. Plaster falls from the ceiling, and the smoldering horsehair embedded in it adds to the acrid smoke. I've always know he was Satan in human form, but now? Backlit by the flames, he's never looked more demonic.

"If you strike me down, I shall become more powerful than you can possibly imagine!" Emmanuel's voice is frantic, screechy.

Sean barks a laugh. It's harsh, but filled with genuine humor.

"Seriously?" he asks. "You're going to quote fucking *Star Wars* at me? That's how you want to go out?" Sean shakes his head. "That line didn't work out so well for Obi-Wan," Sean tells the madman. "Still, perhaps it's best not to take the chance."

Sean lowers the pistol from Emmanuel's head, and fires twice. Emmanuel falls to the ground, and my heart sings out to hear the son of a bitch screaming in such pain. One of Sean's bullets pulverized his left kneecap. The other took him low in the belly. Neither wound is necessarily fatal, but either one will make it hard to get out of the burning chapel.

"You have raised your hand against the Anointed of The Lord!" Emmanuel gasps, writhing on the floor. His voice is raspy from the smoke, weakened by pain and blood loss. "You will burn for this!"

For a long moment I think about all the lives that this lunatic has destroyed with his perversion of religion. My own life, maimed and tortured, but never broken. The torment that he's put me through. The future he'd planned for me. Every tick mark on that scorecard is a point against him, and my heart hardens with each one.

"You... will burn... for this..."

Sean raises the pistol again to put him down, to end Emmanuel's pain. To end the screaming.

"No, Sean," I say, gently pushing his hand down. I stoop to kneel next to the son of a bitch, close enough to kiss him if I wanted to. Close enough to whisper in his ear. *"You burn first."*

Sean holsters the pistol, and we walk out of the chapel, hand in hand.

The silent congregation is still gathered there, but it's now grown larger by two members: the grisly corpse of Brother Lucas lies on a blanket at the bottom of the steps; and Nathan, clutching a huge antique family Bible in his hands, who stands on the small landing at the top. He's watched everything, through the open doors.

He's so lost. So confused. My heart breaks for this little boy. He's been responsible for so much pain, both for me and others. I know he caused the deaths of Daniel and Joshua when he told his father about what he'd seen them doing together, but how can I blame him? He was manipulated, placed in a position where there was no other course he knew how to take. I don't know what to say to the boy, and hold out a silent hand toward him.

"No," he says, shaking his head. "Just go."

Sean's truck rumbles at idle behind the crowd, and someone revs the engine wildly as we go down the steps.

"Come on! Move! Move!" the driver yells through the open passenger window. "We've got about six minutes to get the fuck away from here!"

The ride out – the *egress*, Sean calls it – is a bumpy one, and his big four-wheel drive truck earns its reputation a hundred times over as the big man at the wheel races us into the pitch darkness away from the burning compound. He drives with no lights on, using another set of the same four-eyed night vision goggles that my Sean wears. It's only a short run off road, just a few minutes, but my head bounces off the roof of the Blazer at least fourteen thousand times before we find the other man's truck in a clearing in the woods.

"Thank you," I tell the driver after we put everything in his truck. "I'm sorry, I'm afraid I didn't catch your name?"

For a long moment he doesn't answer, looking back to where roiling, billowing fire still lit the distant horizon, and scrubs fingers through very close-cropped hair. It looks like an unconscious gesture, a habit.

"That was a hell of a thing back there," the man says, looking back at me. "That was as much of a mess as a lot of other places I've been with that asshole. We came out of it, though, and from what I heard on the radio you were a big part of it."

"What else could I have done?" I ask. Sean reaches an arm around my waist, and I lean into his shoulder. "He saved me. I…" I don't know what else to say. I'm at a loss for words to explain how and why, in that moment where Sean was paralyzed by his memories, I knew the right thing to do and was able to do it.

"I think we saved each other," Sean says softly, and my heart flip-flops when he squeezes me.

"Yeah," the driver says. "I think he's right. Well, miss? You were on the op. You fought. You were right there with us, so I think you've earned the right." He holds out his hand to me, completely enveloping my own when I take it. "My name's Angela," he tells me.

On impulse, I slip out of Sean's arm, reach up and wrap my arms around the oddly-named man. "Thank you so much, Angela."

"What kind of parents would name their son Angela?" I ask Sean as we watch the other man's taillights recede in the distance.

"I dunno," he answers, hugging me tightly to his chest. "Not yet, anyway. I think we'll find out when we have kids, though."

Chapter 22

Sean

Saturday Morning, 20 August 2016

Courtney's hand on my knee wakes me in the passenger seat of my truck, stiff and achy, as usual.

"We're almost home," she tells me. "Did you sleep okay?"

"Yeah," I say, scrubbing at crusty eyes. "Where are we?"

"295," she answers. "We're coming into Portland."

I did sleep okay. Huh. That's the first time in... longer than I want to remember. No nightmare. No dream. No... anything.

"Thanks for driving, Courtney." I yawn, looking out the window as we cross the bridge over the Presumpscot River. The sun, still barely below the horizon, paints the sky over Casco Bay in waves of color. Classic rock music plays quietly through my truck's speakers. The display on the radio says it's WBLM, 102.9 FM.

"It's okay. I had my nap earlier," she says. "Once you got us to the freeway, it was no problem for me to take it from there. I want a *real* shower, though. That water was cold back there!"

"Solar-powered water heaters don't work too well in the dark," I say. "But the important part was to get most of the blood and filth off. Would have been even harder to explain than the machine guns on the drive up, if we'd gotten stopped."

"Still. I want soap. And *hot* water. And my father." Courtney looks out at the sky over the water. "It's a new day," she says, squeezing my hand until I think bones are going to crack. The clouds and haze over the ocean are deep scarlet streaked with purple and orange.

"Red sky at morning..." I murmur to myself. I can't seem to shake off the nagging feeling that something's still missing.

"What's that, now?"

"Sorry," I tell her, covering a yawn with the back of my hand. "Old superstition about the weather. Red sky at night, sailor's delight. Red sky at morning, sailor take warning. It's not true, not really, but we get pretty superstitious out at sea."

What am I missing? Something to do with missing. Missing pieces? Missing... children? Hmm. That's part of it, but not everything.

"I'm not awake yet. There's something not quite—oh! Did you see that little girl tonight, Courtney? At the end?"

"No," she answers, pursing her lips grimly. "And

that's something else I need to do today. I need to know that Jennie's okay."

"What about the little boy?" I ask. "Lucas's son, the one that he beat into what looked like a seizure?"

"How did you know about that?"

"I saw it happen. With binoculars," I tell her. "The day I found you, before you got back to the compound. Lucas signed his own death warrant right then. Later? The rest of it just underlined the sentence and added some fancy calligraphy."

"I didn't see him either, no. Or his mother, for that matter." Courtney looks at me, concerned. "What're you getting at?"

"I don't know," I tell her. "Or, not exactly, anyway. But there's something missing here. Missing pieces, and missing children. Missing people."

"There were others I didn't notice, either, Sean." The concern in Courtney's eyes changes to worry. "Did you see my mother? Or Jeremiah?"

"No." I sigh, leaning my head back against the blue vinyl seat. "I should have asked that poisonous little shit when I had the chance."

"Nathan." Courtney shakes her head, sighing, as she takes the Forest Ave exit. "I hope he's okay. He's always—I don't know. He's a good kid, Sean. Or he could be. If he can just break out of this twisted thing. Get away from his father, get away from this whole Church of the New Revelation thing."

"Maybe," I say. "Maybe not. It sounds terrible, but some kids really *are* just born rotten. Where do you think they are, though? Your mother and that greasy shit-weasel? And Jennie and the little boy?"

"They're all together, probably," she answers in forlorn voice. "My mother knows how much that little girl means to me. She's going to blame me for what happened tonight. For Emmanuel's death. *Satan's* death. For bringing everything crashing down."

"Oh, I don't think she'll put it *all* on you. She's going to save at least a little bit of blame for me," I reassure her. "We can start making phone calls today, though. See if they've been found. See if they're okay. State Police investigators should be there already, and they'll *certainly* be involved by the end of the day."

Courtney nods, and a long silent moment passes.

"Hey, by the way," I say as she turns on to our street. "Have I told you yet today how much I love you?"

"No," she replies, blushing and flashing a shy but brilliant smile my way. "I don't think you have."

"Well, I do, you know. Quite a lot." I nod definitely, as if that settles the matter, and my lovely blonde driver rolls her eyes at me as she pulls into the driveway of my childhood home, putting the Blazer in park.

"Why don't you give me a few more details?" she asks, unbuckling her seatbelt and leaning over the center console to me. "Just hit the highlights for now, though, we need to go inside."

One hand on the back of her neck pulls Courtney the rest of the way to me, and her soft lips melt into mine for a long kiss. She shrieks in gleeful laughter as she pulls away, batting my other hand away from her breasts.

"I said just the highlights!" She laughs, then leans back over, pressing her breasts against my arm to whisper in my ear. "You can give me the *full* explanation later."

"Oh, I *do* love you," I say, feeling my face practically crack in half with an unaccustomed smile.

"I know," she replies impishly. "Let's go inside now. I need to see my dad."

"Let's go, then," I say, glancing at the clock on the dashboard. "It's just past six. I doubt anyone's up, and if Bill had to work last night he might not even be home yet."

Leaving our things in the truck to be dealt with later, we climb the steps to the front porch. I hear a muffled voice inside, but can't make out the words.

"Someone's up," Courtney says, smiling up at me in anticipation as I turn my key in the doorknob. When the door opens silently on well-maintained hinges, I can hear more clearly.

My mother's voice. Someone else. A man, not Bill. Someone--

Beside me Courtney is opening her mouth to call out a greeting, and I clap my hand over it just in time, laying a finger of my other hand on my own lips. Her eyes are confused, eyebrows crinkled in a question that changes to fear at the sound of breaking glass, and raised voices in the kitchen.

"You crazy bitch!" That's mom. Who's she yelling at? Not Bill.

I flatten against the wall, creeping to the corner. Courtney follows my lead. I don't remember pulling the Beretta from the holster in the small of my back, but the big Italian pistol is already held in a two-handed grip with the safety off.

"*The wages of sin is death!*" It's a woman's voice, ranting, and the floor falls out of my stomach. "Sin is *death*, and I want to live! Life means *no sin!*" More glass breaks, and I hear liquid splashing.

We've found Heather, and Jeremiah can't be far behind.

A glance behind me shows panic, frantic terror plain on Courtney's face, and I place a reassuring hand on her hip next to mine, before carefully advancing along the wall.

"Heather, please--" Bill's voice cuts off in the sound of a stinging slap.

"Silence, sinner!" Heather shrieks. Bill sputters a response, but it's interrupted by a crash.

"She said *silence!*" I grin viciously as I hear Jeremiah's voice, whistling and lisping through the teeth I broke. Oh, good. You're both in one place. Makes this a lot easier.

Wood floors grow squeaky with age, and this house is over a century old, but I'm more than up to the challenge. The SEALs may have polished my skills at stealth, but this wooden floor laid their foundations years earlier. Sneaking out of the house with a noisy floor and a light-sleeping mother had left my teenage self with a detailed mental map of where to step. Even the heavy boots I wear do not break the silence.

Courtney does not have that map.

Creeeeaaaaak!

"What's that? Who's there?" Shrill, furious.

Fuck. Heather heard it, too.

"I know you're out there!" A pause, then I hear scrambling feet and dragging furniture. I raise the Beretta in a firm two-handed grip as footsteps approach the archway from the kitchen to the hall, but they skitter away again before a target is visible.

"It's Pearse," Jeremiah whisper. "It has to be."

"Oh! Sean!" Heather's voice has changed. Bright, cheerful and sickeningly sweet, this new version is almost more terrifying than the crazy bitch that held a straight razor to her own daughter's neck on Monday. "Is that you, Sean? Welcome home!" You could drown a hundred pancakes with that much syrup. "And my daughter's with you, isn't she? Why don't you both come in here? Brother Jeremiah and I have just been having the most interesting conversation with your mother, Sean, and my husband!"

"He's not your husband anymore, you *cunt!*"

My eyebrows go up when my mother spits the final word at Heather. This must be *really* bad. She's *never* said that word around me before, and slapped the living shit outta me the one time she heard me say it.

"What therefore God hath joined together," Heather shrieks, "let not man put asunder!"

Oh good, the crazy's back. This just gets better and fucking better.

"Heather," Bill says in an overly calm voice. "*You* divorced *me!*"

Another crash, and Bill doesn't say anything further.

"Sean Patrick Pearse! Courtney Elizabeth Dwyer! You two come in here *right this instant!*"

Heather is supermom again, scolding two naughty children who've been running in the house. I risk a glance away from the door, and Courtney's face is stricken with grief, her lips quiver, tears stream from tightly closed eyes. I give her hand a quick squeeze before steadying the gun again.

"And speaking of things joined by God being put asunder by man! We're all so proud of little Brother Nathan. He found strength last night, found his voice! He called us last night, gave us all the news."

A sigh.

She's pleased. With what? What'd that little shit do after we left?

"Why don't you both come in here and we'll talk about it while I fix you some breakfast. You've had a busy night," Nice-Heather says, sweet and happy, but it's Beast-Heather that finishes the thought. "Busy with your filthy whoring and murdering!"

She still doesn't know for sure that we're here. All she heard is just a single creak in the floorboards. For all she knows, it's just the house settling.

"Melissa, honey?" Nice-Heather says. "Why don't you explain to your son and my daughter *why* they should come in here?"

"There's nobody out there, Heather."

My mother sounds beyond exhausted. How long has this been going on?

"I didn't *ask* you if there was anyone out there, Melissa *Pearse*." Nice-Heather whispers loudly, emphasizing my father's last name. Denying that Mom and Bill are married.

"Fine. Sean? Courtney? If you're out there, please come in. Heather's--" Mom cuts off with a gasp.

"Now, now. I didn't tell you to ad-lib." Still Nice-Heather.

"She's going to cut me, Sean!" my mother yells out. "Help us!"

I hear another resounding slap, and Beast-Heather screeches incoherently at my mother's continued disobedience.

Courtney's hand tugs at my shirt, and I glance back to see a tear-streaked mask of horror on her face.

"I can't let my mother do this," she whispers, and I hear Heather cackle madly from the kitchen. "Not after last night. Not this, too." She steps away from the wall, holds out a hand to me. "Let's go in," she says, no longer whispering.

Confused, but realizing that the time for stealth is over, I take her hand. I've missed something here. What don't I realize yet? I tuck the pistol into the front of my pants and pull my T-shirt over it. I have a nagging suspicion I'll need it again this morning.

The kitchen is a shambles as Courtney leads me in. Broken glass is everywhere, and the floor is slick with the mixed contents of wine and liquor bottles. Bill and my mother are prisoners, held to their chairs with at least three layers of duct tape each, going by the empty cardboard cores on the floor.

Bill and his chair lay on their sides on the wet, glass-covered floor; Jeremiah has a knee on Bill's head, Emmanuel's rusty revolver is at Bill's throat. Heather stands behind my mother with the same straight razor in her hands. My mother's eyes are wide, rolling wildly in terror as Heather grabs a handful of hair and slices it off with the blade.

"Hey, there you two are!" Heather's face is pleased, happy. She's completely round the bend, and everyone else in the room knows it. "You look confused, Sean. What's the matter?"

"Hm? Oh. What'd Nathan do last night? After we left?" Keep it calm. Play for time. I can shoot Heather before she can cut Mom, but then Bill dies. If I shoot Jeremiah, then Mom dies. Jeremiah's grin is made wolfish by the jagged stubs of broken teeth. He knows what I'm thinking about. You fucking assholes have put me in an impossible situation for the second time in a week, and I'm sick of this. You will not get a third shot at this. No matter what else happens here, neither one of you is leaving this kitchen alive.

"I'll let my daughter explain it to you. She's listened to the sermons! She remembers, she understands," Nice-Heather titters cheerily, but Beast-Heather's eyes burn with hate, and she rips at my mother's hair again, holding it out tight for the razor. "Go ahead, sweetie. Tell him, and if you miss something we'll fill it in for you."

"The verse, the one my mother recited. It's about marriage." Courtney pauses, looking at her mother with pleading eyes. She's begging to be told that her guess is wrong, but Heather smiles, nods her head encouragingly. Courtney closes her eyes and in a hollow, dead voice continues. "The Bible says The Church is the Bride of Christ. Last night, we broke the link between them. We 'put them asunder.'" Her voice is barely a whisper by the end.

"I don't get it," I say, but I have a sick feeling growing in my own stomach. "So what'd Nathan do?" Courtney shakes her head and shrugs, while Heather cackles madly, still holding my mother's hair taut.

"He preached, Pearse. My little brother found his *voice*, and he *preached*." Glee and pride are mixed with anger and sadness on Jeremiah's face. "The Lord inspired him, and I helped him with the words, and we listened to the whole thing. It was glorious." A rapturous ecstasy tinged with envy pushes all the other emotions aside. "We *all* listened, didn't we, *sinner?*" he hisses into Bill's ear. "Tell my wife and this other sinner what happened."

"You people have some odd ideas about marriage," I say. I know I should keep my mouth shut and not antagonize them, but I can't help myself. "Your wedding got cancelled, Jeremiah. Rescheduled, at least. I think you're going to have to find a new location for it." He doesn't rise to the bait, and again orders Bill to speak.

"They got the call on a cell phone," Bill says, his eyes closed. "They put it on speaker and that little boy... My Lord, Sean, he sounded about eight years old, maybe nine. These two coached him on what to say, and he told the people that without their link to God, to The Lord, they'd be lost. They'd all be lost forever, and they could never stand behind God's throne at the judgement, but would instead *be* judged. That there was only one way to keep their connection to God." Bill draws a deep ragged breath before continuing.

"They followed him into the church, and he asked the last person in to close the door behind them. We heard it, all of it. On the speakerphone. Until the phone stopped working. They- they *screamed.*"

"You see, Pearse? My little brother was a great prophet. He led the flock to follow our father in the path of righteousness!"

No, you stupid fuck. A bunch of other stupid fucks let a brainwashed nine-year-old talk them into a mass grave! That's not prophesy, that's fucking gullibility!

Heather yanks at my mother's head again, leaning down to whisper more insane bullshit in her ear, but my mother drives her skull backwards, catching her tormentor square in the middle of the forehead. Courtney's mother stumbles for a brief instant, flailing to regain her footing. A wet, slippery floor and broken glass don't make it any easier for her.

Like a tree falling in slow motion, Heather wavers first one way and then the other as each foot slips in turn. Her head strikes the edge of the counter top with a sickening thud. For a long, shocked moment nobody reacts, and Heather lies on the floor, blood from her scalp mixing with the other liquid on the floor.

"*Sister Heather!*" Jeremiah panics. I never believed he was the brains of this operation, and he's proving it. He's distracted, lunging toward Courtney's mother, and as soon as his pistol is clear of Bill's body, my right hand flies under my tee shirt while the left pulls the hem up to clear the pistol.

I'm fast, but weasels have good reflexes too, and Jeremiah jerks back to Bill, roughly slamming the muzzle of his own gun against the back of the bound man's neck.

His eyes flicker back and forth between my gun and the woman lying motionless on the floor.

"Sister Heather!"

Heather's shoulder twitches first, then an eyelid. She's no danger, not right now at least, so I keep the Beretta centered squarely on Jeremiah's upper chest. He keeps repeating her name, plaintive and forlorn, while I edge away from Courtney.

Separate the targets. He wants us all dead, but I'm the dangerous one. Our parents are lowest priority; they can't go anywhere. He'll go for me first, then he'll chase down... *no*. I will *not* think about that. I will *not* allow that.

I make it a little less than half the distance to the straight razor lying next to Heather's hand when one eye flicks wide open, followed more slowly by the other. Jeremiah's eyes light up in hope.

"Oh, Sister Heather! The Lord has restored you to us!"

Heather gingerly pushes herself onto her elbows, to her knees, twisting and rolling with effort to place her back against the cabinets under the sink. She blinks several times, rapidly, and I notice that her eyelids are out of sync: the left eye lags noticeably behind the right, and neither seems focused.

"Sister Heather, are you all right?"

"I... think so," Heather answers.

She's slurring her words.

It's barely noticeable, but it's there.

Left eye isn't quite tracking with the right, and what about—yes, the left corner of her mouth is drooping.

Heather's eyes scan the room, pausing on each person in turn. The fires are out. The fey light in Nice-Heather's eyes, the manic rage in Beast-Heather's eyes; both are gone. They're sad now, dull. Old eyes.

"Bill," she says, looking at her ex-husband, taped to a chair, his prosthetic leg missing, lying smashed in the corner. If I didn't know better, I'd say that's regret on her face. "Courtney." And in her voice too, or is it just the slurring getting worse? "Melissa?" Heather's eyes travel over my mother's face, over her hair, mangled and patchy from Heather's razor.

Every SEAL is trained in battlefield medicine, and I've seen a lot of wounds. Injury: blunt force trauma to the head. Symptoms: Slurred voice. Poor coordination and lag from one side of the body to the other. Diagnosis: Heather's bleeding into her brain.

"Sean," she says, and her eyes travel from my face down my arms to the Beretta, and back to my eyes. "Brother... Jeremiah."

I pay much closer attention to her nuances now.

Details are important.

She looked at everyone but him. She looked at me when she said his name. At my gun. The turned down corner of her mouth. That was the right side, not the left. Was that scorn? For whom?

"Yes, Sister?" He's eager, wants to please her. He has no idea what to do. Jeremiah was born to a position, raised to be the next prophet, but he's never actually been in charge of something on his own. He's looking for leadership. She's an authority figure, and he's just a piece of shit. Loyalty to his father has been transferred.

"There's not much time left," she says, her gaze steady on me. Her voice is getting worse, but that's definitely a sneer. Why? And her eyes... "Very, very little, in fact. We must—we must follow. Soon." Heather's breathing is labored, and she struggles a little in pulling herself to her feet.

"Yes. The way hath been prepared for us." Jeremiah glances at Heather, but his eyes never completely leave me, and certainly not for long enough to matter. "And my bride will be coming with us."

Is Heather wincing in pain, or at what grease-weasel just said?

"What therefore," Heather says softly, "God hath joined together..." Her breathing is rapid, thready, and her gaze flicks back and forth from Courtney to me. She's... no way. No fucking way.

"Let no man put asunder," Jeremiah finishes.

"Yes," Heather says, her eyes fixed on mine.

This isn't Nice-Heather, and it's not Beast-Heather. It's just... Heather.

I cock my head, raising questioning brows.

"Yes," she says again, and all the sadness in all the world is wrapped up in that one word.

Heather only needs to cover a few feet to reach Jeremiah, and she makes it one labored step at a time. Her coordination is definitely getting worse, and her left foot drags uselessly behind, echoing her daughter's limp. She drops to her knees beside Jeremiah, still holding his gun pressed against Bill's neck.

"It's time," she says, looking at Courtney, then at my pistol, and finally at my face. "It's time for the sinners to face their judgement."

Jeremiah's eyes light with anticipation—that crazy bastard believes he'd actually survive judgement!—and he points both his malevolent stare and his father's revolver at my Courtney, Heather's hands at his wrist ostensibly helping to steady his aim, but actually keeping the barrel pointed anywhere *but* at her daughter.

Even as weak as she is, Heather acts before I can pull the Beretta's heavy trigger, tugging his hand into her own belly, and Jeremiah's bullet finds its new home not in Courtney, but in her mother instead. Jeremiah's weasel face registers shock and horror, but only for the barest fraction of an instant before I fire.

I shoot him four more times before his body hits the floor, and each bullet adds to the ruin of his head.

Courtney rushes to her mother, skidding to a halt on her knees, but I hold her back until I can kick Jeremiah's gun away from the dead fanatic's hand. Away from Heather's hand, too. Whatever happened there at the end, I don't trust that Beast-Heather won't come back. My pocketknife makes quick work of the tape on one of Bill's hands. Once that's free, he can handle the rest of it, and I use Heather's dropped straight razor to cut my mother free. She's stunned by the noise of the gunshots in the small kitchen, and I scoop her up in my arms while circulation comes back to her after the long, terrifying night taped in the chair.

The danger has passed.

Heather's eyes are closed, her head pillowed on Courtney's lap. Bill sits awkwardly behind his daughter, arms wrapped around her. His own eyes are tightly closed, his mouth and forehead crinkled with the effort of holding back his own feelings while giving his daughter all the comfort and caring he can.

"Courtney," Heather whispers. "My baby."

"I'm here, Mom. I'm here," Courtney whispers back, pushing blood-matted hair away from her mother's face. "Hold tight, Mom. We'll get help. We'll get you in an ambulance, get you to the hospital."

Heather shakes her head weakly.

"No, honey. It's too late for me. It's always been too late for me." The sadness in her tone is heartbreaking. "But I don't hear *him* anymore. I just want you to do one thing for me."

"Anything, Mom." Courtney's blanket promise makes me tense up.

"Be happy, my darling," her mother says, her speech growing more indistinct with each word. Every syllable comes at a terrible price in effort and pain, but Heather's face is at peace. "Be... happy..."

Heather's lips continue to move, but her words are lost in the sound of her final shallow breaths. When her eyes close for the last time, the corner of her mouth curves in the barest hint of a lopsided smile.

"Put me down, Sean," Mom murmurs in my ear. "I'm okay. They need us now."

Bill keeps it together, but only until I'm able to gently lift his ex-wife's head from Courtney's lap and help my love to her feet. He's only just gotten her back, and now he has to let go of her all over again. Courtney buries her face into my chest, tears soaking through my shirt, and I make sure that she's not facing the bodies.

"What happened?" I ask. "When did they get here? Why?"

"They were here already when I got back from the camp yesterday," Bill says after clearing his throat. "From when I took you and the wheels up there. Waiting, inside the house. I wasn't expecting it, and..." He shrugged. Sirens wail in the distance, and Bill looks toward the front door. "Someone took care of that detail for us, I guess."

"Bill was down and out when I came home from work." Mom picks up the story while helping her husband into a chair. "They were looking for you, of course. Wanted to make sure you didn't do anything to disrupt the wedding tomorrow. They figured that old bastard, he made a mistake letting you live, so they were going to correct the mistake. Didn't believe you could be trusted to leave well enough alone."

"Yeah," I say. "In hindsight, it's hard to argue the point." On the floor, Heather's face is relaxed now.

At peace, for the first time in my lifetime, and probably in hers. Jeremiah, on the other hand...

My mother's gaze follows mine, and she blanches at the sight of the dead man. Bill, on the other hand, smiles grimly at Jeremiah's corpse, though I notice his eyes slide away from the body of his ex-wife. Not enough time to process that one yet, I guess.

"Good job, son," he tells me, and I nod a silent acknowledgement as the sirens draw closer.

"Courtney?" I say, gently lifting her chin. "Are you okay?"

"Yeah, I am," she says, and the tiniest beginning of a wan smile peeks through the tears. "For the first time, I think I am. It's over, and I'm safe. And I have you. No matter what else, I have you."

"For better or worse, yeah. I think you do have me," I say, and look up as the sirens stop outside the house. "For as long as you want me, I'm yours."

"Forever," Courtney says, and her smile is finally full. She looks over her shoulder at her mother. "I didn't understand it, not at first. What she was saying at the end. What she *meant*."

"Me neither." Cradling her cheek, I scrub away a tear with the tip of my thumb. "And even when I did, I didn't believe it right away. But she understood, and she was right."

"Hm? What do you mean?"

"I don't know if it was God that joined us together or not. I mean, I'd like to think that you and I made up our own minds. Made our own luck. But I'm sure as hell not letting anyone split us apart. Not ever. I love you."

Courtney doesn't respond with words, but her smile tells me everything I could ever hope to hear.

Epilogue
Courtney

Saturday, 18 February 2017

"Are you cold, Courtney?" Casey asks me.

"Oh no, I'm fine," I tell her. "Thank you for asking. It's actually quite warm and toasty in here. Just the way I like it."

It's an old house, company-owned and tucked away on a corner of the estate near the gate, but the heating system works *very* nicely. Just looking at the snow outside the window makes me shiver. I was so cold, for so many years that it's reflex.

"It is definitely that." Her voice carries so much conviction that I wonder if I'm not over-heating the place. "I hear that pregnancies wreak havoc with a woman's thermostat." She smiles and glances down at my belly with something that might be wistful envy. Whenever Tom McGuire gets around to marrying her, I'm guessing there will be more babies on the estate in short order.

I would love to ask but we're not close enough for me to do so. Not yet. Maybe one day. This is a budding friendship, and it's been so long since I've made a new friend that I'm probably the most awkward person she's ever met. And of course, there's the other minor detail—Mr. McGuire might not *quite* be her husband, but he is *definitely* my husband's boss.

"No, nothing like that," I say pouring her another cup of tea. "It's just habit."

It's only been a few months since my father got Sean a job working night shift security at the shipyard and the oil terminal, but that didn't last. Once my dad's boss saw Sean's resume, she poached my husband – even after five months it's still a thrill to think of that! – and then *her* boss did the same thing, over and over again. I don't think anyone ever climbed the corporate ladder so quickly here, but I'm pretty sure he's done moving up. Mr. McGuire doesn't *have* a boss. Most days Sean works at a desk in the corporate headquarters, but whenever Mr. McGuire travels, Sean goes with him. He's also in charge of the estate security, which means we get to live in this lovely old house on the estate.

"How's college going?" I ask.

"Just fine," she says with a grimace. "Nothing really exciting. I go to class and I study and truth be told, I can't wait for it to be over so I can finally get on with my life. I've been trying to pack in as many extra classes as I can, and I *think* I'll be able to graduate after the summer session." Casey is so full of enthusiasm that sometimes she makes me feel positively ancient. We're not so far apart in age, but her life has been more sheltered than mine was. "I hope everything's okay," she sighs. "This snow, the roads..."

We sit in comfortable silence for a moment, looking out the bay windows toward the gate. Any minute now, our men should be driving through it, and back to us.

"When I talked with Tom last night, he said you guys had some good news, but he didn't tell me what it was! Since they're not back yet, I thought I'd ask you directly," she whispers conspiratorially, leaning over close to me even though we're alone in the house.

Curiosity is obviously eating her up, but I don't mind. I know she means well. As far as she's concerned my life has been this extraordinary adventure, a fairy tale in which Sean plays the part of the knight in shining armor.

It's true, he is my hero, but now I have to share him with her and Tom, sometimes.

"Well, first thing, the State Police have finally closed the books on everything that happened up north," I tell her.

"I was sure they would," Casey says, waving her hand dismissively. "What happened in Portland was *obviously* self-defense. You'd been gone from that horrible place for a *week* before the..." She trails off, not wanting to say the word.

"The mass suicide," I finish, fill in the blank that she's avoiding. "It's okay, Casey. I'm familiar with the term, and I know what happened there."

"Yeah," she says, and this time she's the one that shivers. "But still, it's just so *horrible*."

"It was," I agree. "Very."

It was not Jeremiah's death that had me worried. The Portland Police Department had concluded their investigation quickly enough, and the Cumberland County District Attorney had said in a press conference that it was the most clear-cut case of justifiable homicide he'd ever seen come across his desk.

No, what had kept me up late at night was everything that happened at the compound the night before that.

When the state police came to question us, I thought they were going to be suspicious, but no. Not in the slightest. They came for information about life at the compound, and to tie up the loose threads connecting what happened in the kitchen of our parents' home with the mass suicide. Witnesses remembered seeing me run from the farmer's market in Greenville the weekend before, so *obviously*, I couldn't have been there, and testimony from surviving members of the Church of the New Revelation had confirmed absolutely that I had *not* been back since. At all. I didn't understand that part, not at first.

"Every time I think of what happened there, I can't help but think how much of a miracle it is that Sean found you when he did. Just one week later... " She doesn't need to finish her sentence for me to understand she thinks I would have been a victim like all the others who fell in the collective suicide. "Or, if that guy, that one that came to Portland with your..." Again, she tries to be delicate with a difficult word.

"Jeremiah," I say. "And my mother."

The State Police investigation had concluded that they had come to Portland to catch the runaway and make sure that she joined them in their trip to eternity, and I certainly wasn't going to argue the point. The fires at the compound had been intense enough to destroy almost every shred of evidence that could implicate my husband in anything. The only things left was the shower of empty shell casings around the penance box, but the gun that matches those was locked away safely in the hands of the SEALs in Virginia.

We're finally in the clear, but that isn't the reason for my broad, happy smile now.

"The *second* piece of good news is that the adoption will be final soon," I say. "All the paperwork has cleared, and the judge should sign off on it Monday. The last thing they were waiting on was the State Police investigation to be closed, and then she'll be Jennie Pearse."

"Oh, that's *wonderful* news, Courtney!" Casey's face lights up and she gives me a quick, excited hug. "That little girl is *so* adorable."

"Isn't she, though?" I beam like a proud mother, because I am. Or in a few days I will be, legally. My poor little darling Jennie *does* miss her parents. She cries for them at night sometimes, but I've been taking her to a counselor, and it helps. Helps *me*, too.

I thank God every day that my sweet little soon-to-be-daughter had *not* gone back to the dorm like I'd told her. My clever baby had gone a different direction entirely, and had hidden with Matthew and Sister Andrea.

No, not Sister Andrea. Never again. Just Andrea now.

Andrea's instinct to protect her child had, yet again, been stronger than her brainwashing. When Lucas's shotgun sounded the alarm that woke up the compound and set everything in motion leading up to the mass suicide, Andrea fled into the woods, taking her son and my Jennie with her. They were the only survivors, and it was Jennie's quick thinking and her loyalty and love that convinced the others to tell a story of the terrible night in the northern Maine forest that left me entirely out.

"And how's Matthew's mom doing?" Casey's expressive face shows real concern for Andrea.

"She's getting some help, but she needs a lot more than me. She's at Spring Harbor," I tell her, referring to the psychiatric hospital in Westbrook, over by Exit 8. "They're taking good care of her, and I take Matthew to see her whenever I can. The only thing that worries me is how Jennie will do when Andrea gets out of the hospital and Matthew leaves us to live with her."

"Oh, I didn't even think of that," Casey says. "They're so close." She looks around my living room, as if just noticing that we really are alone in the house. "Where *are* your two little monsters today, anyway?" she asks.

"Sean's mother came and picked them up earlier," I tell her. "She knew Sean was coming back tonight and she swapped shifts with someone so we could have some time alone together."

"Most couples don't have such a full house after only a few months of marriage." Casey laughs. I just smile at her.

"Oh, yes, a *very* full house, and in just about another four and a half months, little Angela will be here, too," I say patting my growing belly.

I'm in on the joke now, and I know that Max Anghelescu's parents didn't name their son Angela. *Our* little Angela will be a girl, though. Fortunately for her, Sean and I will never get to find out for ourselves what kind of parents would name a boy Angela.

"You look so happy!" Casey gushes. "You guys seem like the perfect couple, and you're going to be *such* a good mom."

"I hope so," sigh. I flatter myself that I've learned from my mother's example. I know how *not* to be, but does that automatically mean I know how *to* be?

My mother has been on my mind constantly, since she died. Was the woman that heard the voice of a twisted and brutal God in her mind the real Heather Dwyer? Or was it the woman that pulled Jeremiah's gun into her belly? I only had a chance to meet that woman in the final moments of her life, but I wish I could have had more than that minute with her, cradling her head in my lap as she died. I think I would have liked her. I wipe away the beginnings of tears, unwilling to let Casey see me cry.

Sean's friend Doctor Moloney went over the autopsy report with us, explaining the information-dense medical terminology in a way we could understand. The impact of her head against the counter had caused a hairline fracture in my mother's skull, and broken a blood vessel with a long and complicated name. It wasn't the gunshot that had killed my mother, but bleeding in her brain.

At the same time, the head injury and the bleeding are likely what saved her from *His* terrible voice. And that saved *me* from Jeremiah's bullet. In those final moments of her life, my mother was lucid, and whether or not she still heard *His* commands, she was able to resist them.

Jimmy pointed out something else on the X-ray as well: traces of another skull fracture, much older and long-since healed. A childhood injury, vaguely hoof-shaped. Could the two injuries have been bookends to her madness? Caused by one, and repaired by the other? Could that be why my mother always seemed more *herself* after Emmanuel hit her? Our doctor friend shrugged away the question. Brains are complicated, and we don't really understand them.

He's right, of course. Brains *are* complicated, but they *can* heal, every night brings me more proof of it. Sean's dreams are better now. The nightmares of that terrible alleyway, the ambush that almost killed him, have been getting fewer and ever further apart. At first, it was just *not every night* but that quickly turned into *not every week.*

It's been twenty-nine days now since his last nightmare, so soon it will be *not every month.*

The sound of a big diesel truck rumbling up to the house makes us both turn our heads toward the window. Our men have returned, in one of the estate's big four-wheel drive trucks.

"I'm glad they drove that," Casey says. "Tom wanted to take the Porsche, and I had to work hard to talk him out of that. He thought sure the storm would hold off longer."

The front door opens, admitting a flurry of puffy snowflakes along with two very bundled-up men.

I stand to meet my husband, but he rushes over, easing me back down into my chair.

"No, no, don't get up!" he tells me, and I roll my eyes. "You just stay there!"

"I'm not made of glass, Sean," I grumble at him, but I'm secretly pleased. He's so careful and thoughtful of me, and of our baby. He's going to be a wonderful father. I have no doubt of that. My husband had a great example to follow as a husband and father.

While Sean strips off the layers of heavy outerwear, emerging from underneath a virtual Michelin Man arrangement of insulated clothes, his boss takes a knee next to my chair.

"Congratulations, Mrs. Pearse," Tom says. "I'm so happy for you guys on the adoption. It's wonderful news."

"Thank you, Mr. McGuire. We're glad to be finally closing the books on everything there," I answer. "Casey and I were just talking about that."

"And Tom," Casey cuts in, "we probably ought to be getting back to the house. I think Courtney has some plans for her husband since you kept him away overnight," she says tugging at his sleeve and winking at me. "They have the house to themselves tonight. We don't want to take up their time."

"True, very true," my husband's boss chuckles, rising to his feet again and holding out his hand to my husband. "Sean, good idea on the security plan for that excavation. See if you can't work up a list of names for it. We'll talk about it more Monday, though. Congratulations again, to both of you," he finishes as Casey drags him toward the front door.

"I hope you left the truck running," she says, zipping up her coat and pulling a knit cap down tightly over her ears. "It looks *cold* out there."

"It's nasty," Tom tells her. "Now, let's get on home so we can rattle around in that big empty house all by ourselves."

"I think we can find some way to stay entertained," she tells him with a warm smile and raised eyebrow as they vanish into the Maine winter.

Getting up out of my overstuffed chair is a little more awkward than it used to be. It's not difficult – yet – but it's definitely a preview of things to come. Sean rushes to my side, holding out a hand to help me.

"Oh, stop it!" I tell him with a baleful glare, but I can't hold back the smile that gives the lie to my scolding. "I've missed you," I tell my husband, patting his clean-shaven cheek. "I like this look on you."

"It works better with the whole suit-and-tie thing," Sean says. "I missed you too. It's good to be home."

"So what's this you were talking about?" I ask, setting out plates and lighting candles for our supper. "An excavation?"

My husband tells me all about an archaeological expedition that one of the McGuire Family Trust's foundations is funding next year, and the security concerns are his responsibility. I make the appropriate noises in the right places, but I'm not really following. I'm too lost in my own wonder, my own happiness.

I'm the luckiest woman in the world, and certainly the happiest one, and it's all due to you, Sean Pearse.

I've had enough of listening to my husband talk about work, and in the way of wives with talkative husbands since time began, I shut him up by pulling his face down to kiss me.

"Mom called me and said she picked up the kids," Sean says when I finally let him breathe. He's wearing the naughty ear-to-ear smile. The scar on his jawline twists into something piratical, menacing to those who don't know him and love him, but it melts my heart every time.

"Indeed she has," I answer with a wickedly suggestive curl of my own lips. "*And* she's not bringing them back before Monday."

"Two whole days? Without tripping over toys or stepping on Legos?" he laughs in faux amazement. "What*ever* shall we find to occupy ourselves?"

"Oh, I think we can find *something* to take up the next couple days," I tell Sean, leading him by the hand to the stairs.

"Aren't you hungry?" my husband asks, looking over his shoulder at the romantic candlelit dinner setting I've laid out for us.

"Dinner's not quite ready yet," I say, looking down at him from the third stair. "And I feel like an appetizer first." Sean's eyes light up with anticipation.

"You're right," he says. "I don't think we're going to be bored at *all*."

The End

Also by

Olivia Rigal & Shannon Macallan

Home Bound (A Christmas Novella)

Shannon Macallan

Giving Thanks
A Matter of Honor
Taking Charge

Olivia Rigal

Jade
Ripped
Learning Curves
Flirting with Curves (2 novels, with Ava Catori)
The Curve Masters (6 novellas)
Iron Tornadoes MC Romance (5 novellas)
Category-5 Knights MC Romance (3 novellas)

About the Authors

Shannon is a native of Maine, descendant of a family that has lived in New England since the last time there was a queen named Elizabeth, and has worked for the government, been in sales, and done some technical work as well. These days, Shannon is sick of working for someone else and has decided to take hold of fate and the future by writing.

Shannon is happily married with an assortment of two- and four-legged children which all seem to be surviving nicely, and a variety of plants which are not.

Born in Manhattan, Olivia spent her youth going back and forth between the United States and France. She has lived and studied in both countries.

While still a student, she kept herself busy with a variety of jobs, and has worked everywhere from the famous Clignancourt Flea Market all the way to a Parisian recording studio, with stops along the way as a dog groomer in Manhattan and an assistant in a famous British auction house.

Olivia finally settled in France to raise her family and practice law. When her legal practice does not keep her busy in Paris, she runs away to write novels in her Florida home next to MacArthur Beach State Park.

Olivia and Shannon met in the summer of 2015 and worked on Hold Fast together for an entire year, ultimately finalizing it during the Romance Writers of America 2016 annual conference in San Diego.

Made in the USA
Charleston, SC
19 October 2016